WORLDS AT WAR—

Tannia, Erde, and Occo—Earth's farthest-flung colony worlds. Long [illegible]rgotten by the mother planet, each [illegible]und its own path to survival. Occ[illegible] planet of mystery . . . Ta[illegible]in colonies that ha[illegible]Earth years—but fa[illegible]wenty years earli[illegible]me under Tannia's [illegible]ordveldt, shot dow[illegible]ame first a prisoner o[illegible] professor of the classics, atte[illegible]to civilize his former enemies. Then [illegible] met the beautiful Maggie, a fighter pilot. Drawn together by love, they were eventually driven apart by Nordveldt's past loyalties—until Tannia and Erde were attacked by a new a deadly foe, Occo! And suddenly old enemies became uneasy allies, and Anton and Maggie flew the skies together in a desperate struggle to save both their worlds. . . .

War Birds

R. M. Meluch

A SIGNET BOOK

NEW AMERICAN LIBRARY

A DIVISION OF PENGUIN BOOKS USA INC.

NAL BOOKS ARE AVAILABLE AT QUANTITY DISCOUNTS WHEN USED TO PROMOTE PRODUCTS OR SERVICES. FOR INFORMATION PLEASE WRITE TO PREMIUM MARKETING DIVISION, NEW AMERICAN LIBRARY, 1633 BROADWAY, NEW YORK, NEW YORK 10019.

SIGNET TRADEMARK REG. U.S. PAT OFF. AND FOREIGN COUNTRIES
REGISTERED TRADEMARK—MARCA REGISTRADA
HECHO EN DRESDEN, TN. U.S.A.

SIGNET, SIGNET CLASSIC, MENTOR, ONYX, PLUME, MERIDIAN and NAL BOOKS are published by New American Library, a division of Penguin Books USA Inc., 1633 Broadway, New York, New York 10019

First Printing, August, 1989

1 2 3 4 5 6 7 8 9

PRINTED IN THE UNITED STATES OF AMERICA

PART ONE:

TANNIA

I.

I hurt. I want to go home. The air boils and presses down. I cannot breathe.

In suffering sometimes a pleasant memory presents itself with the hazy veil of intervening time ripped aside, so crisp and immediate and more vivid than when it actually happened that it edges out at least for a blissful moment a reality that is no longer endurable.

I remember Maggie.

We first met in the quadrangle. She was a dizzy thing, came climbing out of the second-floor window, wearing a dress. I looked up and saw this girlish leg sporting a lace garter which served no purpose that I could see except to flash with the flip of a hem, and all else she wore underneath was so little as to be nonfunctional. Young girls' fashions were frivolous that year.

She was dangling out of the window, clinging to the ledge and groping for a toehold, when she looked around and down. Then she saw me. She was probably not so impressed as I was. She hadn't my view, for one thing.

What I looked like—I looked very young, as young as my students, though I was creeping up on middle age; I think it's the lack of extra weight that does it. I am of slight stature, short, though I hold myself erect; I'm not clumsy; and my reflexes are still good. The eyes are gray and too big. My hair is light brown and worn in a short generic cut like most other men who don't want to call attention to themselves. In my most depressed and self-deprecating moments I would describe myself as spindly. In my egotistical moments I am aquiline.

On seeing me the young lady raised a finger to her lips

for silence. And with that she lost her grip on the window frame and fell.

As I said, my reflexes are good. I rushed in and caught her. Sort of. I got under her and we both crashed into the bracken bushes, which were in fruit at the time, so when we scrambled out of the bushes we had crushed red berries and dirt on us. On me mostly. Brackens are, luckily, springy, or we would both have been hurt. As it was she was scratched and I was bruised, mostly from a sharp elbow in the ribs.

She sprang up first and helped me out of the bushes. Brackenberries smeared bright crimson streaks on her pale yellow dress. "Oh, I'm *so* sorry," she said, giggling, trying to brush off my clothes. She only made a bigger mess. "Oh *no!*" she cried, covered her mouth with both hands and laughed. "I'm sorry!"

My senses flooded melianthems. Her perfume. She must have taken a bath in it.

She kissed my cheek and thanked me for catching her. "That was sweet of you." Then *I* felt dizzy. I can't say why. There were lots of young girls on base. Lots of them dizzy.

In this one I sensed the air bubbles were more a reflection of exuberance and youth than of true emptyheadedness. She was seventeen standard and allowed to blow with the trendy breezes. An elfin reed of a girl, she was full of spunk and playful adventure (she had been gated by the dean for it, to explain her unorthodox exit from the dormitory). She said her name was Maggie. Mary Magdalene Collier actually.

I raised my eyebrows. From that she could tell I was faultily familiar with the source of her name. She planted her fists on her sharp-boned hips and announced, "Let me set something straight here, mister. Nowhere in the Bible does it say Mary Magdalene was the adulterous woman, and Mary Magdalene did not wash Christ's feet with her hair. Mary Magdalene was the first person to see Christ after he was crucified, and Mary Magdalene is a saint. Got that? Look it up."

"I believe you," I said, smiling idiotically.

"You're laughing at me."

"You're delightful," I said.

She wanted to know my name.

"Anthony," I said. "Anthony Northfield."

She shook my hand. "Pleased to meet you, Mr. Northfield." Then she said, "Oh, are you *Professor* Northfield?"

I admitted I was—a bit deflated that she chose to overlook my first name. As I said, I was standing before the threshold of middle age, and I *hated* it. I hadn't thought I was *there* yet. Of course, it is characteristic of that particular malady that one imagines himself still attractive to seventeen-year-olds.

I was thirty-two Erde-Tannian years old. (No, I don't feel like translating that into standard right at this very moment thank you very much.) It was within reasonable bounds to say I was old enough to be her father.

Maggie darted furtive glances about the quadrangle and back up at the window. The underage students were on base only under an iron authority. The age of majority on Tannia is eighteen standard, which comes to 15.3846 Tannian (OK, go do your damn arithmetic, you vultures). Minors are treated like children and so tend to act like them.

"Don't tell on me," Maggie begged.

"Of course not," said I.

"I have to run," she said. And run she did. Lace garter flashing.

I still smelled melianthems.

I went on to my faculty meeting, my head in a cloud. My heart is seldom given to fluttering. I kept to myself those days, in my books. I did my work and did not socialize. I still felt very much an outsider here. I had no use for women. Oh yes, they are very nice, but I do believe in honesty in relationships and I was prepared for neither honesty nor a relationship. The girl had made me smile. That was all.

The chairman of my department was not impressed with my dirt-and-grass-and-brackenberry-stained apparel. "New fashion, Northfield?" he said.

"Oh." I looked at myself and tried to make my jacket more presentable. "I caught a girl."

"I didn't know you chased," he said, gave me a sniff—melianthems—and turned without waiting for an explanation. He was not worried about it. I was not exactly known as a lady killer.

My housemate was a ladies' man. I was living at that time with an officer candidate/pilot-in-training. Rather he was living with me. I let some rooms on my top floor to him. His name was Brutus Burke. He was big as a house. He was called, of course, Brute. He played football in secondary school and was on the fleet's team the year we beat New Port so soundly.

We. As if I were really fleet.

Brute and I made an odd set of housemates. Think of every incongruity you can. He was bass to my baritone, hairy to my smooth, ruddy to my pale. (He said I spent too much time in my ivory tower to have any color.) His short curly dark hair and beard continued from his head like roaming moss onto his great chest. He had massive beefy shoulders, a classically tapering torso which narrowed to what the girls always told me was a "cute ass" just before they asked me to introduce them.

He was young, but I looked younger than he did if you didn't look at my eyes. When I first started teaching on base I had the damnedest time getting a drink in the rathskeller and local pubs; I was consistently mistaken for an underaged junior cadet. By the time I met Maggie I looked a little older. Then I got mistaken for a senior cadet.

Except by Maggie.

Burke and I lived just outside the base in a two-story house. I could watch the ships fly over. I'd been asked if I were not afraid a cadet would fly one in my window someday. I said I had faith enough in their poor aim that they would miss completely.

Actually the kids were very good. Morale never ebbed from the euphoria born of winning the war against the Erders against all odds twenty years before; so the kids, those who weren't even born during the war, were very cocky. I could see them cavorting over my house in the airships. Sometimes a T-15 flew over.

In fact my house exists with the understanding that the fleet is not liable for noise damage; and in order to live there I had to sign a waiver in case anything ever did come through the window. Odds were long, and I didn't think it would be such a bad way to go—splattered by a wayward T going mach two.

The Tannian T-15 is a beautiful machine, the only serious rival, mechanically speaking, to anything in the Erden wartime fleet. Old technology, I know, but I'm partial to the older spaceplanes, and she's as solid as anything they have now. You can tell by looking at her she's a hypersonic. Even unswept she has snubby wings, which gives her low rotational inertia and makes a quicker, neater orbital. Those stub wings also make her one of the Swift series—she can't take off by herself. Swifts have to be dropped or boosted. On the ground by herself she's a penguin. She waddles with her subsonic engines, but at mach speeds she's poetry. She's great in space, changes direction fast as an orb, and comes down neat as an airdiver in reentry. But if an engine ever blows out she glides like a brick, so they say if you're going to break something, do it out in space.

I call her "she" because I'm in love with her; can you guess? The T-15 is a legend. But she was touchy and expensive to keep in the air, especially if she did any in-atmosphere combat. After the war the T's costly maintenance and delicacy caused her to be phased out for the stouter Defender—the Flying Cow, I call it. The Tannians manhandle their machines. They needed something sturdy. The T-15 is a pilot's machine. The Defender is idiotproof. The T-15 was the better ship, and I was sad to see her go.

What I was doing on base: I kept the Tannian fleet from sending up unread illiterate slobs. They did that anyway; pilots-in-training have the attention span of a sea cucumber on the subject of classics or any book that has no specs in it. But I was supposed to try to educate them.

They don't know how to read. I always knew when the compact vid cell burned out at the library; there would be a mad scramble for the condensed version on the fourth floor with the foreign-language books. I had a carrel up there. The day before the essays were due they had come thundering up. They saw me and froze in a sheepish clot. I just lifted a brow and said, "Burned out another cell, did you?" And I gave them an alternate assignment in case they didn't read the play—as if they were all going to get through *Romeo and Juliet* in one night.

I used to tell them to write what they would do if they were grounded and could never fly again. But in that case I could expect a pile of one-line sentence fragments: Kill myself. No one had anything constructive to say. Did I really think there was a good answer to that one? I had hoped.

So after my faculty meeting I was doomed to go home to read the essays they tried to pass off on me. Their excuses for *not* writing them were more inventive and thoughtful than their essays. The one I hated was—and there was one of these in every class—the whine, "Professor Northfield, you're not a pilot; you can't understand."

I paused at the office to pick up my messages. I didn't wear a remote. There was no such thing as an urgent message for me. I did not teach science, so I did not need a computer on me. If I really needed one I was close enough to home to consult my core.

I collected my things and walked home.

Burke was there when I arrived, Burke and company, a pack of young pilots talking air/spacecraft. I offered nothing to these conversations. What pilot wants to hear what a classics professor has to say about a Weltraum Ectocraft? So I kept quiet. Except when Burke, as he did sometimes, gave me a wink and a nudge: "A T-15 could fly doughnuts around a Kralle KR-22, ain't that right, teach?"

"Kralle" was what they called the Erders during the war. It means "talon" and it's derogatory. The Erdetechnik KR-22 was the pride of the Erden side, a Swift Class ship like the Tannian T.

The maneuver of which Burke spoke was possible—and had been done once to my knowledge—if the Kralle in question had a canard broken off and one engine out.

"Sure, Burke. Does anyone want coffee?" I said.

They said no, and I decided I didn't want any either. I wanted a *drink*. I retreated upstairs with a whiskey and water.

Voices followed me up. "Why's it called a canard?"

"Because it can 'ardly fly without one."

Very funny. Whiskey and water, hold the water.

I had given up my imported (which is to say Erden) ale. My penchant for Erden ale used to earn me odd looks at the pubs. Just because it's Erden. People still remember the war as if it were yesterday, and Erde is the Enemy.

I should qualify that. To judge Tannia from the spaceport is to see the world through a straw. It's a very narrow view, and this was the view I was getting. Memory persists longer in a spaceport town. The final Battle over Trevane was fifteen Erde-Tannian years ago. Erde was completely normalized by now. But they never forget. No one ever really forgets.

And if this was what it meant to be victors, I feared what memory was like back on Erde.

Tannians despised Erders.

Erders are depicted as vicious, narrow-eyed madmen with hooked noses. I don't know any Erder with a hooked nose. I suppose it comes from the Erden national symbol, which is the eagle. Eagles were brought to both worlds by the colonists, but Tannia has since lost its eagles. As the bird is the national symbol of the Erders they tried harder to preserve theirs. Erde still has eagles.

Tannia wanted a native symbol for its new colony, something from the new land itself. Nice idea in theory, but symbols need a past; they need history and association to give them weight. A brand-new symbol has all the emotional impact of a company trademark—which would have fit Tannia perfectly, now that I think of it. Tannia was almost a nation without a past, its culture shallow as a vid screen. But they woke up in time and are rooting madly for their nearly lost heritage. Which was why they had me trying to teach *Romeo and Juliet* to a bunch of space aces and plane brains.

And their national symbol does have meaning. The founders wanted something less martial than Erde chose, but something noble. They resorted to an Earth import after all: the horse. It was powerful and beautiful. The horse has been a sign of nobility since its first introduction to civilization. A horse could represent war, but it was not a predator. It was a nice choice, I think. Especially when it turned out that the front-running candidate among the indigenous possibilities turns cannibalistic in time of famine. Narrow escape from national humiliation, that.

Rumbling laughter of Burke's friends carried from downstairs. The upstairs rooms were mostly Burke's, but I kept a study up there. I sat over my dismal essays and my whiskey, and stared out the window.

I watched Erde rise over the airfield at sunset, full and blue. The black dot of Tannia's shadow crept across its face like a slow airplane shadow. Midmonth already. Erden eclipse.

I tried to make out which continent was getting the totality, but I could distinguish nothing for the cloud cover.

I had a scope in my bedroom, but that would necessitate going downstairs and passing through Burke and the pilots. I could envision me explaining to them why I was carrying the scope upstairs: "I want to look at Erde."

Sure you do.

No, suddenly I didn't.

They hate anything to do with Erde. Never mind that the Tannians were using Erden technology now, and never mind that the Tannians were going to need the Erders in the face of the new threat, the Occons.

There was already talk of the coming war. We knew—some of us knew—even then, in the late summer of 189, that the war was coming.

And this, as I finally get around to stating a purpose, is my story.

II.

I don't know who I am writing this for. Who will ever read this I am afraid to speculate. I try not to dwell on questions of will I ever see home again and what will be left of it if I do.

Earth. I have decided I am writing this for Earth. Perhaps I will launch a drone toward the stargate with this record, in case anyone there is curious about what became of Earth's farthest-flung colonies.

In that case I ought to say something about the past war before I begin on this one. The first war was called the Erden-Tannian War or the War of 174. At the time it was simply the war, the only war that was, so it had no number or designation besides "the war."

It was in the 174th local year after settlement that Erde invaded Tannia.

We are a double planet, Erde-Tannia, founded at the same time, but we grew rapidly apart, became separate nations. Tannia is a pure democracy. Erde became a constitutional dictatorship. Tannians speak English, of a sort. Erders speak a German-Dutch-English-miscellaneous mélange that can only be called Erden. A five-hour flight and a more than literal vacuum stand between the two worlds.

The climates on both planets are, to put it mildly, limiting. The ice caps are large, the temperate zones small. You can't go too far north, can't go too far south, and on Erde you can't go too far up because the atmosphere thins very quickly. Habitable, arable, Earthlike land is at a premium, and Erders are inclined to feel they have a right to all of it. Superiority is more than a state of mind on Erde—it is an ethnic trait. Not that Tannians are not jingoists and elitists, especially after winning the War of 174, but Tannia has a merely patronizing approach to lesser beings. Erde is flat-out ruthless.

Which explains the attack. There is still plenty of land to go around right now. Our populations are still small, in the millions. But Erde looked ahead and saw whose children would be crowded out.

So Erde started it, almost won it before you could call it a war. It was nearly a simple invasion and takeover.

It turned into a classic David-and-Goliath encounter (though your average Tannian, with the exception of someone named Mary Magdalene, would not understand that reference). Erden overconfidence and technological superiority fell to Tannian spunk and ingenuity.

For the most part it was a clean war, which is to say no nukes except for the spaceship engines that blew up. Erde did try to use neutron bombs, but those did not get through.

Bombs are classified as clean, semiclean, and dirty. Dirty is anything that causes fallout, directly or indirectly, so that includes antimatter bombs. Semiclean are your neutron bombs, if you launch them; if they are fired at you, they are called semidirty. Clean bombs are far from clean but refer to anything in which the destruction does not persist, with the exception of causing fire.

Biological warfare is anathema. Nobody even thinks of it. I hope. I still wonder how the hell my mother got polio. *Polio.*

Both planets were well defended against full-scale destruction. That kind of attack is the least desirable, because one ends up destroying what one is trying to possess. But the Erders tried it in the end when they saw that their attempted takeover was doomed to defeat. If the Erders could not have the other planet, they would burn it.

But Tannia, like Erde, is shielded to the point of overkill, and so the invaders' last hurrah went out without so much as a fizzle. Erde was vanquished. Erders were normalized, which means the two planets became nominal allies with Erde actually under Tannia's thumb. Erde lost its constitution. The Erden Congress is peopled with Tannians, I suppose to make sure such a thing never happens again.

One of the most heinous weapons employed, I think, were the sound bombs. An Erden invention, naturally. Tannians defended by wearing sonic filters, but there were always those who refused to keep them on. Most pathetic were the mothers who could not stand how their infants cried and so did not make them wear the filters. There is a somber shortage of Tannians with a birthdate of 174. Mary Magdalene is on the near side of that gap.

There was a great deal of fiendish technology hurled across the void, but in spite of the modern inventions it came down to a war of pilots.

The use of individuals in combat is a tactic that goes cyclically in and out of vogue, but it is never wholly gone. For a time following the war, pilots were considered obsolescent. Piloting was an antiquated strategy, an idea whose time had come and gone.

The problem with pilots is that you cannot (that is, *we* cannot; I don't know what Earth has been up to) speed up human comprehension. The human brain takes in information at a finite rate, synthesizes it, and makes a decision. The transmission time of that decision to the machine has been shaved down to some nicely thin instants, but there remains that tremendous lag time within the human wetware.

Robots were in fashion, and missiles and satellites, sonic bombs, spread rays, large-scale weapons.

Man was outmoded. Historians will know right away that this is rubbish.

Machines are fast. But machines are predictable. To combat a machine, use another machine. Machines reach stalemate, and it takes a human mind to break it.

Because no matter how advanced the machine mind, nothing can outthink a human being in value judgment and invention. So Tannia put pilots back in the cockpits, and the academy started training pilots again.

And, for all that, pilots are an attractive image. Whether the lawman rides a horse, drives a car, or pilots a plane or spaceplane, everyone loves a daredevil hero.

Why am I neglecting the Occons in this discussion of technology?

Because they did not participate in the first war, and we (we, Erde-Tannia) did not know what kind of hardware they had.

Because Occo is, at the very nearest, twenty-seven million miles away, and it is usually a great deal farther than that. Occo is two and a half light-minutes at the closest, and we are able to receive radio messages only part of the year. When Occo is on the far side of the sun, it is absolutely out of sight, out of reach—out of sight and normally out of mind. We tended to forget Occo's existence until it pushed itself upon us.

Whenever Occo approached twenty-seven million miles, which it does every 1.6 of our years, we of the double planet became nervous.

Occo had never been a paradise, though the Occons claimed otherwise, but things had to be getting worse for them. The already limited communications from that place broke off one hundred of our years ago. Then, shortly after our war, disturbances in Occo's atmosphere became detectable even from Erde-Tannia. A message of concern was sent. The Occons transmitted back showing opulence, bright Byzantine color, richness, fountains, water, water in all the pictures where there could be no water, artful oddly alien-looking cityscapes, stone gardens, colorful buildings with upswept eaves, pagodas, architecture so lovely it did not look as if it belonged to a working city. It looked like a vid set.

The Occons told us our dire readings were mistaken. We did not know why they were lying to us, but we did know the place was a veritable hell. (And I can tell you they are in worse trouble than anybody ever dared guess in his worst vision.) So we knew they would be coming, one of those passes.

In case the records have been lost or obscured, I should say something about the solar system itself.

Earth sent the first survey robot through the stargate roughly three hundred standard years ago. What the robot found was this:

A double star system consisting of a type G5V star of .97 solar masses, magnitude +4.98, orbited by nine planets, and a white dwarf companion.

The companion's orbit is circular, or close enough—not to quibble over a hundred million miles here or there.

The stargate is near the companion, which is 14.33 billion miles from our main sun. It takes a ship ten standard years to get here once it's through the stargate. Not a trip you want to make twice in a lifetime.

But evidently worth the trip once, because Earth colonists followed the survey ship, and we are their descendants.

Of the main sun's nine planets, the survey ship found three capable of supporting life as Earth knows it.

The innermost planet is a lifeless molten blob.

The second planet is Occo, large, heavy, and hot, with a thick, breathable (the report said breathable; I beg to differ) atmosphere, and two very small moons.

The third planet is the double planet Erde-Tannia.

The fourth planet, crater-pocked Iris, has life of a sort, a primitive ammonia-based organism. Life develops where it *can.* I forget the technical name for the life form. Tannians call it frozen crud. It dies at normal temperature and pressure—it boils away. So there is no danger of contamination.

The fifth planet, Augea, became our toxic waste dump.

The outer planets are fairly unremarkable, standard satellites.

And farthest out, with no satellites of its own save asteroids, is the companion white dwarf, so far away, so small, that we mistake it for a planet in the night sky. It is three times the distance of Pluto from Sol. Its only importance to us is that it appears to be the nexus to the stargate.

The significance of the stargate to us is historical, not practical. The stargate is a ten-year journey. The route to it on the orbital plane is positively mined with asteroids, remnants of the companion's own planets. And the population of Earth was already seventy billion when the colonists left, the land 30 percent unusable from poison and bad use. No one thinks of going back.

So the companion sits out there. We hardly know we are a double star system.

We never forget we are a double planet.

But only in relation to Occo does Erde-Tannia become

one unit. Until Occo enters the conversation, one is either an Erder or a Tannian. Absolutely no one calls himself an Erde-Tannian.

The original colonists came here with fifteen ships. Five went to Erde, five to Tannia, five to Occo. Tannia because it was most Earthlike. Erde for its low-saline oceans and because it is beautiful. Occo . . . God knows why Occo. Maybe for its gentler tides. The settlers who became Occons thought they knew something the others didn't, and they weren't sharing.

Erde is the smallest of the three worlds, Occo the biggest. A 45-kilo girl (you don't suppose I'm thinking of Maggie again, do you?) would weigh 82 pounds on Erde, and 148 on Occo, and the Tannian girl who fell out of the window hit me with 97 accelerating pounds. I suppose it was a dumb idea to try to catch her.

The Tannian day is nearly identical in duration to Earth's and divided into twenty-four hours, despite the fact that there are not 360 days in the year, for which that archaic division was originally made. But it was a familiar unit so they did not tamper with it.

Erde's day is shorter, divided decimally. Ten hours is logical. People still have, after all, ten fingers. I might mention here that the only bioengineering done on ourselves was to keep us from falling to tidal sickness. The tidal drag between Erde and Tannia is twenty-three times that between Earth and its moon. We seem to have adjusted. No one falls to tide sickness anymore.

Tannia and Erde orbit each other like Earth and moon but twice the distance apart. Though they orbit around a common axis somewhere between them, each relegates the other to the status of a moon. An Erder will say Tannia orbits Erde, and Tannians will tell you Erde orbits Tannia.

The plane of their mutual orbit is nearly flush on the ecliptic, so Tannia and Erde eclipse each other every fifty-two Tannian days. Both planets call one mutual revolution a month.

To be more precise, here are all the stats I can think to give—in Earth units, since this is meant for Earth eyes:

	Tannia	Erde	Occo
Mass ($\oplus$ = 1)	1.4	.8	3.8
Volume ($\oplus$ = 1)	1.72	.963	4.09
Gravity (G = 1)	.972	.82	1.48
Solar year (in standard years)	1.17	1.17	.72
Distance from sun (in astronomical units)	1.1	1.1	.8
Rotation	24 hours	28.1 hours	20 hours
Pressure at sea level (in millibars)	1,022	848	c. 4,000

Look at the Occon statistics and wonder how anyone could doubt the Occons were in trouble.

We had no idea of the half of it. Had we any inkling of the truth we would have gone in with bombers a hundred years ago. But we didn't know. By 189 it was too late. The Occons were building up their fleet and we knew they would be coming here.

One of these passes.

III.

The night was warm. The base was situated where it was because of the moderate weather, so we had some fine nights. I had left the windows open, and the breezes brought in the scent of native flowers mingled with the imported lilacs. I had the house to myself, as Brute and his buddies were out carousing.

Brute would not be home this evening. He would not be home until dawn unless he could not score, which was highly unlikely unless he was throwing-up drunk. Brute Burke was a young pilot and a prime piece of meat. Brute was much in demand.

His big brown eyes were bedroom eyes, said the ladies. I couldn't see it. And I thought his lips too big, too red, with a self-indulgent pout. The beard he'd grown made him look bestial. "Part of my animal magnetism," he said.

What did I expect from a man named Brute?

I was left alone with my essays and music when the sound of breaking and entering came from upstairs. I might have closed all the windows with the master switch and cleaved the intruder in twain had I thought it a real burglar. But this was a spaceport town, and you don't do that when it is most likely some academy kid's harmless or semi-harmless prank. So I went upstairs to investigate. The noise was coming from Brute's bedroom. It had to be one of Brute's wenches.

I could distinguish a small feminine figure clambering from the webby branch of the acor tree to the window. Well, I decided I would help the girl in so she wouldn't break her neck.

But she made it in OK on her own. She stepped down from the windowsill and immediately tottered on the unexpectedly undulant mattress of Brute's bed, and I went to take her hands to steady her. I think I recognized the scent first, a wave of melianthems. She looked up from the blond mop of hair blown into her eyes and I saw her face.

"Maggie!"

"Oh! You!" She was startled to find me here. "I'm sorry, I forgot your name."

Of course she forgot my name.

"Anthony," I said. I was not going to repeat my last name. I was not going to be called Professor Northfield by a girl I was infatuated with in my own home.

She was wearing a dress, a red one this time, not exactly climbing clothes, a chain of wilted xanthi blossoms tucked in her belt next to her remote, which hung from a lanyard.

She jumped down from the bed. "What are you doing here?" she said, brushing a blond strand from her mouth.

I believe I frowned. The wrong person was asking the question. "I live here," I said dully. "Do you ever use doors?"

"Oh dear," she said. "I got the wrong house." She unhitched her remote to ring up her core and double-check the address.

I had been right with my first thought: it *was* one of Brute's wenches. This distressed me more than I could say. Not her, was all I could think, not Maggie. She was so fresh, so different; Maggie involved with Brute I just could not reconcile. "You're looking for Burke," I said. "He lives here too."

"You know each other!" She smiled brightly, dropped her remote back on its lanyard, and clasped her hands together. Then she took my arm conspiratorially. "You're his friend. You know what he likes. Tell me how I can get his attention."

With chagrin came also sudden relief that nearly staggered me. It hadn't happened yet. She wasn't Brute's. Yet.

Get his attention, she was asking. I cast my eyes to the window. She had appeared in his bedroom at midnight.

That was a very good start. She did not need advice from me. If Brute had been here, she would have had what she wanted, or thought she wanted.

She was waiting for my reply so expectantly it tore my heart.

I touched her cheek, on impulse. It was such a natural thing I didn't realize I was going to do it till my hand was there. I said tenderly, "You will have no trouble getting his attention."

She blushed and giggled. "You really think so?"

"Keeping his attention may be a different story," I said.

"Why? He moves on a lot?"

I had never stepped on Burke's territory before. He could do whatever he wanted to whomever he wanted and I did not consider it my place to judge, object, or intervene. Still I felt the need to protect this one. "To say the least," I answered. I owed her that warning. "As a matter of fact, he is not where a certain other young lady believes he is right now. Brute will break all my bones for telling you that." I imagined the scene: like kindling to an ape.

"But I shan't *tell* him," said Maggie. She patted my arm as if I were a brother and confidant. She announced undeterred, "I'm different from all the others."

"I daresay you are," I said softly.

And I didn't want to see her on Brute's chain.

I set out to tell of the Occon invasion. If I seem to spend excessive time on Maggie, it is because the young lady was much on my mind. And I like to think about her while I am here. And she is the reason I was where I was when war broke out.

And she fired the first Tannian shot before the formal declaration. Quite a few shots. Didn't hit a damn thing, but I guess you could say she fought the first battle, and she was the only survivor of it on our side.

Night again. Burke was home, in bed. I was in my bed downstairs.

I heard rattling of an upstairs window, a stumble, a

thump, Burke's startled "What the—?" A feminine giggle. A mystified male chuckle.

Coils around my gut.

Oh no.

Voices. Giggles.

I stuffed a pillow over my ears and turned on some music.

In the morning I got up, shuffling, to find my bathroom door shut. I am a bit fuzzy-headed in the morning. I should have gone back to bed right then, but I stood there. The door opened. Out came a blond waif, blanket wrapped many times around her slender figure.

She grinned at me. "The upstairs was occupied and I really had to go. I hope you don't mind."

"Of course not."

She scampered away, dragging the blanket with her like an overlong train. "You don't see me."

"Of course not. You're not here."

And oh God I wished she weren't. Maggie and Burke. Maggie and Burke.

I did not see her leave that morning. She mustn't have used the door.

Burke came down jauntily. He had no idea I was aware of anything or that I had a personal stake in this affair. He went to the fridge and stuffed something leftover in his mouth for his usual breakfast, talking the whole way. "You'd never believe it! This *tidbit* comes in through the *window,* falls on the bed . . ."

I tried to look bored so I would not get the whole account. I diligently readied for my class, remembering things I had left in other rooms, inventing reasons to go to the cellar. I managed to miss most of it, but it angered me that Brute's buddies were going to get this whole thing in detail. Like a pearl before swine.

Brute's friends came to get him. I heard the pack of them hooting for him on the front step. He let them in. "Just a sec," he told them. To me, on the fly, he said, "Vote for me, teach."

"I did," I said, and nodded at the screen. It was just waiting for his pawprint.

"Great." He slapped his palm on the screen and the votes went in to be tallied. To his friends as he was leaving he said, "Teach is real smart."

I usually did Burke's voting.

I don't believe there has been a direct democracy in human history since its invention, and even that first time it had excluded women. From then, the populations being governed were simply too large to make gathering every citizen together for a vote practicable. Democracy was always an unwieldy form of government, but technology has finally advanced enough to make the old idea workable again.

The colonists saw their new beginning on Tannia as the opportunity for a great experiment. Every Tannian citizen votes on everything. All you need is citizenship, a verifiable birthdate, a registered handprint, and a registered address with a voting terminal. The legislature makes up a ballot of issues, and every morning at 0800 starting on the meridian, Tannians vote the ballot they find on their screens. If you aren't current on an issue or feel incompetent you can assign your vote to one of the legislators for that day.

Burke usually gives his to me. It's not a legal assignment. Officially it's still his vote. I push the choices and he puts his print on it. Usually he doesn't even look. It's a big joke to him that he doesn't know what he's voting for and that *I* am doing it.

Actual voter fraud is difficult. Forged handprints are possible, but the tally center double-checks the origin of each return, and your address had better match your registration or the Federales come on the double.

In contrast, the Erden colonists opted for efficiency when they founded their world. By popular vote they picked a government that would best ensure their survival and progress. They voted against democracy. The Erden constitution provided for an Autokrat, elected for life. Every ten years there was a popular vote to decide whether or not to dissolve the government. They never did. The Autokracy continued until Erde's defeat in 174. Tannia dissolved the government.

Erde is now a representative republic, but the choices for all major posts are between two Tannians.

* * *

Just as I predicted, Maggie needed no help in getting Brute's attention. He thought she was great fun. However, she would not have lasted a week as his main attraction—for she was not his type—but that he discovered I was more than a little fond of the girl. This revelation put Maggie into a whole new light and suddenly Burke's interest revived to blazing magnitudes.

When he first perceived it, I had said something unwise and revealing. His mouth widened under his black beard. His eyes sparkled merrily, and he sputtered, unable to contain his glee, "Maggie? You? You want Maggie?" He laughed. He roared. He clapped his beefy hands and stalked circles around me.

I was still as stone and pale as marble, mortified.

"You've got to be—you are—" He hardly knew where to begin. This was the mother lode and he knew it.

I had thought I was looking fairly good that day. My black trousers were of a flattering cut, everything trim. I am very slender but with good muscle definition. I thought the way I was dressed was subtle. Not subtle enough. Burke asked if I thought it was mating season.

As he was mocking me I could sense him making a second mental assessment of Maggie, who was heretofore a pale slip of a frilly young thing. Brute liked them busty and sultry. Now he was reconsidering to see what I saw.

Around he went, circle, circle, like a T-15 doing doughnuts around a crippled KR-22 with a broken canard and one engine out. The motion made me queasy.

I stood still but I really wanted to run and hide. If only I could have kept the color from coming and going from my face I might have pulled my dignity from the fire. But he saw that too, and he howled.

He carved me to pieces. He went through my age, which was nearly twice his; my stature, which was nearly half his; my employment, which was nothing next to his; then he laughed and said Maggie was his and I could not have her, not that she would be interested anyway. He slapped me on the back with a great paw and left me devastated.

I saw more of Maggie in the days to follow than I cared

to. She spent more time at my house than did I. I banished myself to the library most of the day, not to see or hear the two of them together, or even to see her in the house alone and know why she was there.

Brute did not let her move in—ostensibly because it was my house, but actually because he still had other girls.

It was not my place to enlighten her. I think Burke was waiting for me to do that. I don't know what kind of bear trap was set for that contingency, because I didn't step in it. And for all I knew Maggie was already aware of the competition.

Burke had a party at my house. I went to the library. I had a key so I could stay after hours.

I intended to spend the night there.

I was up in my customary fourth-floor carrel, deep in my books, when I heard footsteps in the fire-escape stairwell. I looked as the door opened and Maggie popped out of the stairwell.

She wore a green low-cut cocktail jumpsuit over which she had thrown a trench coat because it was cool outside. She was tipsy. She took an empty champagne glass from her coat pocket.

"I was going to bring you a drink, but I wasn't sure the guard would let me in with it." She dropped into the chair next to mine. "So I drank it."

"You look very nice."

"Thank you. You ought to come to the party. It's so much fun."

I hedged, "You're all dressed up. I have nothing to wear." This was true, actually. I hadn't been to a party in fifteen years.

"Oh, nobody cares. Not after this many rounds, anyway." She pulled on my arm. Just that much touch sent my senses reeling. I hadn't done a lot in fifteen years.

She was terribly pretty. She was not dressed for the library. Her jade-green jumpsuit had a plunging halter top, a sash at her small waist, and harem pants gathered at her ankles. She wore a bone ankle bracelet and little strappy sandals. A hair ornament was lost in her artistically disheveled mane. "Please come."

"No. You go enjoy yourself."

She scooted her chair closer and looked over my shoulder at my work. "What are you doing?"

"Translating *De Tanniisch Schlacht.*"

"You know Erden that well? Won't it make you go blind?"

"I don't think so."

"I wish I was that smart," said Maggie. "You aren't even using a dictionary."

I am a thorough man. When I learned the other nation's language I learned it flawlessly.

"It's a military book," I said. "It's fairly cut-and-dried."

I was trying not to look at her but her perfume was getting to me, melianthems. My heart sped up, and I felt warm.

I was becoming thankful that Maggie had drunk the wine and not I. I was feeling intoxicated without it.

It was pleasant up there with Maggie beside me, asking about my work.

She got into everything like a curious squirrel.

She put a bubble in the reader. The image of an Erden fighter appeared. It was an old hydrogen-powered scramjet. She asked why the wings were swept forward. She asked how a hypersonic engine worked.

"Voodoo," I said.

"No, really," she said.

I started cautiously. It was as difficult as explaining relativity. Air acts weird moving faster than sound. It doesn't act like air—which only makes sense because the engine doesn't look like an engine either. It has no moving parts.

But I was not too much surprised to see Maggie following what I said.

She got into a book of spaceplanes. "What's that? What's that?"

She wanted to bone up on them so she could impress Burke. That was her original intent, but she got caught up in it and the interest became genuine and independent of Burke.

We unscrolled plans and spread them out all over the

floor. She'd taken off her shoes, was crawling around on all fours in her party outfit.

Green silk drew smoothly across her thigh. She was not wearing underwear. Some sound escaped my throat, and I drowned it in a fit of coughing.

She was not big-chested, and down on the floor, leaning over, her top fell loose and you could see from here to Occo.

We were alone in the great building, which was dark but for the warm sphere of light around us.

Maggie was asking why mach five was the dividing line between supersonic and hypersonic.

What?

"Difference between fast and real fast," I mumbled.

"Anthoneee," she giggled. She had her shoes on her hands, and she danced them on my shoulder. "Are you sure you don't have a bottle stashed up here?"

I suppose I sounded drunk. My answers were getting stupid. It was hard to concentrate on spaceplanes.

Finally she announced that she was going back with all her newfound knowledge and show off to Burke.

"Don't," I said. "He'll know where you've been."

"So?" she said. It did not occur to her that there could be any jealousy between us. I don't think it entered her head once that I could be a sexual being, that I had any feeling that way. I don't think she saw me as a man at all. She regarded me as some other thing, neither male nor female, an academic eunuch. I was simply a smart friend.

She kissed my cheek and scampered back down the stairs.

She forgot her shoes.

I came home in the morning. My house and Burke were in ruins. I dropped Maggie's little sandals on his chest. "Your girlfriend's."

He grunted. "Thanks. That's real good of you, teach." He went back to sleep.

I avoided my house when I knew Maggie would be there, but I came home one evening too soon and found her still there. She took my jacket for me. A note fell from my pocket. She retrieved it. It was a love note from one of the bubble-headed teens in my junior academy class. Maggie read it, laughed, intrigued. ''What's this?''

''Oh. I get those all the time,'' I said absently. I took a few more from another pocket and crumpled them. There was never any place to throw them away. ''My students.''

''The girls fall in love with you?'' she said. She thought it was hysterical.

I became depressed.

Then came the final bomb. Two bombs. You would have thought I couldn't feel the second one for the first one but this was not so.

The first one came from Maggie. She and Brute Burke were to marry.

The second blow was that the Tannian fleet was putting the T-15 back into commission and Burke was going to be flying one.

As I've said, the T-15 was legend. The T-15 was what saved the Tannians' collective butt at the Battle over Trevane. Brute Burke got to fly one, and he never missed a trick to rub my nose in that fact. He knew I admired that spaceplane, and I knew he liked to torment me, but I didn't know how cruel he could be till he came home and dangled the set of twin keys on one blunt-tipped finger and said, ''Why don't you take her up, teach?''

''Why don't I swallow a live grenade,'' said I, clearing off the coffee table. Then I made for the stairs.

He pursued me. ''Who's gonna know?''

''I think they'll know,'' I said. ''I've never flown a T. I've never touched a T.''

''Like falling off a bike,'' said Brute. I had reached the stair, but he stopped me. His hairy arm was over my shoulder. The keys were jingling in my face.

I lost anything like composure.

''Go to fucking hell,'' said I. I ducked from under his heavy arm and *ran* upstairs. I locked myself in my study. My heart didn't stop pounding for half an hour.

I think I might have cried.

IV.

To distract myself I walked out to the training field, as close as I was allowed, to watch the planes take off. From the edge of the field I saw only the launchings, an endless conga line of them, not the landings, so one had the impression that nothing ever came down. They just went up and up.

Added to the usual parade of hardware, I saw a booster take up a brand-new Airdiver. Once up, Airdivers really *don't* come down. They remain in space and make only occasional forays into the upper atmosphere.

Most ships are specialized like that. One ship cannot be all things. Put all available equipment on one machine, it won't get out of its own way.

I like spaceplanes better than spaceships. Vessels designed exclusively for space are less aesthetically pleasing than the aerodynamic ones, *I* think.

What comes to mind in particular is one prototype spaceship which we on base called the lost golf ball. The thing is a joke, trouble-plagued from the beginning. Cadets see it coming and they yell, "Fore!" It was constructed in space, because its hull is quite fragile and also because it's powered by matter/antimatter engines, which are popularly called matter/what's-the-matter engines. M/AMs are not permitted in atmosphere, where the smallest accident could be cataclysmic. The fleet is lucky one hasn't blown up.

The lost golf ball was one of the projects which the military, having sunk so much money and effort into development, was determined to make work no matter what.

I would like to see them send the damn thing against

Occo. One could hope anyway that the Occons would die laughing.

The Airdiver is not without its problems either. Because of some stupid Tannian antitrust laws, the body was designed by someone other than the builder of the in-atmosphere powerplants. Well, a supersonic's body is part of its intake system, I am sorry. You just don't stick an engine on a fuselage and expect it to fly.

Erdetechnik and Weltraum never had those problems before Tannia nationalized the companies and split up their departments.

But technical superiority isn't everything. Tannia won the war, and Tannia was making the rules now.

After the Airdiver went up there was a lull in the take-offs. I soon saw it was because there were maneuvers going on over the plain. I tried to see.

I always wished I had field glasses, but I felt self-conscious bringing them, so I just shaded my eyes and squinted at the specks in the sky.

Someone was pulling a monkey-back maneuver.

As a battle strategy the monkey-back was no good any-more; everyone knew how to get out of it. But the cadets saw it in a vid or some such thing, and they all had to duplicate it.

The first pilot to do a monkey-back was an Erder flying a KR-22. No one was ready to defend against it. Tannian simulators had thrown their full repertoire of attacks at their pilots, and this one was not among them. The trouble was that a simulator would not simulate an Erden KR-22 lowering its alighting gear while it was flying. Because the KR's underpinnings are not even "alighting gear." They're "parking gear." KRs land in a wind barrel, not on wheels.

The monkey-back is an in-atmosphere, subsonic technique. In the maneuver, the attacking ship moves in above its victim much too close for either ship to fire. The attacker drops its gear and actually executes a three-point landing on the victim's wings, then goes into a dive. When this was first done, the victim trustingly waited for his ship's collision-avoidance system to counteract the move, only to find too late his engines overcome by the double payload. By the time the attacker launched itself off the victim's back, the victim had too much momentum and not enough altitude to pull up.

You see, collision avoidance only keeps you from having scenes like in old movies and vids. You know the kind. The villain closes in; the fleeing hero peels off and the chase vehicle, be it car, plane, missile, or motorcycle, hurtles headlong into a mountainside. That can't happen in modern ships. The computer collision avoidance won't let you crash. Unless you are pushed by a monkey on your back.

The move was a favorite of the Erder ace Nordveldt in the war—back when a favorite Tannian evasive maneuver was letting an Erder draw too close to shoot. The Erder would put his struts down, and down they went.

To these kids, practicing it now over the plain, it was a game. They rolled out so easily they looked as if they were playing tag. They were so used to the monkey-back as to render it ineffective. It was the shock of the thing back in 174 that made it deadly.

Tannians are nothing if not adaptable. They had better be.

I do not know who will win this Occon war. Rather I am afraid to call it.

To comfort me I can always remind myself I was wrong the last time, when I was sure Erde would be victorious.

I returned home and found a strange little man had parked himself outside my door. He had come in a motorized vehicle, which should have tipped me off immediately. Powered private vehicles are not permitted on base. My house stood on military land. I owned the structure; the land was leased. This man had a motor car on Fleet property.

I climbed the steps but made no move to open the door, not with him standing there. His eyes I can only call beady. He had a wilted mustache, a bony little frame, and an imperious bearing as if he were the king of the system—or had a ramrod up his tail. He demanded, very officially, to know where I had been.

I told him I had been watching planes.

"Oh, I see," he said and scribbled in the notepad he carried. I noticed he also wore a recorder pin on his collar, so I could not figure what he could be writing longhand. His tone and the recorder and the scribbling irritated me. I put a hand on the top of the notepad and pulled it down so it tilted away from him. He looked up from it in shock that I should dare do such a thing. But I was more offended than he. I said, "What does that mean, 'Oh, I see'?"

"What's your interest in the spaceplanes, Professor?" he said.

"I like them," I said shortly. "What's your interest in me?"

His lipless mouth twitched. "Now, I don't like that insinuation."

"I don't very much like yours," said I. "Who are you?"

He was someone I should not have been arguing with, as it turned out. He flipped open the badge of a Federal security officer. I had been provoking the Federales. Plural. They are always plural. They hang together like maggots.

His name was Gortz.

I let go of his notebook. He drew it back in protectively as if my touch had soiled it.

A fingernails-on-blackboard kind of person. His quick persecuted eyes narrowed at me, and his hatchet slit of a mouth approximated a smirk at my sudden silence and properly quashed insolence. He'd hated me instantly for balking at his interrogation. Never mind that he had set me up to resist. Maybe he'd come here hating me. I don't know.

One actually pities this sort of weasel, unless he is after *you*.

He pocketed his identification. "Let's go inside, shall we?"

"No," said I. This was my home, and I made it a practice not to take in anything that might have an accident on the carpet.

The mustache worked like a dying caterpillar. Paranoia flamed eagerly in the beady eyes. "Why? What are you hiding?"

"What do you want me to be hiding?" I asked agreeably. "I'll see if I can't find it for you."

If this was a witch hunt, by God I would give him witches.

He wanted to know what I was teaching my students. Was I trying to influence them. He asked about my housemate, Burke. He warned me that he had already questioned Burke and my answers had better match. I was not afraid. I know Burke, as much as he enjoys sticking pins in my skin, would never betray me to the Feds even had I been guilty of anything. Blackmailable secrets were to be treasured and held over my head, not thrown away on the likes of this.

But my answers did not match Burke's. My answers were preposterous.

I started making up things.

Gortz's eyes grew wider and wider and he sucked in all the scandal, pen scorching his notebook as he madly scribbled.

When the logs of his pyre towered high enough I threw in my torch. I told him that according to my source something had just taken off from Occo.

The notebook slammed shut and he sputtered, turned off his recorder. I thought he would have a seizure. He turned on the recorder again and said, "How did you get access to such information? Who is this source?"

"You," I said. "I got it from you."

He was stone-faced.

I continued, "I know what a launch window is, and I know what time of year it is."

Most people think Occo in conjunction is the dangerous time. It is, but it's not a launch date; it's an arrival date. Occo was in a launch window at present. If they were to send anything to Erde-Tannia this pass, they needed to launch it right then. My guess was that Tannian surveillance had seen something go up from Occo this time.

I told Gortz, "There's always a security crackdown whenever something awful comes from Occo, and this is as blatant a crackdown as I've ever seen. You came here looking for a security risk. You found it. You ought to turn yourself in."

He turned off his recorder, backed it up, and erased the last seconds. He tucked his notebook under his armpit and parted menacingly from my company. "We'll be in touch, Anton." We. I told you the Feds are always plural. And that angered me, his calling me by my given name, as if I were an Erden menial. I didn't go in. I went for a walk. And I made sure I could not account for my time.

I received the summons the next day. It was only from the board of the academy, so it was not as serious as it might have been. The military administrators of the base are a little more skeptical of intelligence coming from the Feds. The academy was, however, in no position to ignore the report that appeared in the board's box the next morning. I was called on the carpet before all of them. I nearly lost my position.

I was wrong to be so blithe in this situation. As I walked to my summons, I saw Occo still shining in the morning sky after the sun was up. No one was going to be in the mood for sarcasm.

Occo is visible from Tannia as a brilliant star. Unlike a normal planet, it twinkles. It has reflectors, hundreds of kilometers across, to turn away some of the irradiation.

As I walked to report to the board, Occo overhung the horizon, signaling my doom if not Erde-Tannia's.

The chairwoman informed me that in the report, the agent Gortz had said I humiliated him. That I was out to get him and make him look ridiculous and undermine the effectiveness of a legitimate operation. I could deny none of this. The person in question needed no assistance in looking ridiculous, but I refrained from saying so.

The report further stated that I had not said one true thing. Whether Gortz deduced that himself or tried to turn in his report to his superiors and was laughed at I had no way of knowing. Either way, he was now aware that I had fed him a feast of offal and he had taken it home.

It was easy to be contemptuous, but I had made a bad enemy.

Perhaps something in the very scathingness of the report, the overkill of the attack, raised the board's doubt, but they—in their infinite tolerance, they let me know—decided to give me another chance.

"We will overlook this incident this time," said the chairwoman. "But be advised, more discretion is in order for academic personnel on this base."

"Yes, ma'am," I said.

"And Anthony." She addressed me as she would a servant or a schoolboy. "Staying away from the planes, aren't we?"

The phrasing was so patronizing that I answered in royal plural, "We are."

"Have a care there," said the chairwoman.

"Yes, ma'am."

Autumn came. The bright malevolent star that was Occo drew near and moved on, and it began to look as if we would be spared for another pass. Some of the tension lifted from the base. Some of the paranoia of the Federales slacked—at least I heard no more from them that season. The pilots were a little disappointed, I think.

I went for a walk in the early morning through a park of imported trees. The leaves were changing with the season. A mist hovered over everything, muting all the colors. I like these woods.

It was cold. I wore a jacket and scarf. I kept my black-gloved hands in my pockets, because my long fingers turn to ice in the short days and don't thaw out till spring.

We were at 28 degrees north latitude. (We—we on base.) Tannia is tilted 22 degrees on its axis, Erde 24. Erde is more off than Tannia—yes, there is a joke there.

The wealthy houses are on the equators of both worlds.

I liked the northern woods, even if my fingers froze.

The place was thick with chattering birds. The birds were changing too. Most of them are green or brown throughout the summer, turning brilliant like the leaves in autumn, then brown and white in winter. Farther toward the arctic they turn pure white.

They seemed to be liveliest early in the morning when few people were about. I thought I was alone.

Then from somewhere beyond this stand of trees I heard a female voice that must have been a bicyclist coming up behind a runner call out, "On your left."

Later I saw Maggie with her bicycle on a side path. She gave a big smile and waved hugely with one arm, and she came pedaling over.

She dismounted to stand on one pedal as she coasted up to me. Her nose was red, and there was a sparkle in her eyes. She hopped to the ground and walked her bike alongside me, chattering.

She was saying that she was thinking of switching over from engineering to fighter pilot training. "But Brute doesn't think so."

I looked over her small agile form bundled in a long bulky sweater. "I think you would be a fine pilot," I said.

"Wish Brute thought so," she said.

The word of a professor was not going to contradict the Brute Burke, so I said, "Go get tested and find out once and for all. It can't hurt."

She shrugged and pushed her bicycle. She switched the talk to other things. Her mind moved like a swallow's flight. She said she was going to be eighteen standard this month. She was going to run out of the dorm so fast it would make the dean's props spin. She couldn't wait to get herself an address and vote on something.

She seemed such a child to me. The brilliant ones tended to remain children longer. Not just bright. I mean brilliant. It would explain Maggie's giddiness. I had had several geniuses come through my classes, and they all lagged behind socially. Even when they were making a concentrated show of maturity, theirs was often the blustering forced confidence of an uncertain child rather than true calm maturity that comes of simple age.

And they never seem to catch up. Always behind or wide.

I thought of this while Maggie was chirping. I had already perceived a razor mind under all the bubbles. She would never be like other women. She had a Peter Pan streak. She would always chirp.

She was talking about the falling leaves.

I, out of left field, said, "I love you."

"What?" said Maggie.

It came out just like that. God knows I hadn't intended it to.

I was cold, with my gloved hands jammed in my jacket pockets, just standing there, and blurting I love you.

She got mad, I think. No wonder. I don't blame her. She was engaged. To Brute. Maybe I wanted her to be angry with me. I don't know. I walked away, shoulders hunched.

In a minute I heard the kickstand go down and her footsteps running after me. I felt her palm hit my back. Smack. It was nothing near hard enough to cause injury, though she capable of some power with her skinny arms; it was mere expression of wrath. I wished she would *hit* me. She sounded furious. "How dare you!" she yelled. Smack. "How dare you!" Smack. Smack.

Indeed, how dare I.

Burke got me for it. This time, Maggie told on me. Burke had been waiting for this. He pummeled me a lot harder than she had. Of course. I had made a move on his fiancée. He was within his rights. It was even legal. "Friend, huh? Friend, huh?" He loved it. He had been dying to do it. We had never been friends.

Then he packed up most of his belongings and moved out. He left a lot of his things behind, giving lie to his righteous anger. He would be back. This was not a true break. Except for Maggie. Maggie was gone from my house. I felt relieved and empty.

One thing about Burke and me. Burke the big, Burke the strong, Burke the rugged handsome, the pilot, the Don Juan. Why he needed to hurt me and why I let him. Because Burke was jealous of me. And there was no depth for him to crush me sufficient for him to feel even.

V.

Winter had come. Outwardly all my bruises had long since healed.

I had never ventured into the base's war museum, and I don't know what possessed me to tour it that day. I don't like museums. Too many ghosts. The past leaps out and makes me uneasy, because I believe in ghosts. I never admit that aloud, because it is not a rational thought. It's not a thought, actually. It's more a feeling, so on that supposition, I guess it is allowable to be irrational.

All pilots are superstitious.

Once inside I settled into fascination for a time, because the place was filled with beautiful machines. And naturally it would not have been complete without a T-15 and an Erden KR-22. This I could have anticipated, but when I saw which ones were on display I stopped dead.

They wren't mere examples off the assembly line or reconstructions. Oh no, not these. These two war birds had names.

I saw the broken canard and the black on the wing of the KR-22, the molten metal solidified into a shapeless glob over the one engine cowling, and I must have gazed at it a full minute without comprehension until realization sank in. This was the previously mentioned KR-22 that the T-15 had flown doughnuts around. And next to her was the T-15 that had shot her down.

I bent over to look underneath; morbid action, that. If she was who I thought, I had to see it. A fast landing by a ship never meant to land. A rough ride without a canard.

The belly was ripped. I stood up, blinked. This was it.

Black soot covered the KR-22's name, so it was not visible, and it was written in Erden anyway: *Die Sturmschwalbe.* The *Storm Petrel.* Named for a bird that lives its life on the wing. A restless spirit.

I was so shocked to see it I just stared. I felt a little sick.

A voice I knew sounded from behind me. "Ought to call her *Kiwi* now."

That was Burke.

I did not turn around. "I didn't realize this was here," I said without tone.

I shifted my stare over to the Tannian ship. That had been a magnificent machine and magnificent pilot. Hal Halson. A pig of a human being when not in the air/space. In the cockpit of a fighting spaceplane he was someone else entirely. A gallant knight of the skies. He'd died ten years before in a training flight with a cadet. His license had been yanked and he was drunk as a skunk at the time. He'd been thirty standard years old, twenty-five Tannian. His liver already needed replacing. Is there anything more wretched than a grounded pilot?

Both ships were battered. The problem with the Erden KR is that it is optimistic. A fine fighting machine, but one small injury and you don't go home again. It presupposes that the battleground will be friendly territory at the end of the fight. It counts on winning. At the Battle over Trevane it counted wrong.

A KR normally puts down in a wind barrel. This one had gone in the drink. They say any landing you walk away from is a good landing. Especially from ships designed not to land at all. And, looking at it then with that canard off, I could not see how it had ever been done.

Or why.

I stared at her rather some time. Burke's voice came again from behind me. "Just a shell, teach. They took her guts out. She's got no engines."

I shrugged. "Didn't think it was going anywhere."

There was always something a bit horrid for me in beholding stuffed creatures—once-living ones. There they were, a couple of birds, gutted, stuffed, and mounted, and quite quite dead.

"Pity," said Burke.

"Pity," said I.

My house was very large with Burke and Maggie gone. Except for the encounter at the museum I didn't see either of them anymore. And even then I hadn't actually *seen* Burke, because I never turned around. Our paths never crossed, a schoolteacher and a pilot.

And without me around to revive his rivalry, Burke's interest in Maggie waned. And finally he left her. This I discovered in the middle of a late winter night with an insistent pounding on my door when Maggie showed up at the house looking for Brute.

I had been asleep. I wasn't going to answer the rapping, but I heard Maggie's voice crying out for me and for Brute alternately. All the windows were closed or I suppose she would have used one of those.

I plodded downstairs and opened the door to the blustering chill wind, and there she was shivering in an oversized black fur. She was overly made up and wearing a long string of pearls around her neck and some silly-style shoes that require one to master the art of walking on razor blades. She was dressed at the height of young fashion, shivering on my doorstep, looking for Brute.

I, sleepy-eyed, tousle-haired, in nothing but a bathrobe—I wear nothing to bed—just stood there.

My door, programmed for a brisk entry, had only a three-second delay. It snapped shut between us.

I opened the door again and held it open.

"He's not here," I said.

Maggie nodded. "I guess I didn't really expect him to be."

She stood in the doorway. Wind whisked snowflakes on my bare feet. The door whirred in mechanical imperative to shut itself.

"Can I have some coffee?"

I squinted at the clock for the time—oh dark hundred—looked down at my bathrobe. "Not very decent," I said.

She burst into tears and wailed, "This whole bloody

affair isn't very decent for God's sake Anthony let me in!'' She said it all strung together like one sentence.

I let her in.

She trailed me into the kitchen, where I put on the coffee water, she in her black fur and silly shoes and I in my bare feet and robe. Coffee making was a serious operation here, not to be trusted to automatons. The wizards of modern efficiency with their boiling water on tap and quick brews would leave us nothing to fumble with in desperate or awkward situations. This situation was fast becoming both.

I said something about heartbreak. Maggie said it was her pride more than her heart that was damaged now that she thought about it. It had seemed a grand thing at seventeen to be a pilot's girl. She was eighteen now, older and wiser, and over all that. She was going to be a pilot herself.

"A pilot rather than a pilot's rib," I said. A woman named Mary Magdalene could not miss the reference.

She nodded. And there the conversation died. It didn't just die. It went into rigor straightaway. Maggie leaned against the robot oven twisting her pearls so that I thought she would break the string, except that I guess they are engineering pearl strings to withstand that sort of thing. I can't figure what else long strands of beads are for. Me, I was watching that coffee as if it required all the concentration of brain surgery.

I would have felt more secure if I'd only had some clothes on. Shoes would have made a difference. My eyes drifted up to the ceiling, down to the floor. I turned my head to the side. I inhaled to speak. Didn't.

Maggie developed a sudden intense interest in my plants on the windowsill.

I scratched the side of my nose. Took up the coffeepot. Put it down. It was not anywhere near done. I left it there, turned around, and said, "Um, do you think we might be more comfortable on the couch?"

"Good possibility," she said very seriously, a serious crease in her young brow, with a serious adult frown.

We went out to the parlor in silence. I thought we would fall into each other's arms, but we didn't. We sat on the couch. Not at far ends, but not exactly together.

Now what?

I thought I had made it rather clear that I wanted to hold her. Or didn't she think she was sure? Or hadn't I been clear at all? If I made a stupid move and mauled this girl when that was not what she really wanted at all, I would never recover from it. I cursed my long hiatus from dealings with women. What if I was mistaken? I kept my hands on the couch cushion.

I talked idiocy. She talked idiocy back. We wouldn't look at each other.

She kicked off her shoes and crept one stocking foot over to my bare foot, and we played tentative games with our toes. And talked blather.

I had a clock with an analog face. She, accustomed to digitals, asked how I told time with it when it only went up to twelve. I explained it to her.

Finally she said, "This is ridiculous. I'm saying one thing on the floor and up here I'm talking about your bloody mantel clock."

I stopped talking, shifted to face her, took her hands and held them in both mine, and looked into her eyes. Our gazes kept shying down, but we managed to look at each other at last. I started to put my arms around her and take her to me, then I stopped, pulled away, and said, "Go home."

Maggie put up a protest. I reminded her who she had come here looking for.

"What? Who? Him? Not really," she said. "Not really."

She didn't see why she had to go. I told her she just had to was all, and I got up.

"You're gay."

"No."

"I'm ugly."

"No."

"You want me to stay." Maggie tugged on the belt of my robe for me to sit back down.

"I swear I do," I said into her eyes.

"Then what is the problem?"

I took her shoulders and lifted her from the couch. I had trouble thinking of what I was saying with her scent flooding my nostrils, and I had to concentrate to keep from babbling. I start showing a trace of an accent when I am very drunk or very tired. Yes, an Erden accent. ''You don't know me. You came here on a rebound. It is an obscene hour of night. You're probably not thinking clearly—I know I'm not. I am probably acting like a perfect ass—''

''You are.''

''And so.''

''Let me stay.''

I was ushering her steadily toward the door. She brushed against me, glanced down. ''Anthony, you really really really don't want me to go.''

''I know.''

''Then why are you doing this to me?''

''You might not feel the same tomorrow,'' I said. And that was the real reason.

''I'll take my chances,'' said Maggie.

''I'm not just talking about protecting *your* feelings if you change your mind. I can be hurt too.''

That slowed her down. She had never considered that. ''I didn't think men felt that way.''

''This one does.''

''That does it,'' she said firmly. ''I won't change my mind.''

''Tell me that in the morning,'' I said and touched the door panel.

''Can I have my shoes?''

I was so quick to be rid of her I had forgotten she'd taken them off. The door shut itself.

I went in and fetched her shoes. I opened the door again. It shut. Maggie turned around and slapped it. ''What is with this thing!''

''Put your shoes on.''

She held on to me as she balanced on first one foot, then the other. She stalled at the door. ''And what if I do?''

''What?''

''Tell you in the morning, that is?'' she said coyly with her pearls pulled across her lips. She made sideways with the eyes, and gnawed prettily on a pearl.

I hit the panel and bundled her hastily out the door. ''Then I'll fuck your eyeteeth out.''

* * *

The door chimed at sunrise. I had just cleaned out the coffeepot and put new water on the heat. I took the pot off and answered the door.

There she was. First time I had ever seen her make a civilized entrance, I think. Nearly civilized. She jammed herself into the doorway before it could shut itself in her face. "I've come to have my eyeteeth extracted," she said.

What more can I say?

VI.

Maggie claims I lied. I did not do what I promised.

"I didn't?" I thought I had.

"I have never been there, but this feels suspiciously like love," said Maggie.

OK. I lied. Do you know what hour it was when I said that? "So I brought you here under false pretenses. I could still make good."

"No you couldn't. You are too gentle and too caring," said Maggie. "You're different."

This last comment I took as a barb. "I know that," I said dryly.

"But you're thin-skinned, Anthony. It was supposed to be a compliment."

"Then I thank you."

Maggie nestled under my chin, grinning under her blond hair like the cat who ate the canary, and hugging me. My well-trampled pride was puffing up nicely.

"Tony—"

"Don't ever call me Tony or I'll beat you."

"You wouldn't," she said.

"You won't call me Tony," I said.

"*An*thony. Have you ever been in love before?"

"Yes."

She slapped my chest. "You're supposed to say no." She thrust out a pouting chin and planted it on my sternum. She puffed her bangs from her eyes. "I haven't."

She said I was the best she'd ever had.

"Maggie, I don't care."

All right, yes, I was lying again. But she didn't have to say that.

So here she was in my bed, giggling and grinning and blushing and snuggling close. I missed my first class. My next one was starting and I didn't care. I was wondering if I should make another attempt at brewing coffee.

"Anthony, have you ever killed anyone?"

That took me off guard. It was a while before I could answer. I thought it was hardly appropriate conversation given the circumstances.

She explained, "I was thinking about becoming a combat pilot. I'd have to be prepared in case I have to do more than fly all this terrific equipment around. I haven't the vaguest idea what it must be like, and I don't know anyone who does. I mean, it can't be like the simulators." She moved her finger. "That's it. Someone's dead."

All I had to offer was very pat and very simpleminded, but it's what I believed. "You take an oath to defend your country. From there you must have complete faith that your admirals and your government would never send you up unless absolutely necessary."

"I'm ready to defend my country," said Maggie. "But . . . trust the judgment of a democracy?"

I laughed. "That's not very Tannian of you to admit, Maggie."

"*You* don't trust the system. I've never seen you vote."

I never told her I don't *have* a vote. I only did Burke's. I let the point slide.

"Then I guess it comes down to whether you're willing to stake everything on 'My country right or wrong.' "

"Now *that's* not very Tannian," said Maggie.

"And it won't exonerate you in a war-crimes trial in case you lose, but I still think it's a legitimate philosophy. If you don't have that attitude, the fleet won't put you in a plane."

We continued this talk for a few hours. I missed every one of my classes.

In the end, Maggie went in to see about becoming a pilot.

Maggie is a sandbagger. The reason she was able to follow my explanation of hypersonic aeronautics that night in the library was that she already had subsonics well under her belt. She could build an engine. I didn't know it but she had been in an engineering track at the academy. She already had an air pilot's license and had hours enough for a commercial rating, though she never applied for it. I didn't know either that she had ridden horses competitively. She had done all kinds of things I did not know about.

"I was a spoiled little kid," she said, shrugging.

I was impressed. So was the Fleet. They took her on the spot, midterm.

Following that morning I was in heaven. Poor Maggie was running into difficulty. I should have foreseen this.

She came over to the house early one day, when she was supposed to be in class. It seems some schoolmate of hers had commented, "A step down for you, Mag—from pilot to schoolteacher."

"What did you do?" I asked.

"I hit her," said Maggie.

Maggie hadn't just hit her. She'd punched her with her fist.

Luckily the other woman was a pilot-in-training also, who would rather die than admit she had been hurt by fluffy little Maggie, so the incident went unreported.

I can't say Maggie was exactly unhappy, but all was not well with her. She did not tell me all the incidents. I could tell she was withholding stories from me.

Maggie was a born astronaut. The limiting altitude for astronauting on Tannia is eight kilometers. When the time came, Maggie passed her solo perfectly. There are two types of combat pilot: air and space. You have to learn to function in both media, but in time you show a preference, like handedness.

In the atmosphere the major problem to be overcome is not thrust—you have more than you can use—it's friction. Up to mach one, drag increases in relation to the increase in speed by its square. Go twice as fast, you face four times the drag.

In space, you go as fast as your engines will carry you, unimpeded by anything but your own mass and the crush of acceleration.

We don't have faster-than-light travel. We don't have

anything approaching anywhere near light speed. Except of course the bend in space called the stargate, which brought the colonists here.

Weapons only go light speed, the fastest of them. And the speed of the ship firing does not speed them up. Light speed plus 77.99 kilometers per second is still light speed, and that's a law of nature, Jack.

Maggie is a spacewoman. She likes weightlessness. She likes being able to jump sideways. She likes instant turns.

And space is, in some ways, more forgiving.

Open-house time came around again, a recurring event on base almost as dreaded as an Occon pass. It's one of those PR days the military abhors but needs to keep the program popular with the taxpayers.

At the influx of civilians, any military person who could get away with it ran for cover (''I mean, what do you *say* to a civilian?''). Everyone else polished their buttons and their smiles, and shoved me at visitors: ''Talk to them, Northfield.''

I managed to kick lose in time to see Maggie run through her space trials.

The place was overrun with parents and spouses and children and curious voters, so even I was allowed in the command center. At least I walked in unchallenged.

Maggie was doing her orbital.

I heard her amplified voice come over com: ''I found your Occon bogies. Please advise.''

The return message from ground control stated, ''No bogies, Dagger Nine. You're alone up there, Collier.''

A hesitation, a nervous return: ''I am not alone. Is this a test?''

Annoyed and pressured in front of an audience, the ground controller sent, ''Collier, the screen is blank.''

The screen was projected big as the enormous wall for all visitors to see. Maggie's was the only blip.

''Then what are those?''

The projection on the screen flickered as Maggie turned on a camera and relayed the image down.

What Maggie saw filled up the wall.

Those were Occon surveillance drones. RAM-skinned

passive recorders, they weren't sending out any signals to be detected by ground control's instruments.

A gasp whispered through the gallery, and my blood stopped. Maggie had blundered into a swarm of Occon spy machines.

Ground control barked, "Arm yourself, Collier. Code red. Repeat, code red. Your guns are operational. Get them!"

Every single hair on my head felt to be on end. The code is never spoken unless the emergency is real. Otherwise one refers to "the unmentionable code." The ground controller had spoken the unmentionable by name, so there could be no mistake. I was not watching a war game.

A superior officer snarled to a subordinate at the same time, "Scramble some real pilots, now!"

Meanwhile Maggie commenced shooting Occon drones. On the big monitor one could see them being picked off one or two at a time.

I stood up, wanted to shout. There was too much noise. A sudden war situation, and an officer was commanding, "The civilians will leave the premises."

Maggie didn't have her jammers on. That was so *we* could track her. It left her open to anything else that wanted to locate her. Add to that she had her transponder on. Might as well have been wearing a big sign that read, "Shoot here."

After a short delay, as if it finally penetrated the robot brains that they were being shot, the flock of them abruptly started to run. Machine minds do not lag that long. Someone had recalled these orbs. Someone else was out there.

I was up in the gallery where I couldn't shout loud enough to get through to Maggie, but I heard the words I wanted to say sounding in my ears as if there were a microphone in my brain, broadcasting. The voice belonged to Maggie's instructor, the Tannian ace they called Brass Ones. "Turn off that transponder, for God's sake! Look out for the escort, Maggie!" To the controller, whom he slapped, he roared, "Get that goddam signal off her!"

"What escort?"

The one that had to be there.

All at once, a red line appeared on a monitor's screen, extending from a blank part of the screen to Maggie's blip. Someone else was shouting, "Laser, Maggie! You've been pegged!"

Maggie's voice: "Oh shit!"

Abruptly the camera image spun around and around. She'd been hit, her ship sent whirling like a top.

"Her life support is out," a controller said matter-of-factly.

VII.

I held my breath. Something tore and fell away inside. Some part refused to believe.

A controller coldly clicked off the whirling image beamed from Maggie's camera. Replacing it was the instrument display. The blip that was Maggie's ship was still there, and it was firing, spinning and firing once every turn like a pulsar.

Maggie . . .

Someone finally got a ground camera aimed and resolved, and projected the image on the big screen—Maggie's ship turning like a yappy dog chasing its tail and barking up a fury.

Wider angle showed the elusive target of the spinning ship's once-per-revolution fire. None of the other instruments were picking it up, but it showed up on camera. The invisible menace was revealed.

An Occon fighter.

Not a drone, but a spaceplane, smooth, black, tracker-invisible. Occon characters on its hull read: 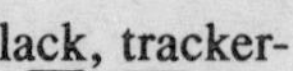, which is a number, 2734.

It had shot Maggie from three thousand kilometers away. It moved in now, nearly on top of Maggie's ship.

It easily avoided the crippled Dagger's shots.

A controller spoke. "She must have suited up. That's not autofire."

Oh God. Oh God.

Brass Ones bolted from the room, vaulting over some people clogging the doorway on his way out.

I overheard pieces of a hundred exchanges, sifted out the important ones.

"—Can't we get a shot at that thing from the ground?"

"He doesn't read on anything. We can't sight."

"We've got the goddam *camera* on him. Sight from that!"

As if the Occon had overheard, the enemy ship glided behind Maggie's ship.

"Is that craft dead? Can we shoot through it?"

NO!

"Unknown. Someone said it's not autofire."

Meanwhile the ground controller was trying to raise Maggie. "Dagger Nine, come in. Are you operative, Cadet Collier?"

Silence from com. Either Maggie's transmitter did not work or she was not taking time to respond.

Answer, Maggie. You're alive. There's a maniac down here who wants to shoot through your ship. Answer, Maggie!

"—What about a fixed-point X-ray laser? What kind of ship is that cadet in?"

They still wanted to shoot through Maggie to get the Occon.

"Hard body. Negative on the laser."

"Damn."

Fuck you!

A voice sounded on the com. Not Maggie's. Male and foreign. A question.

Someone demanded of the ground controller, "Who is that?"

"The Occon."

And Maggie's transmitter blistered to life with a spate of obscenity. She launched every weapon she had at the Occon, missiles, beams, everything. Her ship looked like a sparkler.

But her computer sight must have been out, because nothing hit.

The Occon evaded the barrage lazily. He transmitted something else and withdrew.

By then our ships would be coming out of the atmosphere. I doubted they would catch him.

I was feeling faint, my head light and swirling, not quite connected. I had heard Maggie's voice. Death had passed her by. Guards were hustling me with the rest of the civilians out of the control room. I let myself be evicted. There were so many civilians on base it was a simple matter for me to get myself conveniently lost and end up where I did not belong.

I trekked across base to the landing field in time to see a Harpy Class ship put down with the wreck that had been Maggie's Dagger in its clutches.

Brass Ones appeared in the hatchway of the Harpy, a heroic brass-plated strutting little turkey cock of a Tannian ace doing what I should have done. He guided a drunkenly staggering Maggie down the ramp. The ground was solid, but Maggie's brain was yet spinning. She stepped out with a Coriolis-ly placed foot, careened into Brass Ones, who righted her again.

I tried to hop the fence. MPs stopped me, but Brass Ones looked over at the noise and shouted, "Let him through."

I ran in to the Harpy's ramp. Brass Ones bundled Maggie at me. "Your puppy, Professor?"

I grabbed her and held her.

"Your puppy needs a bath."

She had thrown up at zero g. Leave it at that.

Anyway it would be a while before I could take her home. The military would be here any second to snatch her away for debriefing.

I thought Maggie would be traumatized. She was fighting mad.

"I want that ten-forty'd son of a bitch! Did I hit him?" "Ten-forty" is a Tannian curse of uncertain derivation. "Did I hit him?"

" 'Fraid not, Maggie."

She flailed in my arms, fists clenched. "What did he say to me? Does anyone know Occon?"

"That was Erden, Collier," said Brass Ones.

Maggie yanked her chin in, scowled, eyes floating to the left, snapping back to center, floating left. "Erden! He was Erden?"

"No, dear. Your ship had 'Erdetechnik' stamped on its hull, and you were swearing in two languages." Those are the only Erden words every Tannian knows. And some words do double duty. Erden for "damn" is "damn." "He thought *you* were Erden."

"How dare he? What did he say?"

Brass Ones' eyes slid to me. "My Erden is rough. Why don't you, Professor? Did you hear it?"

"I heard it."

"What did he say!" Maggie shrieked.

I answered, "First the Occon asked if you were alive. After you assured him you were alive and bilingual he said, 'Come back, puppy. Come back when you are a dog.' "

What became of the ships which were scrambled to chase the Occons was classified information. Here is what I learned long after the fact:

The presence of an Occon fighter of small size (one man, or two in tandem) and limited speed (he was clocked at thirty kilometers per second) in our space indicated that the Occons possessed what Tannia did not, a spacecraft carrier, or mothership as some call it.

The Tannian squadron had a good idea where the Occon mothership was lurking. They calculated the vector from the Occon drones' flight, then took the time between Maggie's destruction of the first drone and the time when the drones started to run—fourteen seconds—and halved that. From that they guessed that the mothership, the brain for those little drone nerve endings, was seven light-seconds distant—two million kilometers.

Two million klicks is a very long haul, half a day one-way, and the pursuit ships had no insurance that what they sought would stand still for them. They had no idea of the mothership's configuration, its firepower, its speed, or what it could carry besides one fighter and a flock of robot spy drones. It was imperative that the squadron get a look at it at least, disable or capture it at best.

They did not do any of that.

They never came back.

Maggie's career was pretty much made. No one bothered pretend but she had full wings in the bag. You would hear officers figuring squadrons and assume Mag would be in one of them. "Let's see, when Collier gets out of the academy . . ."

"They'll probably want Collier over at Trevane . . ."

As Brass Ones told her, "For a girl, Collie-pup, you've got balls."

I'm guessing they also told her she could do better for herself on the personal front, because, next, Maggie wanted to make me a pilot.

She tried to coax me into the program even though I was thirty-eight standard years old, close to thirty-nine. She was all enthusiasm for this scheme. She hovered about my shoulder, chattering as I stacked logs by the fireplace. We had a fondness for wood fires in the evenings. "You're not too old," she said. "I checked. But you have to start this year. Your reactions are fast. You could be rejuvenated. You already know everything they teach in ground school. And you love spaceplanes, Anthony. You could learn to fly. I know you could."

"I can fly a plane," I said without much expression.

She was surprised. She hadn't ever guessed. She had just assumed I couldn't. Everyone assumed that because I didn't, I couldn't. Logical enough. But *cannot* can mean *unable* or it can mean *not allowed.*

After she was done being shocked she was overjoyed. "Well then, you've got a big start! Why don't you enroll?"

"I can't," I said.

"Why not?"

I put down a log, straightened up, and faced her. "Maggie, what brought this on?"

"Nothing!" she said too ingenuously, surprised that I should think anything at all had brought this on. What in the world could I possibly mean?

"Are you ashamed of me?" I said.

Hearing it spoken, she could not hide. Her eyes dropped to her silly shoes. "I guess I am," she admitted, near tears. She was ashamed of being ashamed.

I think my eyes hit the floor too. I wanted her to be proud. And I could never make things right for her. It's why I avoided women, why I should have left her to her own life.

She drew in a great sniff and cried, "Why don't you

defend yourself? You just let them look down on you and they call you Kiwi and you let them—how can you? Either you're far above them or a coward.''

''And which do you suppose I am, Maggie?''

She bit her lip.

''Answer that, Maggie.'' It came out a command. She was not used to hearing force from me.

''If you entered the program they couldn't say those things.''

''You did not answer me.''

''You didn't answer me! Why?''

I did owe her an explanation.

I brushed soot off my hands and made her look up at me. ''Maggie. I can fly. I can fly a fighter. At the Battle over Trevane, two years before you were born, I was a pilot. I was an ace.''

The focus of her eyes—they were blue today—seemed to turn inward for a moment, and her lips moved as if pronouncing my name, Anthony Northfield. Then she looked at me and shook her head. ''I never heard of you. I know all the aces.'' She pouted, then her brows contracted. ''Though—'' The name must have sounded familiar suddenly, but not enough for her to place, because it was not quite right.

''Anton Nordveldt,'' I amended.

They Tannized my name when I came here. With the proper accent it does not sound as close as it looks in print. No one ever blinked at my Tannian name. You could hear the two spoken in the same sentence and not connect them.

Maggie's hands went to her mouth, and the blue eyes got very very big.

I was an ace. On the other side.

I was the Kralle in the KR-22 that Hal Halson's T-15 did doughnuts around.

''And if I go near another spaceplane they have orders to shoot to kill.''

VIII.

The last time I had anything to do with women was back in 179. I had been out of prison for two years by then and at great pains to eradicate any trace of an accent from my speech. I was teaching at the academy, trying hard to fade into the Tannian woodwork. I was succeeding. And was very lonely.

I stopped into a local pub one evening and saw two young ladies who apparently worked out of there. I heard them speaking in Erden.

I must have cranked my head around and looked, because no sooner had the man at the table told them to take their trade elsewhere than the taller one caught her companion's eye and cocked her head toward me, and they closed in.

They pulled up a barstool on either flank. They made me an offer in Tannian. I answered in Erden—not what I had meant to say at all. I had meant to say yes. Instead, like a sanctimonious creep I asked how they could do this to themselves.

Their eyes widened, first at hearing their native tongue, then at the rebuke. We got hot at it—hot angry, not hot passionate. The taller one asked what *I* did for a living. I told them I taught at the academy. She said I was no better and started off in a huff. I said, "Where are you going?"

She said, "What's it to you?"

I said I wanted to hire one of them.

She said since I had reminded her of her native pride she wanted nothing to do with scum who would buy woman's flesh. And out they went.

I gazed perplexedly into my beer.

The barkeep said, "Whatever you said, you sure told them, mate."

But I hadn't meant to. I was not a puritan, and I don't know what got into me. I had not yet accustomed myself to doing without, and I really did want one of them since the moment I'd heard them speak.

As if I had conjured her, the younger one came back. She perched on the edge of the barstool like a bird about to take flight again. "I can't afford to turn down a customer even if Hilda can. I'm at the Braxton. Ask for Heidi."

I caught her wrist as she started to leave again, asked her to stay.

I bought her a drink. Several. We got nostalgic. She started humming a folk song which was more to the national heart than the militant blaring Erden national anthem. She crooned a few words. I started to hum along, then said, "Stop, stop, you'll get us thrown out."

She started to speak, still in Erden. I interrupted her. "In Tannian. For one thing, we have to learn. For another, we're making people nervous."

My Tannian was nearly flawless by then. Hers was heavily accented. "I can't. I can't this language learn."

I said, "Maybe if you spoke it instead of Erden you would learn. You're not trying."

I had more to say, but the barkeep butted in here to agree with the first words of ours he overheard that he could understand. "That's right. If you tried, you could learn it. See how well he learned yours."

She stared at me. Slowly she said, "They don't even know you are Erden." Shock and disgust filled her eyes. Blue eyes.

The barkeep hadn't known. He had thought I was just an educated man. He backed off gingerly. My face was burning.

"You don't tell them," said Heidi. "You don't even let them know what you are. And you criticize what I do!" She got up, started away.

"Heidi!"

She looked.

I, quite forlorn, said in Erden, "I was Anton Nordveldt. What can I do?"

"Tell them." She motioned with her head to the Tannians in the room.

"I can't."

Her blue eyes smoked. "Then I am not the only whore in this room." And she left me.

I was going to make one more try, got as far at the front steps of the Braxton, and I turned around. I'd had nothing to do with women since. Till Maggie fell out of the sky.

"Maggie? Mag?"

She backed away. "You're a Kralle."

This annoyed me. My past profession might not have been easy to guess, but my nationality could not have been all that obscure, not to her anyway. "What did you think this was, a speech impediment?" When I am sleepy or distraught the accent comes through. What I actually said was: *Vat did you thenk dis vass, a speesh ampediment?*

"An Erden nanny?" Maggie whimpered hopefully.

"Oh, I had an Erden nanny all right." I took her arm rather more roughly than I had to, sat her down, and told her just who I was.

I remember the eve of the invasion. There had never been a war, so there were no veterans among us. We were all young. But we were drilled and ready and we knew what we were there for. And we were so sure of ourselves. If I could ever be so sure of anything again! We were so *right*.

And when it was over we had lost. Anyone who had come to Tannia in command of a warship was tried for war crimes and convicted—those of us too stupid to go underground.

Die Sturmschwalbe was a one-man ship. That made me commander of my vessel.

I believed in my own innocence and thought it would protect me. I went on believing right up to the time the cell door shut in my face.

I was paroled after three years. And I was still on parole when I told Maggie who I was, what I had done.

Maggie came around. It was too late for her to decide I was a monster. She decided an enemy ace was better than a nice schoolteacher. Her fear faded and she started asking questions again.

She was still a little bit dubious.

"I thought Erden pilots wore diamonds in their teeth."

"I have a diamond," I said.

It is in the lower molar on the right side. You can only see it if I grin from ear to ear—something I hadn't done much in the past fifteen years. I grinned for Maggie.

"But you can't see it," said Maggie.

I explained that the diamond was not just a fashion with us. In case of a crash'n'burn and all that is left of you is your teeth and your diamond, they'll know who to weep for. The diamonds and their distinctive flaws are all registered at home. Mine says that I am Anton Nordveldt.

She giggled. "So we're being taught Tannian lit by a Kralle?"

"There is no Tannian literature, Maggie."

"English, then."

"That's about the size of it."

English is Tannia's national language, but Erders are better versed in the English classics than are Tannians.

Tannia had only in the wake of the war begun to realize that it had no culture, unless you count its pop culture, which is all flash, instantly pleasant, throwaway, and ultimately meaningless and unmemorable. Tannians have no heritage. No depth. They are flat-souled beings, artistic mayflies.

They woke up when they won the war and went to take possession of Erde. The whole normalization force must have stopped and gasped, like vandals in a cathedral suddenly aware of the presence of divinity. On Erde they found everything they had let slip away from them. All the art and wealth of thought from "that obsolete and faraway place" called Earth.

And suddenly they wanted to teach Mozart and Beethoven and Shakespeare and Descartes and Aristotle in Tannian schools. Tannian kids are going "Huh?" but they're getting it anyway. Enough people were seized by the sudden need for a history that almost faded away in the face of the usable, the immediately relevant, the ephemeral, the pleasurable, the faster, brighter, newer. These people yawn after three seconds and say, "What's next?" Teaching them was an ordeal.

And finding teachers was a trick. Erden nannies are in demand now on Tannia, and Erders do it to have employment.

So teaching was the only job I could get. It was in the terms of my parole that I not take a job away from a Tannian. There was no way in hell a Tannian could do what I was doing, so I thought my position was safe.

Maggie wanted to tell everyone who I was. I said no. She said I was silly and ought to let her. I barked at her that I forbade it. Only I think I used the word *vorbad,* I am not certain. Whatever it was I said, Maggie snapped to right quick. She told no one.

My last flight on the *Storm Petrel* came back to me. My engine was on fire—actually its coating was gone and the carbon was oxidizing. Carbon becomes stronger instead of weaker under heat unless it is exposed to oxygen. My engine was dissolving. My squelch system was failing, and I was hotfooting it, so to say, out of the atmosphere to kill the fire. I didn't make it. Fortunate, as it turns out, for the integrity of my hull was in question. But at the time I was making my best effort to get home. My port canard had sheared off and my ship was bucking like a live thing. That's when saw a T-15 in my port viewer. In my starboard viewer. Port. Starboard. Port. Starboard. Hal Halson doing doughnuts round my ship.

Hal Halson who died in a drunken crash'n'burn with a sixteen-year-old girl.

I looked at what I'd become. Not so bad as Hal. But I could not say I'd done all right. Spaceplane pilots don't do well on the ground. I had weathered the transition tolerably, almost tolerably. I tried. Or maybe I didn't. Why else did I take a position on a military base? Near spaceplanes? I was tempting fate. Because fate was inevitable.

Storm petrels never land.

* * *

After the fleet assured itself that all Occon craft had been driven from Erde-Tannian space, the war games resumed, to make a public show of unconcern. The fleet projected an image of having everything under control.

Brute Burke was a full pilot by then, and he won his division in a T-15.

Burke was a pig like Hal Halson. With a difference. Halson was an honorable man in the air. Brute was a pig wherever he went, and he should not have been in the air. He should not have been allowed to touch a space-plane. Still, I was beginning to confuse the two, so that they were inseparable in my mind. Whenever I tried to picture Halson, the only face I could see was ruddy and black-bearded and fleshy. It was Burke.

I was crossing the green going home from class when he saw me. He was with a group of other pilots. "Hey teach!" he called. "Stop over at the coffee shop."

"No thank you, Burke."

Fresh from his victory in the war games, he came striding over to me on his tree-trunk legs. His pilot friends were waiting for him in an impatient knot, wondering why he was bothering with me. He swung his heavy arm around my shoulders. "Come on. I'll buy you a doughnut."

I said nothing, merely made a small motion no, my face frozen into a neutral smile.

"Some other time, then," said Burke. And he saluted me in the sloppy way Tannian pilots greet each other.

I returned a loose approximate salute, wryly.

Burke grinned and returned to his friends. His eyes were not grinning. Because I'd scared him when I did that. Because he knew. I had given him an Erden salute.

When I came home Maggie met me on the porch shrieking, "I told him to get out! He won't get out!" He. Inspector Gortz of the Federales.

I should have been expecting him. A security crack-down always coincides with an Occon threat. There had been a major Occon threat, and the woman I was involved with had been in the middle of it. Of *course* Inspector Gortz was in my house.

He had no right to enter without my permission, and I told him so. He waited till I threatened him before he produced the court-ordered permit. He leered and asked me to repeat my threat.

I don't like being set up. But you can't fight the Federales. *I* couldn't fight the Federales. My work permit was provisional. Even my freedom was provisional. I was on perpetual probation.

So I let the inspector root through the house. I told Maggie to make herself gorgeous while I started dinner—the most expensive thing I had, and I broke out a bottle of fine wine. Maggie comes from money, so we had some exquisite things in stock. I put a cake in the upstairs oven in what used to be Burke's rooms. Aroma of baking pervaded the upstairs, and downstairs savored of sizzling karranel steaks. I set a table for two, lit a fire in the fireplace. Maggie made her entrance looking *edible.* She put together some elegant canapés and brought them out under Gortz's nose.

The thin pale man with drooping mustache never ate like this, and not with a pretty young woman. That kind eats alone and out of a bag. He made cow eyes at the food, told Maggie it looked good, and, upon being ignored, he left.

The next day the chairwoman of the board of the academy called me in. "You are . . . living . . . with a student."

It startled me that this should be news. Maggie and I had been together quite some time. It startled me that it merited comment.

"I'm not living with her," I said. Maggie still maintained her own residence in the pilots' colony, though she was not in it much, only as required. "I sleep with her. We also fornicate."

The chairwoman received this like a wave of bad odor blown in her face. She blinked, then she continued properly, "Bad policy. You know you are not to . . . sleep with your students."

"She's not my student," I said. "And she never was."

"Eh?" She made a hasty check of the records and saw

that I spoke true. She had just *assumed.* As if it were inconceivable for there to be any reason for a young woman to be with me unless she needed a grade. "How did you meet, then?"

"She fell out of the sky into my arms."

"A man in your delicate position ought to mind his place."

"I am all too aware of my delicate position."

"Then you will understand ours." She always hid behind some mythical plurality of authorities when making decisions, so as not to be alone and accountable.

"Can we make this fast?" I asked. "I have a class."

"You have time, Mr. Northfield," she said.

"I—" I started to question, being on that particular afternoon rather slow on the uptake. Then I understood. I had only to hear it said.

"You are being suspended, Mr. Northfield."

The sinking sensation was upon me before my mind could catch up. "Until when?" I asked cautiously. This could be nothing more than a slap on the wrist. Surely.

"Until we tell you."

That was academese for forever.

"That is all, Mr. Northfield. You may go now."

Go. Absolute limbo. In outer space without a ship.

Go where?

Inspector Gortz paid me another visit. He informed me that persons without an occupation relevant to the base or to the academy were not to reside on the grounds of said properties. Said I, I was still employed of the academy, I had been suspended, not fired, now get out before I report him for harassment and incompetence.

I should not have threatened him like that. Never ever threaten a paranoid. They are more dangerous than your most formidable rival.

And never talk confidently to the Federales. I told him I had not been fired, therefore he could not touch me. Naive me.

The field where the T-15s are hangared is protected by a computer-guarded fence. You can't get over, under, around, or through without a gate key.

Burke waylaid me on a walk through the bluebell wood. He knew I had been suspended, and he knew I came here when I wanted to think. It's the Kralle in me—strict schedules and always predictable. Brute was swinging a gate key on his fat forefinger, and it flipped off and dropped to the path at our feet. "Oops," said Burke and did not pick it up. He stepped on it as he walked over it. He didn't look back. He left it on the bricks.

I just can't let a key—especially one to an airfield—lie on the ground. I suppose he knew that. I picked it up. Of course he would not take it when I tried to hand it back to him.

He casually told me his soloing schedule. Every other Ascendingday at dusk, Burke took up a T-15. Now, if he just *happened* to be jumped in the air, naturally he would be compelled to defend himself.

"That's quite lovely, Burke," said I. "If you lose you lose, but if you win you were only defending yourself. Whereas if I lose I lose and if I win I lose. It's my neck all the way around."

He shrugged his beefy shoulders. "Hey, teach, you touch a plane you never land. So why should I put my ass on the line? You either fly or you don't."

"All the risk is mine."

"Yeah." He nodded. "So is the choice. Nobody's putting a gun to your head."

"Why should I?"

"*Don't* then, Kiwi. I knew you weren't a real pilot."

The other shoe fell. Or, as a more accurate analogy, they chopped off the other testicle.

I was fired. I could have expected that.

What I couldn't expect was what happened to Maggie. She came home—my home—in tears. She'd been dropped from pilot's training. She had passed all the tests. More than passed. They would not keep her because fighter pilots should have no "doubtful associations."

That's me again. A doubtful association.

This was more crushing than anything that had happened thus far. It was bad enough being a grounded pilot, but I had been directly responsible for grounding another pilot. My fault. And I loved her. I couldn't touch anything but it fell apart.

I let my head fall back. "That's it. That's it. That's it."

I told Maggie to leave me.

"No!"

"Do, Mag. Because, you see, it's not really up to you."

"Oh no! You're not leaving me. You can't live without me."

"This is true, Mary Magdalene," said I. "I'm committing suicide the fun way." I went to my room and retrieved the gate key. Maggie recognized it for what it was.

"You can't fly!"

"*Mayn't* fly, Maggie," I corrected her. "I can fly."

IX.

Maggie pointed at the gate key. "Where did you get that?"

I told her Brute had been pushing me to fight him ever since he learned who I was, and I had just run out of reasons not to. I caved in. "I accept."

Maggie said, "They'll throw you in prison."

Implicit in that statement was her faith that I would win. Either that or she did not understand what losing entailed. She had survived a shooting. Kills are usually more thorough.

I also counted on winning. "It will be worth it," I said. "I can't live this way."

"Anthony, stop this and marry me."

"They've yanked your pilot's clearance."

"I don't care."

"You will. If I can't be a hero for you I can at least be notorious for you."

"I take it back. I love you any way you are."

"And it's not just for you. You know that."

I put my things in order. Maggie followed me, stepping on my shadow all through the house. I think she was talking. My thoughts were shut tight so I don't know what she was saying.

I was thinking of the odds.

It was to Burke's advantage that he had flown a T-15. Much as I admired the craft, and I had fought against one (and lost!), I had never been in one. The T was, however, modeled closely after the KR-22, with which I was intimately familiar.

He had youth—for what that was worth. My reflexes

were always like lightning and even slowed might be faster than Brute's.

I had the weight in my favor for once. In identical ships my mass would be a good thirty kilos less than Burke's.

My sense of equilibrium is all natural. They say I was born with a gyroscope in my ear. Burke had real gyros; they were implants. I don't know which is better. I only know I've never lost a direction.

My major advantage was that I had done this before—fired under fire. I had been shot at. Oh yes, the simulators are perfect. They feel and look exactly like the real thing. Only they can't simulate the clutch factor, the knowing that this time is real and you can really die and really kill.

I had killed. The first time you are never sure you can until you actually do it. Or fail to do it. Do you know what it takes to make a person kill his fellow human being?

And I had the discipline. We are a rigid society. Erders are ashamed to show emotion. We were expected to keep them in order. So I knew how to suppress for the time the overwhelming need to beat Burke's ass. Trying too hard is certain defeat. So I went very cool to the airfield. Cold, Maggie said. She called me a Kralle. That startled me out of my otherworldly state for a moment.

I had gone back to 174. It was the Battle over Trevane and I was going to meet not Brute Burke but Hal Halson, who was *not* going to do doughnuts around my ship.

At the same time it was also Burke. My tormentor. He'd slept with my woman. Is that the most primitive reason in the world to kill a man? Close, I suppose.

Maggie brought me back to real time, and I became aware of what she was saying. She was still begging me, if I loved her, not to go. "You don't have to do this. I don't care. I'm much older than when I said those things."

"You never said anything, Mag," I said gently.

"I'm much older than when I thought those things. Please, please, Anthony."

I touched her cheek. "Maggie, don't stop me."

"Could I? Really?"

I nodded. "But don't. I'd be a caged bird."

She cried and kissed me. "Damn you. Damn you."

And as I opened the gate she didn't try to hold me back. The gate shut between us. She waved.

I walked briskly to the hangar as if I were exactly where I ought to be.

A voice challenged me. "Aren't you on the wrong side of the fence?"

My insides seized up for a moment, but I recognized the voice. Burke. I flipped the gate key he'd given me into the dust. "You lost something."

He fell in step with me.

As we neared the hangars my pace slowed. "Burke."

He turned.

"Don't," I said.

"Scared? I'll finish you off quick."

"You're untested."

"Oh ho! Don't be so generous, teach. *You're* fifteen years rusty. I don't think you have the proper grasp of this situation. *I* almost didn't ask *you*, considering what a one-sided slaughter I expect this to be."

My second thoughts evaporated and my enveloping cloak of cold settled back around me. "Very well."

We had arrived at the hangars.

As I went in, some of my coldness slipped. I saw her. She was calling my name.

An artistic machine wants a delicate touch. I have been accused by someone in a position to know of treating my spaceplanes better than my women.

The T-15. The Fleet almanac lists her rather dryly thus:

> ***Contractor:*** *Tannia National Defense Corporation*
> ***Power plants:*** *two Chrysalis turboramjets, convert at speed into scramjets. One X2R space rocket.*
> ***Accommodation:*** *pilot only.*
> ***Dimensions:*** *span spread 14 ft 0 in, fully swept 12 ft 0 in, length 25 ft 1 in, full height 14 ft 0 in, height swept 12 ft 0 in.*
> ***Performance:*** *(estimated) combat speed at S/L clean Mach 3, max speed at altitude more than Mach 15, no ceiling, absolute velocity in vacuum 20 mps, supersonic range 3000 miles, hypersonic range indefinite, unrestocked endurance 36 hours.*

Armament: *four fixed forward-firing beam guns; two beam cannon turrets with hemispherical firing range; two programmable space torpedoes carried internally. Torpedo bay cannot be opened in atmosphere.*

The T-15 was also retrofitted with a bionic firing mechanism, but neither Burke nor I could use it. Thought-activated controls must be customized to the individual pilot. Human brains don't come off an assembly line, so there is no universal way to plug them into computer hardware.

Naturally I had not been brain-mapped for an interface, and Burke could not use his because I made certain that I took his ship.

I climbed into the T, sat there a moment, felt a rush inside. I ran my hand lovingly across the instrument faces. Everything was where it was supposed to be. Just like my *Storm Petrel.* I touched the controls until they felt right. Sense of *déjà vu* was enormous. I inhaled the familiar machine smell which stirs me as the scent of melianthems does.

I fitted the helmet and mask to my head. I had no suit. If the cabin pressure went, so did I. That was all right. I did not care too much if I came back from this one, as long as I won the fight.

The twin keys were in place, waiting for me. I started her. The atmospheric systems came on. I felt her come alive under me, sensed the deep pervading thrum of nascent power. Outside, the antinoise transmitters killed the roar, making the ship more stealthy, but in here I felt a rumble.

The hangar opened to sunlight, like an eyelid opening to me having existed so long in darkness. It was a rebirth.

I needed to fly. It's a drive, like sex—you don't die without it, but you wonder sometimes if you are alive. When I dream of flight I feel a resonance with something elemental, like the memory of angels before the fall, as if, as Socrates held, souls once had wings and yearned to have them back again.

Maybe I wasn't as good at checking my emotions as I thought I was.

I was able to bluff the computer ground controller easily enough. At my request it obediently sent a drudge to slide me onto the launch rail without a challenge.

Countdown. The Chrysalis turborams engaged. I could feel them gather strength like a crouching cat. Boosters roared, and my ship began to move along the rail. My heart pounded with the acceleration. The land blurred past the ports. At launch speed I felt the lift like a billowed sail and my T shot off the rail. I was airborne.

Flying. Really flying. I turned a few loops for pure joy, dove and soared. I swept her wings back and blistered the air. I decided I *like* swing wings. *Die Sturmschwalbe* had been a fixed-wing craft. Hal Halson had unfixed one of my wings.

The T-15 is all she's cracked up to be. I spun her in circles. My com came to life. ''Nice doughnuts, teach.''

Those weren't doughnuts. He hadn't seen doughnuts. ''Watch these.'' And I looped around his T.

I couldn't see his face, of course, and he said nothing. But I knew, *knew* he was shocked. Perhaps he caught his first scent of death, the faint thought that maybe he was in over his head. But he did not offer truce.

I had gotten up first. Burke's first mistake. I could have planted him on the launch rail. But I let him get up. My first mistake.

We were blazing over the airfield. ''Field'' is imprecise designation. It's a whole damn prairie, bounded on the far sides by ocean and tundra.

We climbed, streaked over the clouds. I saw a pilot's halo, a shimmering rainbow in a full ring all around me as the sunlight spread its colors on the clouds. To see it signifies to the superstitious pilot (and we are, we are) a good flight.

Good for which of us?

We had fired no shots yet, still dancing and feinting like boxers.

The T-15 is fully defensible against itself. This would be the art of this confrontation, shooting a T with another T.

Engines are easy to target on, so they are heavily defended with dispersers. I could forget about hitting those. The vulnerable points on a T-15 are where the weapons come out: the forward gunports, the turrets, and the torpedo bay in the ship's belly. But as soon as a laser sight lands on one of those points it activates a reflector, sends the beam back into your own gunport—right where *you* are vulnerable. It can't do that with a torpedo, but a round of beam fire can usually take out one of those before it reaches you.

I made a few experimental feints. As I suspected, Burke had studied my recordings and he was waiting for me.

Well, I had studied my recordings too, and I was aware now of my old habits, so Burke did not hang me on any of those.

And I had studied Burke's training records. Did he think I wouldn't?

A rule of tactics: if it doesn't work the first time, it won't work the second time. If it works twice, don't use it a third because you have taught it to your opponent by then. Burke was always one to beat a line to death. And Burke thought rules only applied to everyone else.

I think he tired of our bait-and-wait game, because he suddenly shot up into space. The rules change in the *weltraum.* He knew I had no gyroscopes. He must have thought that would be to his advantage. If so, he guessed wrong.

I know which way is up even when the word is irrelevant. Put me in a centrifuge, I'll die or throw up before I lose my way. Ask me to pin a tail on a donkey, I'll get him. I didn't lose Burke. I can find an ass's ass.

Burke was not as good as he thought he was. Not as good as I thought he was. Maybe he just failed to realize how good you have to be to be an Erden ace. Who did he think I was? I caught myself inflating myself. I reminded myself to be careful now not to err in overconfidence.

He moved directly under me. I thought I was going to get a torpedo up my turret—the torpedoes were operational in vacuum—but he rose beside me. I didn't know where he was going, then I realized what he was doing—trying to. He thought he was going to do doughnuts around *me.* Stupid. Really stupid. No one does that to me while I have a whole ship.

I waited till he was over me and I sent a beam into his downside turret freehand. Without the computer-aided sight I hadn't activated his autodefense reflectors. My shot melted his downside gunports.

He left off his maneuver. He was no Hal Halson. No match at all, really. I was disappointed, but it was my turn. I did doughnuts. I did spirals. I got in behind him and gave him a push.

He was right. It comes right back to you. I was troubled by the vague sense that if this was the best the fleet had to offer—a top-graduated cadet who could not even hold his own against an aging ace—then we—we, Erde-Tannia—were going to be in trouble with Occo. But this was not foremost in my mind at the time.

I was exorcising all those humiliating demons of the past fifteen years, and I did everything to him.

But too soon Burke was scrambling back to the atmosphere at a velocity I could not safely overtake in reentry. His angle would take him over civilian airspace, where I could not shoot down at him without endangering the populace.

He was *running*.

I needed to get under him or let him go. With that came my first taste of fear. I had assumed this encounter would end with one of us dead. That Burke would run for safety and I return to land still alive to be arrested unvictorious had not crossed my mind.

This must not be. This was worse than death. I needed to get him. Now or never.

I armed one of my torpedoes and sent it after him. A spray of beams from his top turret detonated it before it was even close. Burke's top turret spat a steady string of beams behind him. My only chance was to get him in the belly where his beam turret was out.

To use either torpedo or beam I had to get under him.

It was too late. We were almost in the atmosphere. I would burn up if I tried to overtake him. If I fired a beam down at him and missed I could hit someone on the ground.

I was hurtling perilously close to the grasping planet with its thick layer of air; my computer was telling me my course was bad. It advised me to chart a reentry window. Too shallow an approach and my ship would skid off the atmosphere like a skipping stone on the water.

I was shallow and Burke was getting away.

I armed my other torpedo. A warning light told me that the automatic bay closing was imminent. I hit the override and held the door open.

I aimed my torpedo and let it go. It missed the reentry window, bounced, ricocheted off the atmosphere and right up into Burke's belly.

I wonder if he even saw it.

X.

Burke came down in a shower of meteors, red and white in the evening sky.

I came down to a squadron of Federales shooting at me. They did not demand ID; they did not say halt. They opened fire. I knew who had sent them.

I had a crazy urge to take them on. It would have been a turkey shoot. I ran.

I took them once around the great prairie. They were cops, not—no matter what they tell you—soldiers. I tried to return to base but they would not let me at it. I had outsmarted myself; I had left them so far behind that when I tried to come back they were still there to cut me off.

Then I used Burke's trick and made straight for civilian airspace. The shots stopped but the pursuers hung on. I tuned to the police frequency in time to hear a voice I knew shout at them to shoot, shoot, shoot. My pursuers answered that we were over a city.

"Shoot! That's an order! Shoot!"

Gortz, gone finally and absolutely mad.

He told them that I was carrying bombs and intended to drop them, so they had to get me despite the risk. At this the chase ships resumed shooting.

And I took my T back up to speed. The Chrysalis turborams converted into scramjets and I left the police ships as if they had been standing still.

My stubby wings were glowing. I could have gone forever like this. The T-15 is nearly a perpetual motion machine at this speed. The air itself wants rid of you, as if it is sneezing you along.

Gortz radioed ahead to another Federal station, ordering up another squadron of police ships to intercept me.

I didn't know what I was going to do. I wanted to blast that little man, but he wasn't in the air so I couldn't get at him. He was shouting orders to others from a safe place on the ground. I wished I did have a bomb.

Then a military squadron rose in my path. Flying Daggers. They demanded an ID and surrender. I gave them both. They told me to cut speed. I did.

A new set of Federales moved in, shooting. Luckily the squadron leader of the military Daggers was a colonel, which trumps a neurotic inspector, and she told the Federales to cease fire at once.

I let the Daggers flock in around me.

Then Gortz was yelling at me on the military frequency, "Halt! Halt! Halt! Put it down! Put it down now!"

I radioed back, "Where?" That for the military's benefit, so they would know what kind of man was after me.

"Put it down right there!"

"The civilian police will disengage communication," sent the colonel.

Gortz tried again. The colonel calmly told him he was cluttering the frequency, which is a serious charge on these worlds.

I liked the colonel's voice, crusty, unflappable. She reminded me of the search-and-rescue captain who had pulled me out of the water when I crashed *Die Sturmschwalbe* into the Tannian Sea.

"Dagger One to pilot of the T-15, are you still there?"

"I'm here."

"Well," the voice drawled, "where do you want to put it?"

"I am open to suggestions."

"We have a barrel, or you can take it back where you got it."

"I'll go to yours," I said.

The coordinates were sent into my guidance system, and we all turned like a school of fish toward the Daggers' home base at Trevane.

Landing is inherently the most dangerous part of flight. And the T-15 has two faults. One, she can't fly slow, and two, which is really an offshoot of one, she can't get up or down without help. On the ground she can't get out of her own way. And coming down, well, as I said, she can't go slow.

One thrill left before I was back on the ground. The wind barrel.

The base had the machine fired up and waiting for me. I could already see its roaring maw.

Sometimes the cadets balk here on their first training flight. It is, I suppose, like landing on an aircraft carrier used to be. The kids go white-knuckled and can't even let the computer bring them in. They have to go out in space, summon a Harpy to snatch them in and bring them down.

I started my approach.

The Daggers fanned away from me—to the dismay of the Federales, who thought they were letting me get away. The police ships moved in.

Well, let them try to follow.

My radar locked on the wind barrel. The computer said I was good. I transmitted my speed to the barrel. Green light.

Into the barrel like a bullet in reverse. I could feel the drag thicken around my ship, the winds roaring past. The computer indicated forward motion at zero. On went the clamps. The wind barrel's computer linked with mine backed off our speeds in unison until I felt my ship sag on its restraints and sink into its cradle.

I was down.

Quite down. I had the dull sensation, the emptiness that overtakes you after all the howling winds have died, when you listen to the silence and wonder, What is that?

Had I just blinked? It was not possible that I had already gone up, fought Burke, and come down.

I was on the ground. And still sinking. That is the problem with going up. It's such a bloody long way down.

Finally I stirred myself and opened the hatch, jumped down. My legs were unsteady beneath me.

At the end of the barrel I could hear a soldier talking to the operator. "You should've heard him. Damn civilian cop shrieking on the military band, 'Halt halt halt!' "

The soldier looked up as I reached the mouth of the

wind barrel, commented to me, "Don't know where he expected you to park it."

"I guess he had some opening big and windy enough." I climbed down and let him arrest me.

"Nicely done," said the barrel operator of my entry.

I had done well, no superfluous moves. It is a simple maneuver, one move done right the first time. Kids want to clutter the process with adjustments. They want to *do* something.

The Dagger pilots were coming in. They and the operator became a little hysterical to learn I had never flown a T-15 before. They wore fear-after-the-fact expressions upon learning that some neo had just flown into their wind barrel at speed, and now he tells us he's never even flown a T.

I told them I had landed in wind barrels before.

Those who had not caught on yet were confused. No other Tannian craft lands in a wind barrel.

But the Erden KR-22 used to.

Someone said, "You're a Kralle." And then, because "Kralle" was a general insult hurled at anyone you hate, he sputtered to clarify, "I mean a real one."

Said another, "Really?" The Dagger pilots were all young and curious. It was a convivial arrest. "What'd you fly?" they wanted to know.

"A KR-22. *The Storm Petrel.*"

Someone barked a laugh. "Ho boy."

"Oh *shit,*" said another. The way he said it I had a feeling I was on collision course with a surprise—something like a land mine.

I wasn't too concerned. The euphoria of the damned had me. It was hard to be upset about anything when I was futureless anyway.

The wing commander, the colonel, came over. "Nordveldt, isn't it?"

"Yes, ma'am."

She asked if I was part of the Erden insurrectionist movement known as Erde Shall Rise Again.

"No, ma'am. Completely private crime."

She said she understood there was a fatality.

I confirmed this was true. My cheerful guards sobered up.

"Let's go."

The base commander was coming out to investigate. Still at a distance, as she was coming across the airfield, I sensed something familiar in the matronly figure.

"Oh *shit,*" I said.

Thomasina Wright. Admiral now.

She'd been a colonel when I shot her down.

Of all military bases I'd chosen to put down here. I *knew* Thom Wright was at Trevane. Where was my brain?

I managed a stoic facade as she approached. She made a civilized show herself. She walked over phlegmatically, as if the admiral were simply taking a little stroll and not confronting the renegade Kralle who'd almost killed her in the war.

Her plump face was smooth, her hair prematurely white and pulled straight back.

"How have things been for you, Kommander Nordveldt?"

"Not good," I said.

She nodded. *Evidently.*

I couldn't help glancing down, a quick move, but one of those gestures you never never get away with, like glancing at your watch while someone is talking to you. You never get away undetected. Lady Thom saw my furtive glance.

"Everything functions, thank you," she said crisply.

I blushed. I'd done a lot of damage to Lady Thom's plumbing when I planted her ship in the ocean. I wondered, didn't dare ask, if she had children.

"Delayed posttraumatic crazies?" she asked.

"No, ma'am." I never suffered from flashbacks.

"What then?"

"A simple murder."

Her hairless brows lifted. "Hardly that."

"An unsimple murder."

"Don't ever make an admission like that, do you understand, Kommander?"

"Yes, ma'am." But I didn't.

To the others she barked, "The rest of you did not hear that. Strike it from your memory. When those pea-headed civilian badge-flashers ask, you heard no admissions of any sort.'' Then to me, more quietly, a comment: ''This is peacetime. You're pretty bad at this.''

''Yes, ma'am.''

The Federales swarmed in. They told the military to hand me over. They told the military I had carried bombs over the cities with intent to drop them.

I looked to the MPs who had me under guard and said, ''I would have, too. The Feds showed up just in time.'' The MPs all started laughing. Ts don't carry bombs. The Federales wondered what was so funny.

I was shuttled back to my own base, where Brass Ones kept shaking his head. ''I'll be damned. I'll be damned.'' He was envious, I think. He wished he could get away with a stunt like mine. But the fact was I hadn't gotten away with it. I'd just *done* it. And now I faced the consequences.

At my trial the prosecutor asked my state of mind when I killed Burke.

I froze. Not because I had been about to prevaricate. I'm sometimes too honest for my own good, and this was one of those times. I knew my answer would hang me.

Before I kill someone I have to dehumanize them. That's what the propaganda corps does in wartime, makes it palatable to kill the other side. Tannians pictured Erders with beaked noses and bared teeth, and called us Kralles to make it easier for Tannian soldiers to kill us. Same thing.

I could have claimed blind rage, said it was a crime of passion—which was how my defense wanted to handle it. Tannians understand an *affaire de coeur;* they can pity a jealous lover.

But my state of mind when I killed Burke—I had assumed a war mindset. I was cold as you please.

I said I didn't know how to explain.

The prosecutor told me that one of my shots had hit a residential neighborhood, that I had murdered an innocent bystander as well.

I felt the bottom of something drop out and leave a great hollow inside me. All the little hairs became cilia and my skin tried to creep away. I croaked, ''I didn't.''

I thought back. I hadn't, had I?

Weapons are classed self-limiting, fixed-target, or infinite. Self-limiting is anything that loses lethality with distance, bullets for example. Fixed-target are laser-type weapons that have one-point lethality and are harmless farther or nearer. Infinite weapons are beam guns, which continue until they hit something.

A T-15s beam guns are infinite, which was why I could not fire down on Burke as he was running away from me back to land.

I reran the duel in my mind. I hadn't shot down. I had been expressly careful not to shoot planetward.

I told the court I had killed Burke, I didn't care if I died for it, but I would not go with that other death on my head. I had not shot down.

They asked how I could know. There were many shots fired.

I told them I knew.

I was certain the wild shot could not have been mine. I felt icy as they replayed the computer reenactment.

It wasn't mine. I exhaled.

But it wasn't Burke's.

It was the Feds'.

Gortz on the stand said that the shooting had been necessary.

I guess someone forgot to explain my joke to Gortz, because he told the court that I had confessed to intent to bomb New Calais.

An awkward silence gripped the courtroom before someone broke the truth to him: Ts have no bombs. Gortz said that the fact made no difference; I had threatened to drop bombs and he had believed me.

Another squirming silence ensued before the MPs pointed out to Gortz that I had made the jest long after the fact, when I was, in fact, in custody.

And Gortz steadily became unraveled. He launched into an insane monologue and we all just watched, slipping down in our seats and pretending we weren't here. He ranted things so painfully preposterous that I believe Gortz's testimony was what made it impossible for the court to sentence me to death.

I wish I could tell what exactly became of him but I

don't know. He retired from the Federales after the incident. I wasn't in a position to follow up on his fate.

They threw me in prison, of course.

The sentence was solitary confinement for the rest of my life, with no parole.

I would still be in that solitary cell if Occo hadn't swallowed a Tannian invasion force without a trace, as thoroughly as a black hole, leaving Erde-Tannia critically short of trained fighters. But that was years later, and I could not see that far.

All I could see was the ocean tide's incessant rise and fall outside my solitary window.

PART TWO:

ERDE

I.

Someone once said they ought to shoot all the pilots after every war. Heroes get lost in peacetime; there is no place for them once the shooting stops.

What I would have done after the war, if I'd had my way, would be to pilot the Life Ship. Rescuing people and rushing aid to disaster zones is something I could have managed nicely. But there are only sixteen pilot slots on the Life Ship, and several hundred Tannian vets who wanted them. With me in prison for war crimes, guess who didn't get one of those sixteen positions?

Now with one count of premeditated murder to my name, committed while I was on parole yet, I could forget about seeing any position ever again, not even within prison walls. I was sent there to rot.

There are those who wanted me dead. But that's not the way the justice system works on Tannia. The death penalty is not used as a deterrent, nor even as justice really. It is a simple removal. Although I was incorrigible in that I would probably do the same thing given the same situation, it was a singular little situation not likely to arise again, so that killing me would serve roughly the same purpose as closing the cage after all the birds have flown. But I was spared reluctantly.

Said the judge, "This is not the old Earth Wild West, Mr. Nordveldt. We do not call each other out for duels in a civilized society."

And being a civilized man, he did not believe in the death penalty either. He simply locked me away. He sentenced me to sixty years for retribution's sake. Not to teach me anything—I learned no lesson in that solitary cell—but to make those outside feel better. As I still had twenty-eight years left on my original sentence, I figured I would be more than two dozen years dead before I was free again.

There were those who thought I never should have been let out the first time. Parole, they thought, should not be granted in the case of war crimes. War crimes—that was what the Tannians called what I did for my nation. All I had done then was what every other Erder was doing—fighting for our country. I had simply done it too well to be forgiven. Some Tannians thought I never should have been freed, or given a job. Now at last in their eyes I was being punished.

If I learned anything it was a sense of the rightness of what I had done. After all those years of servitude to Tannia, spiritually castrated, I finally reclaimed my *self*—my pride and my right to self-respect. I realized I was allowed outside only so long as I was meek and without integrity and I swallowed their abuse.

I rediscovered rightness.

I also rediscovered prison.

The first time I was in prison I wrote a chronicle of the first war. I had no idea then that the Tannians would ever let me out. I wrote in Erden. The work has never been translated. I started to, never finished.

Now I was in prison again and I found I could not write. I started. I put down: "It is the year 190. I have 59 years, 426 days, and 5 minutes to go and someone has glued the hands to the clock face."

That was my watch, the one with the hands. The wall clock was digital. Damn Tannian lack of grace. I smashed it on the fourth day. I tried a hunger strike but it didn't last. When one is confined, eating is the highlight of the day.

The prison was a big facility. The colonists had built it amply sized, anticipating population growth. But the Tannian justice system evolved not to rely heavily on incarceration. Jurists look upon imprisonment generally as unwieldy and self-defeating, preferring to have felons work off their sentences in community work, payment of fines, or service to their victims.

So for now the spacious building was like a tomb. I

was the only inmate in the solitary block. From my high window I could see the yard where the others exercised, but so distantly that even a shout arrived as nothing more than a shout, without form, the edges that would make it a word blurred past recognition.

And I could see my home, 768,000 kilometers away. I watched it creep through its phases night after night, fifty-two Tannian days to complete the cycle. And seeing Erde full in the night sky became an Event, quite as exciting as the arrival of dinner.

The Erden eclipse I saw every month, a black dot moving across her blue-white face. But, twenty-six days later, for a totality to occur here at the prison during the Tannian eclipse was so exceptional that when it happened I nearly blinded myself stealing glimpses of my homeworld swallowing Tannia's sunlight.

Erde is actually more than three and a half times the size of Earth's moon, but at twice the distance it loses most of its splendor. Yet even for its diminished profile there is still quite enough of Erde to effect a total eclipse, because our sun appears smaller than Sol.

I had a premonition of disaster during the total eclipse. I passed it off as the natural unease one gets at the dying of the light. But I remember during the totality looking toward the sun and seeing next to it a very bright star. What you see when the lights go out at midday is not exactly night. It is a sky you never see any other time. You see the heavens near the sun. I saw a bright star. It was Occo just coming past superior conjunction.

And I started waiting for Occo to appear as the evening star. Keeping track of Occo became one of the things I did. I watched it climb to its greatest elongation, then sink back toward the horizon and go under as it came up on a pass.

A pass is the local term for an inferior conjunction of Occo. At the pass Occo comes its closest to Erde-Tannia. Seven days after the pass a launch window opens. In theory, Occon ships could shoot out to our orbital path and intercept our planets in seven days. It had never been done, because the turnaround time is unfeasible—it's a very very very long voyage home. Seven days after a pass is a great launch window for a one-way trip only. So we had become accustomed to ignoring it.

I was up before dawn, watching for the morning star, when the alarms sounded. I thought it was a prison break. Oh good, I thought. This should be entertaining. I might even acquire a companion to yell down the hall to in solitary block when this was finished.

I looked out my window, saw prisoners running. It looked like the whole inmate population stampeding toward the gate. I saw guards running after them.

On second thought, it sure looked like some guards had caught up, but they were still running, running *with* the inmates.

I sensed the planes before I heard them. I have a heightened sense for when someone has a sight locked on me, and I knew all at once: My God, we're going to be hit.

I screamed to the guards, "Open the door!" But they were all gone, and here came the Occon spaceplanes.

Had they pilots they would have realized they'd made a mistake—that this heavily guarded and isolated installation was a prison, not a military base. But these were robots and they struck where they'd been told.

I was bouncing off the walls of my little cell when these things came out of the sky.

The first thing I thought was nukes. If I ever get hit by nukes I want to be at ground zero. I mean I want to be hit on the head by the bomb. Death by radiation ranks with slow dismemberment among my least favored ways to die.

I saw the plane, saw the drop. Hell, it was going to be close. Good.

I shut my eyes, held my breath, waited to be flash-fried. But I heard the blast. Not close enough.

I looked out the window. No mushroom cloud billowed up.

High explosives. Not nukes. I changed my mind. I didn't want them close.

Bombs dropping. Prison alarms blaring. I bouncing from one side of my cage to the other, jumping like an omro. I kept expecting the door to open. Surely some fail-safe system would let me out. But it didn't. I was going to be burned or boiled in here. All the personnel had fled, leaving me here half underground. This great mausoleum was going to be my literal tomb.

Then the sound stopped. All became still.

No one returned to assess the damage. My meal did not come. My water tap did not work. This was worse than the bombs. I was going to die here without water.

I heard distant reports like the muffled booms of fireworks that carry over the hills on Founder's Day. The attack was still underway. Perhaps when the bombing was over someone would come back.

I heard the robot spaceplane coming. I don't know how I knew what it was going to do. But then again, what else does one do with an empty attack plane that can't go home? One-way tickets all, the Occon ships had no means of being retrieved. And Occons would not want them to fall into our hands intact.

The spaceplane empty of bombs had one last explosion left in it.

That's when I became unhinged, utterly.

I lost my nerve. First time in my life. I started screaming.

The plane dove, howling like a Stuka.

The impact took the lights. The explosion brought down the walls. The ceiling of my cell buckled—I didn't have to see that to know it. Rubble piling around me, on me. My window filled in. Things fell on my head. Me scurrying wall to wall, till one fell in.

A deep roaring sound, the groan of a building in its death throes. The whole structure growled. Another crack overhead—great chunks of stone; how many stories was this wing and how many tons were piled over my head?

The metal doorframe of my cell bowed. The door popped off its locks.

I ran to it and opened the door.

With that the ceiling fell in before and behind. I flung my arms around my head as the earth rushed in. Pouring sliding rubble. Dust and darkness. Eyes filled with dust, tears. I cringed against the doorframe, the earth closing in.

When all was quiet again I discovered I could still breathe. I could not see. I could move, but not far. I felt around gingerly. Every touch brought a tumble of pebbles.

In the blackness my groping fingers attempted to read what had happened. The doorframe had held the avalanche off my head. It moaned from the enormous weight it bore. The door had dammed up the slide on one side. The debris itself, twisted beams and great stone blocks, had jammed against the doorframe and strangled off the onslaught on the other side. I had left to me a space the size of a coffin. There were no openings that I could find.

I was buried alive.

II.

Because my coffin-sized pocket in the ground was so dark I thought I was sealed in entirely, but air leaked down from somewhere, a cool draft, and the dark was perfect only because night had fallen. The night was eternal. Come morning the barest point of light glimmered through the piles of rubble overhead.

The day was longer.

The silence had returned and stayed. No one came, no guards, no food, no water.

The breeze that found its way down was hot.

The omros came for me. ''Omro'' is shorthand on the first Tannian surveyors' report for ''omnivorous rodentoid.'' The creature was never renamed. No rodents were brought from Earth, and judging from the omros I can see why.

Omros came for dinner. The old joke—they stayed for dinner. At least *I* had the decency to kill *them* first.

The quiet above persisted. No one was going to come looking for missing convicts. Not for Anton Nordveldt.

I was wrong. Maggie came. I heard her plaintive voice like a song. ''AAAnton! AAAnthoneeee!'' in a minor dissonant key.

I started yelling. Maggie came nearer. A pebble dropped on my head. I screamed, ''Maggie, don't step there!''

''What?'' Maggie came closer.

A rain of debris dropped, filling in the space around my feet like a grave. ''Maggie, don't step there!''

''Where?''

"I don't know!"

A few minutes of hysterical "Maggie!" and "Anton!" exchanges elapsed before one of us thought of something more coherent to say. I told her the ground over my head was not very stable. She said she would go get help.

It was soon after I heard Maggie dash away that an engine started up. I thought perhaps there was a rescue crew on the premises, but as the machine started to roll I knew from the sound that it was an earth-mover.

I started screaming again and absolutely no one could hear.

I can't believe what I did then. One of the stupider things I have ever done. I lost my voice.

I screamed so much that when the earth-mover shut down and Maggie came back amid others, I opened my mouth and nothing came out. Not a squeak. I could not make a sound if my life depended on it—which it most certainly did, because a man was saying he was going to doze the grounds. Maggie told them I was down here somewhere, and tried to make them believe it while I was yelling soundlessly.

"Anton, tell them you're alive! Say something!"

"Come on, lady, we got a deadline."

The workers were anxious to get out. Radiation is a kind of voodoo, and you can't convince some people there isn't any once they get it in their heads that there is. This man wanted to get his job done before his nuts fell off.

Maggie was insisting, "No, no, you have to find him! He must be hurt."

Someone came nearer, tromping heavily. Trash fell on my head. He stomped all around, while Maggie begged, "Be careful!"

"Where?" the stomper said. "Where?"

My glimmer of light shadowed over and I saw a bloated eye peering down. Then a pinpoint of light beamed straight into my eyes. I jumped, I waved, I whispered, "Here I am!"

He saw me. The light beam clicked off. He stood up. "Yeah. He's dead. Roll it."

* * *

I screamed. No sound came out.

Panic does things to you. It froze my brain. I was looking for something with which to make noise. I must've had my brains in a bag. It was Maggie's voice that brought it back to me. I stuck my dusty fingers in my mouth and gave the most eardrum-rupturing whistle a human being ever produced.

"Anton!" Maggie cried.

Wolf whistle.

"You heard it! You heard it! And you heard it!" Maggie cried. "You start that earth-mover, I'll have *you* down there for premeditated murder."

The earth-mover did not start up again. The next machine I heard, and I did not hear it until it was very close, was a low-vibration, nearly noiseless miner's rescue vehicle.

A collection of military officers came to me in the hospital to offer an alternative to going back to prison after I recovered—a commission in the Tannian fleet with a promotion.

It seems Tannia had a sudden dire need for trained pilots and would dredge anywhere to get them.

At first they said they would let me out for the duration of the Occon conflict, then afterward, if there was an afterward, we could discuss what bearing my service would have on my sentence.

I told them no.

I placed less stock in the generosity of a grateful nation than I did in the generosity of a desperate one. I told them to talk now and talk fast. And *that* was when they offered me a pardon and the promotion.

Truth was I'd have done it had they said they would not take a day off my sentence. I was so wild for the chance to fly again that the mere mention nearly made me leap at their first offer. But I hadn't forgotten how negotiations go, and Fortune had them in a bind, so they agreed.

I thought it very funny that because of what I had done—kill Burke—I got to fly again. The Tannians never would have enlisted my aid if I hadn't proved that I could still fly, that I was still fast, and I could still outmaneuver the best of their academy's new class. Crime paid with interest.

I ought to erase these paragraphs lest someone in authority have second thoughts.

Should ever someone actually see this.

The only thing left bewildering me was, since I had made such a bad enemy in the Federales, whose idea was it to let me out?

The answer left me no less bewildered—Admiral Thomasina Wright.

"Lady Thom" Wright is the same vintage as I pilot-wise. In years she is older. They say she is descended from the inventor of the airplane, but those records are lost, so it's just a story, though it makes a good tale.

Lady Thom shot down more spaceplanes than any other Tannian pilot in the war, and she has more assists to her credit than any other pilot on either side.

I shot down Lady Thom.

That does not make me a better pilot. For anyone who has not heard this story, Lady Thom was tricked. It was war and my side was losing. We do things we would rather not.

Thomasina Wright came upon my squadron in her ship, *Shrike*. The wise tactic when attacking greater numbers is to take out the tough guy first. That would be me. She went after *Die Sturmschwalbe*. Only I wasn't in it. I was in the unmarked novice plane next to it. She moved in and I planted her.

She lived. The only one of my kills who lived. (It still counts as a kill. The *Shrike* died.)

A chronicler tried to paint me devious colors. Lady Thom was very gracious and said no, no, it was a legitimate trap and she should have known. She realized as soon as she was *in* it that something was wrong, but by then I was taking her apart.

And she was the one who told the Tannian military authority to get one of its most competent pilots out of a cell and back into a cockpit.

With a promotion yet. In the Erden fleet I never ranked higher than lieutenant kommander, which is the equivalent of a Tannian major. The Tannians made me a lieutenant colonel for this war.

First thing they wanted me to do was hunt up some other Erden aces.

I was very dubious of this assignment. Many of my old comrades had gone into hiding to escape prosecution for war crimes. I did not think it my place to find my fugitive compatriots for the Tannians.

My commanders told me to offer them a full pardon and a commission.

Pardon implies wrongdoing, I said, pushing my limits.

And they let me push. Exoneration then, they offered.

Shocked by my easy victory—like the haggler who thinks he has priced himself out of the market till the buyer quickly says ''Sold!''—I became a little concerned.

''You're desperate,'' I said.

''We are desperate,'' they admitted. ''But you must help us. *Your* planet is in peril too.''

I already had enough clues to make my own conclusions, but I wanted them confirmed. For example, the Occons were using clean bombs. That said to me they meant to invade and move in. You don't dirty a nest you intend to occupy.

''So, it's time you leveled with me,'' I said. ''You forget I have been kept very much in the dark. Tell me what I don't know. What has Occo got?''

And they told me what they hadn't told *anyone* about the last launch window, things the Tannian civilian population did not even know, and why they were so bloody short on pilots that they made a convict a lieutenant colonel and sent him out to recruit fifteen-years-rusty enemy veterans.

At the launch window, Tannia invaded Occo. It was a covert operation. The Tannian electorate did not know about it. The military by necessity has a certain autonomy from the democratic rule. The military is only accountable come funding time.

So without consulting the general public, the military sent a fleet to Occo.

A preemptive strike, they called it then. We call it a debacle now. They lost the whole invasion force.

* * *

My Tannian commanders asked if I now understood the situation. I said I was afraid I did. They told me to get ready to leave for Erde.

I went back to my house to look up everything I might still have on my old comrades-at-arms, something that might help me find someone who did not want to be found.

My house was strange to me. It had been impounded at my arrest and shut up for the past two years.

I was rooting through old chests when she tumbled in through the window.

She was still bright blond, though she'd cut her hair very short, and she wore a military flightsuit instead of one of the frothy outfits I remembered. She toppled off the bed and onto the floor, looked up at me. "I'm not AWOL," she said. "I just didn't take time to put on anything decent. I probably stink. Tough." She picked herself up and hugged me.

Maggie hadn't changed at all. She still had what I saw in her first and needed now because I had lost it entirely—her *joie de vivre.* Joy. And her young eyes. She would have them until she was a hundred and one.

The two years had changed me. When you're lean it is easy to become severe. Hatchet-carved planes had hardened my look—the kind of age the rejuvenators can't heal. Even Maggie gasped as she drew back from her hug to look me over. I looked like an Erden officer, aloof and rigidly straight. I think she was afraid of me.

Of course, Maggie had been unfaithful to me while I was incarcerated, but no one had expected me ever to be let out. She was a high-spirited, very young, and unmarried woman. I had anticipated this.

Still I played the part of the wounded lover. I told her I had to think about it before I took her back—I suppose so she wouldn't regard me cheaply, like a dog you can beat and still it crawls to you in adoration. That is an admirable thing in dogs; in humans it is rather despised.

Maggie couldn't believe it. She was crying. Said she loved me, she was sorry, please, please don't be angry.

I turned my back on her.

"Kralle!"

I snapped around, startled to hear that out of her. And

she was hitting me. Not the way Maggie could belt when she wanted to do damage. Just punching my arm in anger at the Kralle she wanted out of me, the way she had hit me when I first told her I loved her.

I let her cry about it for two days. I never made pretensions at sainthood. I had actually intended to let her go on a week, but I had had enough. I was also afraid she would recover enough by then to tell me to fuck myself when at last I got around to forgiving her.

We hadn't much time together before I was to leave for Erde. Maggie helped me go through heaps of old letters and mementoes, news stories and things I had forgotten I had.

She was looking over my shoulder when I found a picture of a woman, still young. Why did I expect her picture to age with me? No paint, no fashion, but she had a savvy sophistication Maggie lacked. The woman in the still was worldly-wise and old for her years, as Maggie was young for hers. Not as physically *pretty* as Maggie, but she had a way, even in an inanimate picture, that strikes one as beautiful. She was shorter even than Maggie, with long unkempt dark hair, and her dark eyes gazed from the picture with intelligence and smoky raw sexuality.

Maggie's eyes were lilac today. I could tell from her uneasy shifting that she was about to run for the dark brown lenses in a moment.

"Who's that?" said Maggie.

It was obvious who she was, because she had signed her name: *Love, forever, Israela.* Maggie wanted to know *who* she was.

"My wife," I said.

"Your what?"

"She's dead, Maggie."

And I gazed out the window, remembering things.

Maggie's voice sounded small. "You're so far away from me, Anthony."

I shrugged. It was true. I was captive of a sadness I could not express.

"Do you really want me here after all?"

I paused to consider a lot of things.

She mistook the pause. She thought it was reluctance to admit the negative, when in truth I was weighing things, especially the fairness of asking her what I wanted to ask her.

She got up, moved toward the door. If I let her go then and I went to Erde on my mission, I knew I would never see her again.

After such a long pause she did not expect to hear: "Marry me."

She whirled, stared. "You mean that?"

It should have implied a lot that I could not express right then. At least I hoped it did. I felt as if I were calling from inside a block of ice from which I was waiting to thaw. But I simply wasn't thawing, and it was imperative I find some warmth and get out of here, because Maggie was walking out of my life and I fervently wanted her *in* it. With all my frozen heart.

"Yes, I do," I said quite coldly.

"Anton, are you stuck in there?"

I never loved her more. "Yes."

"Then yes."

"Yes?"

"Yes."

So we married in the spaceport the morning I left for Erde, alone.

III.

There's an old saying, older than Erde I'm sure, that runs, "You can't go home again."

I remember Erde as the sun always shining, green fields, glittering canals, pale blue mountains capped in white, skies like a blue-white diamond, cool breezes, verdant scents, vine-laden trellises hung with an exultation of blooms, perfumed gardens, terraces of colored stone, music, cozy cottages in the outlying zones—how quickly the flowers grow in their blink of a summer.

—I dream about snow. I would give anything to see snow again. To be cold—

Nothing was exactly as I remembered it, even the things that had not changed. There was a strangeness to the most familiar places.

Erde looked as if it had lost a war. Cities which had been built with charming forethought were overrun now with Tannian afterthoughts cropping up in the most inharmonious surroundings like weeds growing in a once well-ordered garden. And our proudest, most artistic creations, the grand hotels, the music gardens, were left to rot as symbols of an arrogant rule overthrown.

Symbols, shit. They were beautiful.

One of the reasons I had not come back here after the War of 174 was I did not want to see how my mighty home had fallen.

I had arrived on Erde alone. I told my Tannian military superiors they must cut me loose if this mission was to have any hope of success. Erden aces in hiding are not going to come out and talk to a man in the company of

Tannian MPs, be he the reincarnation of the Autokrat himself.

So they let me come solo but assigned me a strict rendezvous when a Tannian military escort would take me and any volunteers I uncovered back to Tannia at the next Erden eclipse. One had just passed, so I had forty-four Erden days for my task.

There are 365.14 Erden days in an Erde-Tannian year, but those are long days in a long year, so you mustn't think it is similar to Earth. I had forty-four Erden days to find my old comrades.

Miss the rendezvous, the Tannians told me, and they would come after me. Run, and they would track me for the rest of my days.

I overheard a Tannian MP scoff as I parted from them, "We'll never see *him* again."

I glanced back. The MP was very tall, square-shouldered, and too handsome, with blue-black hair smooth as a helmet, like a child's plastic doll. He curled a thick lip at me. I would make a point of saying hello to him upon completion of my mission.

Besides the veterans of the War of 174, I was authorized to recruit Erde's underground military. Erde had no legitimate armed forces—Tannia had outlawed all military activity on Erde after the war—so I was here to enlist the illegitimate one.

There was a shadow organization known as Erde Shall Rise Again for its mission and motto. If you hear people asking for a man named Ezra, you've probably heard them asking for ESRA.

The organization's existence was only half-confirmed rumor, a group of diehard loyalists who went underground to maintain some kind of native military presence on Erde in hopes of liberating her one day. ESRA added to its numbers the disaffected Erden youth who have grown up as second-class citizens under the Tannian rule.

Rumor said also that ESRA was actually in possession of sophisticated weapons, including spaceplanes, and had training camps dotting the Erden highlands, places where Erde's pervasive network of transportation tunnels did not go.

If these revolutionaries were as well trained as rumor

had them, I was empowered to pardon their transgressions against the treaty and give them commissions in the Tannian Fleet for the defense against Occo.

But where was I to begin to look for people who did not want to be found?

I hopped an underground for Center City.

The underground train tunnels riddle the planet like worm holes. You need never go outside to get anywhere on Erde. You could spend your entire life indoors. Shops deliver through chutes in private homes. Private train cars access the transportation system underneath every domicile. The trains glide on superconductors and take you anywhere in the world. Anywhere probably but where I wanted to go.

First place I wanted to find was the hideout of Admiral Pieter Wilhelminazoon Griesmann. The admiral of Erde's wartime fleet was still at large. He had been my commanding officer in 174. If anyone knew the whereabouts of ESRA, he might, or know who knew.

He was, of course, in hiding too. But he was not very difficult to hunt down, which made me wonder why the Tannian authorities had not arrested him long ago.

I suspect now that he'd rolled over on the rest of the fugitive Kabinet, and the Tannian Feds had closed one eye on Admiral Griesmann.

Griesmann was an ace, but I don't know if the criterion was the same for him as for us, or whether his targets were baited tigers declawed and taken to a safe place for him to finish. If my suspicions sound mean and petty (he had more kills than I), it is true I do not *want* him to be a true ace. If there is the slightest doubt of the veracity of any of his achievements I confess I will be the first to point out and magnify them. He is not my superior anymore; I can say things I bottled up while saying "Yes sir" during my Erden service years.

Admiral Pieter Wilhelminazoon Griesmann was a swine.

There.

Why did I just glance over my shoulder for Politzen?

When I arrived at Center City it was raining. It had

been raining for three days, and the streets were rivers. No one but former menials was outside.

You can recognize the menials on sight. They go around looking embarrassed. Tannians called them slaves and liberated them but did nothing to change their attitude. Elevated menials are more comfortable dealing with Tannians, because dealing with people of superior station is soothingly familiar to them. With other Erders you can see them trying to become invisible. They cringe if they have to sit next to you on public transports. The one I sat next to on the train apologized. But they have to sit because the Tannians will take legal action against everyone who is sitting while a former menial is standing, so they sit and try not to be obtrusive. They start to open doors for you, stop, wring their hands and hunch into their collars. They want you to know it's not their own will—they haven't got one—but they are under orders of the new regime. And we understand, because they were born to take orders from whoever ranks highest. The few menials who do find their own heads and turn arrogant turn up dead. Understanding has its limits.

In the gray flowing streets of Center City were a scattering of forlorn menials getting rained on in penance, and me looking for the admiral. I waded to the worst side of town.

Every society has its underside. The more refined, civilized, lofty, ordered, and rigid, the higher the highs, the lower its dregs.

Both Erde and Tannian have their gutter sides, but they are different breeds. The bottom of our barrel is much deeper than theirs.

There is a part of Center City where you can pay someone to hurt you, or whatever else you want. The things people want to do or have done to them are without number, but they were all to be had in Center City. I had an idea I would find the admiral there. While his mother was still alive he made some show of decency, but with her gone, the reins were cut, and I was sure dear Pieter had bolted for the bottom.

"Griesmann?"

The smuggler looked at me hard. Unlike Tannians, he

was not deceived by my young appearance and small stature. He smelled a killer. "No. No Griesmann," he said, so emphatically I know he knew.

I said, "My name is Anton Nordveldt. I'm looking for Admiral Griesmann."

He paused. Less sure of himself, he said, "No Griesmann."

"Have someone tell him I'm here."

I checked into a decrepit hotel under an assumed name. My payment chit would betray my true identity, as I intended it should. I gave the fake name only because people trust what they must uncover over what they are told outright.

No one called, but the next contact I made was not as reluctant as the smuggler. The underground had verified who I was by then.

I was aware from nearly the moment I arrived on Erde that I had a tail. I assumed it was one of ours (ours—Tannian!). I thought the Defense Ministry had at the last minute become twitchy and changed heart about trusting me loose without a leash.

But either Griesmann's spies did not detect my tail or Griesmann was not afraid of Tannian authorities, because he allowed someone to give me his location.

His hideout was right down the street from my hotel. I could walk.

I could swim. It had not stopped raining, and passage outside was becoming treacherous.

At the given address I found an antiques shop. I went inside to the back and up the stairs to the third floor. I was looking around when a young man in a worker's apron came upon me. He was slightly startled but recovered at once and said, "Wrong way. You want down."

I hadn't seen any stairs leading down. I opened my hands in confusion. The young man led me down one flight of stairs to the second floor and pointed at a waiting lift. I hadn't seen any access to it on the first floor—because, as it turns out, there wasn't any. "There," he said. "*Don't* press any of the buttons. Just say 'Down.' "

I walked in, smelled death in this box. The control panel was as antique as anything in the shop. *Don't press the buttons.* I jumped out. I marched back up to the third floor, grabbed the young man, and dragged him down and into the lift. "Escort me."

He sighed. "Down," he said.

The doors shut; the lift descended. When the doors reopened without event my guide shot me a wry look, but I did not apologize for doubting him. I stepped out, and watched how he made the return journey. "Up," he said, and the doors shut.

I was alone now in a garish vestibule of colored lights and black-and-violet plastic walls, luridly dim, and decorated with someone's idea of art or a twisted satire of it. Pieces of things, no wholes, all thrown together in perverse compositions. Baby dolls, lots of those, clowns with chipped-paint smiles and recorded laughs, bird bones, wrappers. A baby doll in a bird cage with her hand in her panties. An omro with bird wings still half feathered where its ears should've been, its stiff paws holding a party horn.

I took a few steps and a carousel started up, blaring hideously merry music, things with awful grins going around and around. Hologramic cupids floated past me, through me.

At the far end of this funhouse, two great plastic Grecian-style pillars framed a doorway. The four panels on the double doors were painted into tarot suits: leaves, hearts, bells, acorns. On the queen of hearts I recognized the face, Kommissar Wilhelmina.

Next to the doors was a purple bell cord. I reached for it, hesitated.

Don't press the buttons.

I looked back for the young man to tell me what to do, but he was gone, the lift doors shut. I knew how to make the lift rise, but I did not know how to make the doors open. Damn.

I pulled the purple cord.

Nothing shot at me. I don't know what sounded inside, certain I didn't want to.

An androgynous computer voice from the autoguard said, "Welcome. May I ask who is calling?"

"Anton Nordveldt."

"Please verify."

"What verification do you want?"

There followed a very slight pause as the computer made a selection at random. It decided on a quiz. "On the third day of the first dekan of 173, you failed inspection. What was wrong with your uniform? You have thirty seconds to reply."

I glanced around for guns, gas jets, or trap door, some macabre consequence in case I failed this test, which I was about to. What happens in thirty seconds?

Pinpoints of sweat broke out on my skin. I remembered the incident in question. I did not know the answer. Seconds dwindled.

"I don't know," I said.

Thirty seconds elapsed.

I heard a click.

IV.

I held my breath, crouched to run.

The doors opened.

"Anton!"

The wave of perfume hit me like a fist. Musky, spiced, it stung my eyes. I squinted to see him—pale skin, a great expanse of it, fat as a seal and pink as a domestic pig, eyes painted like Cleopatra queen of the Nile. He was wearing a silk robe and nothing beneath. Red tint made his straight-line mouth into a little cupid bow. A naked young boy next to him held a tray onto which Griesmann set his crystal goblet. Then he shooed the boy away, "Bring us something better than that."

He waved me in.

I hesitated in the doorway.

"Anton, you're wet. Take your clothes off."

I told him I was fine.

How could my former commanding officer open his door and stand there with his painted eyes and painted mouth, his silk robe, and present to me this appalling silk-and-satin room furnished with scrubbed and tinted nymphet boys, and dare not blush? If this were a fantasy of mine and I were to act it out, I damn certainly would not let another living soul witness it.

He grabbed one of his boys by the ass and said to me, "Can I offer hospitality? This one?"

I shook my head, choked out something inane like "This really isn't a social call."

He let the boy go. "You always were one for the boring creatures." For so he referred to women. Yes, I admit an incurable weakness for the boring creatures.

"How is your lovely wife, Israela?" he said.

Admiral Griesmann hated my lovely wife, Israela. "Israela died in the war, and you know that."

"Ach, one cannot keep track of the tragedies."

"You were at her funeral." And I hadn't been.

"Ach," he lamented.

Women, Admiral Griesmann always maintained, had no place in the cockpit. Women fighters were trick ponies, nothing more. Israela had been an aberration of nature, to his way of thinking. He'd been at her funeral out of duty, and I believe he even managed a few crocodile tears for the news media as he awarded her posthumous medals.

The boy returned with a carafe of thick red liquid. Griesmann poured a glass, offered.

I declined. It was blood.

"Ach, still the little officer, Anton, The war is over."

"The war has just begun," I said, and his plucked eyebrows lifted in interest.

"I didn't know you were one of the ESRA people," he said.

"I'm not. Tannia and Erde are both in danger now. Tannia did something stupid."

"We always knew that, dear."

"I need to find some people."

"Anton Anton Anton," he said in descending pitch. "Am I a directory service?"

"ESRA for starters."

"Ezra who?"

A coy pervert, just what I was in the mood for. "Erde Shall Rise Again," I said. "How can I contact them?"

"No such thing."

"Why did you ask if I were one?"

"No such thing as an organized Erde Shall Rise Again movement. Just people who talk about it."

I presented an officer's rank pin with insignia of a phoenix rising from the ashes of a fallen eagle. The Tannians had confiscated it. 'What's this?"

He brushed my outstretched hand aside with a bored motion. "Kids."

"Kids?"

"Yes. A toy in a game of theirs."

"Admiral Griesmann, that is not just implausible, it's patently weird."

He smiled at me, sipped his glass of blood.

I said, "If such a thing as ESRA existed I should think you would want to know about it, or be behind it."

"I would. But it doesn't exist."

"Aren't you the least bit curious about this?" I shook the insignia.

He did not even look at it. "No."

I pointed out the odd fact that every year fifteen million Erdefrancs' worth of industrial supplies which could be used in war manufacture disappeared on this planet and remained unaccounted for.

"Accounting errors," he said.

"Accounting errors?"

"Now don't go imagining more than there is here."

"I would have thought it bore investigation."

"One doesn't go checking for zebras unless one has evidence that there is a zebra around. Otherwise what use is there hunting zebras on Erde?"

"I smell a zebra."

He chuckled as if this were a joke.

"All right," I said, giving up this line of questioning. "Do you know where Gerhardt Recht is?"

"Gerhardt Recht? I do not know. If he is not dead he has not bothered to inform me."

This I believed. Gerhardt Recht would not communicate his whereabouts to Pieter Griesmann no matter what Griesmann used to be. "What about Kitty Hawke?" I said.

"Why would you want to find Kit? Masochistic streak, Anton?"

"Where is she?"

"I haven't the foggiest."

Lie.

"Nina," I said.

"Nina is *dead,*" he said as if it was stale news. It had the offhand ring of truth. "Anton, this quiz is so boring."

"Corinna."

"Chemically altered on the permanent side." He snapped his fingers. One of his boys placed a small container into his open palm. He flipped it at me. It was full of red tablets. "Put one under your tongue and let it dissolve. Don't swallow it, its a waste, and don't take the whole bottle at once, you might find Corinna."

I set the container aside. "Reid."

He overreacted, launching into the histrionics of being stabbed.

It was not as if I had truly shocked him. He had to know I would ask for Reid. At the end of his act he pouted his red lips. "Bitch!" he said and refused to help me. I could not ask about anyone else. "I'm so tired of this game," he said.

So was I.

But I left with something more than I'd had before. I knew now that Erde Shall Rise Again was real. Griesmann's place had been crawling with zebras.

Slight digression here. After Reid's name shut down my inquiries, there was a bit more conversation, all of which had nothing to do with my mission. You see, I left Griesmann's with more than information.

One of his nymphets caught my eye for its extreme youth and for the fact that I could not tell if it was a boy or a girl. Stark naked and I could not tell. I need an anatomy lesson.

I was in the habit of ignoring other people's life-styles, and I can wink at depravity, but something, I don't know, perhaps marrying Maggie, changed my outlook. At least subliminally I must have been thinking of cooing slobbering babies and little toddlers; and the quasi word "Dada" had become weirdly appealing.

I saw this child, so young as to be ambiguous regarding gender, and my stomach turned over. I swallowed the sourness.

"Want her?" said Griesmann.

Her—that meant nothing coming from Griesmann. He'd called Reid a bitch. "Yes," I said. "To go."

He told the child to get dressed.

As I waited I asked, "What is the answer to the question your computer guard asked me?"

"And which is that?" he said.

"Why I failed inspection back in 173. What was wrong with my uniform?"

"Oh, my dear, I just didn't feel like passing you."

I left with my new companion, who turned out to be a girl, which is probably why Griesmann parted with her so readily.

I took her to the nearest children's shelter. She saw where we were headed and started screaming and hitting me. As we were on a crowded underground it made for a hell of a scene. When we got off the train she changed tactics and tried to be provocative, succeeded only in being completely pathetic. She wiggled her undeveloped, not-even-adolescent body at me. She said she was full-grown mentally and emotionally, and knew everything.

"How old are you?" I said.

"Eight and three-quarters."

When you're eight, quarters count. That's about ten (excuse me, ten and a *quarter*) Earth standard years. As I hauled her bodily to the children's shelter, she threatened me with revenge, death, lawsuit, and she would tell Griesmann!

About then I remembered why I usually mind my own business.

But, for the love of God, eight and three quarters.

End of digression.

It was encouraging to note that my tail had not moved in and asked me what I was doing playing social worker when I was supposed to be recruiting fighter pilots. If the Tannians had not let me entirely loose, they were at least leaving me a long leash.

Not long enough.

I got pissed and turned on my tail. He ran, and I became the tail. I chased him cross-country, nearly to the mountains, then I turned again abruptly and lost him.

Free to continue my search unobserved, I devised a new tactic. As I had no idea how to find ESRA, and I very much wanted an anodyne for the dull sick aftertaste of Griesmann, I decided to concentrate my search on an individual. I wanted to see Gerhardt Recht.

* * *

Gerhardt Recht emphatically did not want to be found. His record was a trail of dead-ended investigations. There was simply no sign of him.

Gerhardt Recht was the handsomest pilot ever to take to the *weltraum,* so all the women, including my first wife, told me. He was two meters tall, blond, fair-skinned, athletic, and deep-voiced, with eyes of bright blue. When they make the war vids they always have the most handsome actor play Gerhardt. Gerhardt Recht inspires admiration on either side. He was always a gentleman.

He was also conscientious and efficient, which explained why, if he did not want to be found, he could disappear completely.

And the likes of Pieter Griesmann would have no idea how to find the likes of Gerhardt Recht any more than omros know the ways of sundancers.

I could not figure where to begin my search when all others had failed. Then I remembered another pilot, Nina, since dead. During the war (while Nina was still married to Rutger Forquet) in a little café and under the table, I spied Nina's hand on Gerhardt's leg. And he let it stay there. So the gallant Gerhardt was not perfect after all. I was relieved to know that. I said nothing. It wasn't my affair.

After the war, Nina went underground like everyone else. For years she lived under an alias, Liza Rosen. When the authorities caught up with her she took her own life rather than go to prison.

She left behind a son, Erik Lizazoon. That was the kind of name unmarried women give their children. I double-checked. Liza Rosen had no husband on record and Erik had no father on record. Evidently Nina/Liza had given her husband, Rutger, the slip at the same time she was escaping everything else in her past.

I put one and one together and did something evil. I put a trace on the outgoing calls from Erik Lizazoon's com, then I planted a note among Erik's messages saying that his father was seriously ill to the point of death.

A call went out from Erik's com immediately. I could not pick up the conversation, because the call established a secure data link.

Now there was nothing inherently odd about that, because the man Erik contacted was the kind of person whose calls were routinely shielded.

Erik had called a high-powered Erden industrialist, Heinrich Corneliszoon Hardt.

I looked up Heinrich Hardt's file. There is a Tannian file on every rich, influential Erder. There wasn't much in it. Heinrich Hardt shunned publicity. His age was right, forty Erde-Tannian years. He had married his young secretary, Darla Rijn. (I checked the date of his wedding—it was two years after Nina/Liza's death.) Heinrich Hardt and Darla had two small children. Seventeen-year-old Erik Lizazoon was nowhere mentioned in Hardt's file.

I paid Heinrich Hardt a call.

Hardt lived in a secluded villa in a river valley where no train tunnels accessed, not even primitive roads. I needed a vertical-takeoff-and-landing craft to get there. Hardt had a private stable of them. I had to rent one.

The VTOL descended amid firepines and golden hollies and came to rest on the thick golden-brown wild grass.

The house was red brick and amberwood with a blackwood trim and tile roof. Wood smoke curled from a chimney.

I did not need to knock. They had seen the VTOL come down.

On first sight I did not know the man who came to the door, but he gasped when he saw me.

Then a great fist closed on my shirtfront, slammed me up against the wall. Heinrich Hardt was so mad he could barely snarl. "You did that to my son! You little Kralle, I'll break your back!"

It was Gerhardt Recht, altered absolutely, and mad enough to kill me. And he would have, but I launched, strangledly, into the sincerest of contrite apologies and told him it honestly was a matter of life and death.

"Whose?"

"Ours. Everyone's."

He let me drop. It was a half meter to the floor. Luckily I was used to weighing more; the thud was not so jarring as it might have been.

A young woman appeared from an inner chamber. "Who is it, *liebling?*"

She was beautiful, a soft-voiced, slender woman holding a toddler by the hand. Mistress Hardt. Darla Rijn.

Gerhardt made a flimsy excuse to his young wife and hustled me into a private den.

"She doesn't know," I said when we were alone and out of earshot.

"No. And she won't." That was a threat. "She means the world to me."

"They forgive, you know. After they get done looking at you as if you had three eyes."

Gerhardt gave a dry smile with his altered mouth. He was calming down. "I don't think I could endure that look," he said. "Voice of experience, Nordveldt?"

I nodded. "I married again," I said. "Last week."

"Congratulations."

"Thank you."

"This is a dim honeymoon," he commented.

"I know. My wife understands. She's a pilot."

"Well, that's consistent."

"We've already survived two Occon attacks."

"Two *what?* What are you talking about, Occon attacks?"

As I suspected, those incidents had been hushed up here on Erde because they were embarrassing to the Tannian military. So Erders did not know there was even a threat. My mission was going to be very difficult. I was here to recruit pilots, but first I had to make them believe there was a real danger. I must've sounded like Chicken Little.

Gerhardt listened, dubiouser and dubiouser.

Then I told him of the Tannian amnesty offer.

Yeah, right.

What had I said about someone looking at you as if you had three eyes?

"Anyway, it doesn't matter, Nordveldt." Gerhardt covered his brow wearily and slumped into a chair. "It's too late for that, sincere or not. I'm already free. I have respect, love, a position, wealth. I'll lose all that if I come forward now. I would rather live in suspense the rest of my life than make the ax fall myself."

I could see how he'd gotten away with it this far. Physically he was transfigured past any whisper of recognition. He must have had vertebrae removed, because he was shorter. The timbre of his voice was different; he'd had his vocal cords shortened. His once-straight blond hair was brown and tightly wound in springy little curls. His once-Roman nose was wide and flat, his lips thicker. His skin was sallow instead of ruddy fair. A purple birthmark blotched his elbow, and a sprinkle of moles dotted his skin. Someone had paid attention to details. He even had white spots on his front teeth as if from a childhood fever Gerhardt never had when his teeth were forming. He'd rounded off his square jawline, and one ear was cauliflowered as if he'd used to wrestle in school. No one would think to check such an obviously uncorrected man for cosmetic alterations. Funny, all the flaws were added. The natural Gerhardt was perfect.

With all the physical blemishes, he still possessed that personal magnetism. I bet he still had to shake the women off.

But he was not the patriot I remembered.

"I have a good life, Nordveldt. You're asking me to compromise that. I love my new life and I won't give it up for anything."

"Not for the safety of your planet?"

"I don't believe that."

"Don't or won't?"

"Doesn't matter."

"I see. To hell with Erde. To hell with everything else as long as Recht's little world is happy."

His silence said loudly he did not have to answer that.

"All right," I said. "Can you tell me how I can make contact with ESRA?"

He stiffened. "I have nothing to do with ESRA. If it exists, I don't want to know about it."

I refrained from saying, "You've gotten good at that."

He said, "I don't want a revolution. I just want to live my life like a normal human being."

I stepped back. "Thanks," I said, for nothing. I started to go, turned. "Oh, I found you by guesswork. Nothing I think anyone else could repeat. I think your obscurity is safe. I only guessed that Nina's son was yours."

"What in two worlds made you think that?"

I told him what I had spied in the café seventeen years ago. He paled. "Who else knows?"

I shrugged, "No one because of *me.*" It was not something I would repeat for idle entertainment.

He sounded grateful. "You're all right, Nordveldt. You're one of the few who were."

"I thought you were too," I said dryly and let myself out.

Everything else in my search was turning up blind. My forty-four days were slipping away, and no one would talk to me about ESRA. Tannia's profile dwindled to a sliver until the eclipse was one day away.

And I had reacquired my tail. Fine, I thought. This is why I'm not making contact with ESRA. Come eclipse my Tannian superiors would get an earful—the MP with the lacquered hair included.

With one day left I still had hopes, dim ones, of finding Reid. Reid the little warkapten.

Reid is Reid's only name. He scrapped the Wolfgang Amadeus part a long time ago. No one except his violinist mother ever called him anything but Reid anyway. He said once, and I laughed, "Why couldn't she call me Johann Sebastian, Ludwig, *any*thing!"

Remember I said Hal Halson was the best who ever flew? I lied. It's Reid. Better than Halson, better than I, better than Lady Thom, better than all the greats.

But Reid had been pulled from duty halfway through the war. Just when he was on his way to breaking the record (held by Admiral Griesmann). I think Reid really did have the record, that Griesmann's was padded, but you know how I feel about Griesmann.

Why Reid had been grounded I hadn't learned. I assumed it was a personality conflict with a superior. Reid was easy to be jealous of. And someone had done his worst to him.

Reid was a fanatical pilot. They may as well have killed him as ground him.

And cut off their own proverbial nose in the process. We could have used Reid at the end. While Tannia was hammering us, Reid stayed retired on one of his estates.

Reid had been enormously wealthy. Immeasurably. He owned half of Erdetechnik before it was nationalized—nationalized by Tannia, not Erde. When we lost the war, Reid lost it all. Well, most, at least. Reid got lost too.

Tannia confiscated his lands, his accounts, his holdings, which added up to billions with a b. We are talking Erdefrancs here, not Tannian trade units.

I like to imagine Reid got away with a million or so, tucked in a valise, and headed for the mountains, but from what I know of billionaires they seldom have liquid capital floating around in those amounts. Of the mountains part of my speculation I was on firmer ground. Reid had a horror of closed spaces. That's why he ran instead of facing a war-crimes trial as I did. Since he had not participated in the war to the end, Reid's sentence would not have been very severe. But he could not tolerate the prospect of even a moment in confinement.

Only a cockpit is not a closed space to him. It was an extension of himself, enabling him to climb into infinite freedom.

On the ground even the plains were not open enough for Reid. He had to have a head up, above any obstacle on the horizon.

So I rented a landskimmer and was meandering through the mountains, killing time really before eclipse, when my tail passed me.

Sometimes I am very slow on the uptake. This time I put all the pieces in order and I followed him.

He led me to Reid.

V.

As I approached the house set high in the hills, a big kite passed overhead, a man hang-gliding. The kite wheeled and dove, pivoted in a perfect stall, caught an updraft, and rode the wind heavenward.

The rider alighted on a rock spur and pushed off again, skirted the crags, and mounted up the cliff face, turned an inside loop.

That had to be Reid.

When I arrived at the lofty house, the valet, who had been my tail, let me in. I had time to look around before Reid showed.

A towering space extended over me, the ceilings immensely high. The rooms were spacious without seeming cavernous. Instead, they felt *open,* with no doors between them, only wood blinds, and strategic turns to divide them. There was nothing in Reid's house that closed or locked.

Great expanses of windows and skylights had no panes, only energy barriers that screened out rain and pests but let through the crisp breezes. There was a lightness to everything, decorated in seaside colors, sea blue and sand and shell pink, all uncluttered, from the hand-woven rugs on the woodbrick floors to the fresh-cut flowers, which abounded.

A waterfall spilled through the center of the house, from the highest part of the high ceilings down to a brook that disappeared under the floor.

I guess Reid had gotten away with a million or so.

I walked out to the terrace, leaned on the white rail. The sun was bright; only a bleary streak of milky cloud wiped across the pale thin sky. The mountain air was bracing cold. My skin roughened; I didn't care.

The gods must have had such a view from Olympus, of blue mountains striated with white glaciers, and purple shadowed valleys. Glistening ice flowers clung to the rock slope. The delicate tickling sound of wind through bell trees carried from the lesser heights.

I thought, How beautiful is Erde and this place like the high crag of an Erden eagle.

I want to stay.

A shadow crossed over me like a great bird. The loud snapping of wind in fabric closed and the shadow loomed large. I retreated inside.

Reid landed on the terrace with his enormous kite.

He slipped out of his harness. The valet took his rig, and Reid came in, sweaty, his nose and high cheeks windburned red. He smiled, taking off his gloves. "Anton. I've been waiting for you. I'll be right out. Make yourself at home."

I already had.

The valet brought me tea.

Reid reappeared barefoot, wearing black silkine corduroy trousers and a plain-spun natural fiber sweater three sizes too large. He curled into the end of a sofa and hugged a pillow. "You look good, Anton. Everyone else has gotten old, fat, or dead."

He was nervous as a bird, closing his hands on the pillow to keep himself still. Nervous energy sparked from him. He was as I remembered him, big-boned and too slender, with deep-set dark eyes and dark hair—lightened now by a few threads of gray. Deep hollows couched within his collarbones. He could have used more weight. His big hands looked oversized.

There was no sign of women. Reid never liked them. Whether he preferred anything else was never known for sure. Reid was private as a cat. Rumor only assumed because he disliked women that he liked men.

There was no sign of any companion at all except the valet, and Reid was not one to fraternize with the help.

Actually it was hard to picture Reid with anybody.

His was a sexless house. Nothing overweeningly masculine, nothing specifically feminine, like a work of art, it just *was*.

What Griesmann could not tolerate about Reid was that Reid wanted nothing to do with Griesmann. Reid spurned Griesmann and Griesmann never forgave him.

What Reid actually said was: "If you were the last mammal in the universe I would marry my right hand."

But I think that says more for Reid's discretion and self-respect than it does his preference, which to this day I don't know. Reid could keep some massive secrets.

I told him why I had come. The Tannians were willing to forget what he'd done during the war if he would fight for them now against Occo. I thought Reid would jump as I had at the chance to fly again.

But as I said, Reid had a positive horror of confinement. He said no. No way.

I assured him he would not be arrested, not detained even an hour.

"No."

"They'll let you fly."

"Oh, Anton," he said, reproach in his voice as if I'd struck below the belt. I had. "It's a trick," he said quickly. And trying to change the subject, he offered a small gold box of crystalline powder. He dabbed his finger in and put it under his tongue. "It reacts to sound. I'll put on the music. Feels like flying. Next best thing."

"How about the real thing?"

"God. God."

I dangled flying before him like water to the dying. I was cruel. He could not refuse me.

He did.

He pressed the pillow against his face. I heard his muffled voice through the cushion. "I—can—not—be—locked—up."

To give him some idea how urgently sincere the Tannians were I said, "Reid, they are willing to recruit the members of ESRA."

"Serve them right," he said, unconvinced.

"Reid, I have in my pocket a pardon for the pilot of the *Manta*, identity unknown, if he will just fly for the Tannian fleet."

"Let me see that."

I took a datacoin out. He magnified it and read. "My God."

The *Manta* was one of ours (ours—Erden). Anything that dark and monstrous had to be the product of an Erden mind.

It was called *Manta* because the ship looked like one and it moved like one. It is an unsettling shape, I cannot really say why. It's not as if manta rays were some elemental terror, a predator from the dawn of man which might linger in the race memory. But the *Manta* does strike fear in the heart. I had seen it in my viewer once, a great looming triangular shroud with a tail and two projections in front, and flexible. I think that was weirdest of all. I'm used to rigid-body craft. This thing looked alive. Variable-camber wings could curl under like a goose's wings coming in for landing. No ship is absolutely rigid; all spaceplanes bend, flex, and stretch to some degree, but not so you are really aware of it. This actually undulated.

Gravity waves have yet to be discovered. I should say by the mainstream of the scientific community they have yet to be discovered. I've heard the *Manta* was powered by antigrav pulse, enabling it to enter the atmosphere like a massless object—which almost needs to be true, because the *Manta* had no heat shield. It was a soft body. It could shoot into the atmosphere but it could not follow at speed. Friction and the *Manta* did not get along.

I saw it once during the war, come flapping like a nightmare. I turned tail.

A compatriot and I ran from it.

"Do you know who the Manta was?" I asked. So we called the craft's anonymous pilot.

"He died."

"You know that?"

"Everyone knows that."

"I mean do you personally know that?"

"Of course not. I never knew the Manta."

No one did. No one could say whether the craft was a privateer or a secret weapon, a special commission of the Autokrat or what. I don't know who built it or if it was ever at any time sanctioned by the Erden Field Command or any other branch of the government.

The *Manta* appeared late in the war, out of nowhere like some kind of interstellar Zorro, and it was hailed as a savior. But it was too late by then. The *Manta* was just one ship, and one ship could not turn it around for us.

The *Manta* continued its attacks on Tannian ships after Erde's surrender and armistice. Rumors are various: that the Manta was a private citizen ignoring the armistice; that the Erden Kabinet had given secret orders for the craft to carry on while giving public disavowal; or it was a secret weapon gone renegade, refusing orders to cease fire.

The official story remains that none of Erde's official agencies knew anything about it.

The *Manta* had been a revolutionary design. Somebody had access to some cutting-edge technological research. The builders took a path not chosen by the mainstream and came up with a hell of a spacecraft.

I had heard the story Reid was telling me, that the Manta died. I also heard that the Manta had become a member of ESRA but that no one in that organization knew exactly *which* member he was. It is said that when ESRAns meet one another they immediately think of two questions: "Is this a Tannian infiltrator?" and "Is this the Manta?"

"How did he die?" I asked. "Allegedly?"

"He broke up over Mardra." Mardra was the last battle of the renegades. "Strayed too close to the atmosphere." Reid tugged on the tufted corner of his cushion. "There is a legend from old Earth of a man with wings of wax who strayed too close to the sun. For here we need a new legend, a winged being that strayed too close to the ground and got stuck and could never fly again."

Such sadness when he said it. . . .

He got up, went to his wide window, gazed out at the boundless vista, his big hands clasped behind his back.

"For those who dabble in piloting and then can walk away I have nothing but contempt. Those who tramp around on hallowed paths, who have split the air and heard the voices of angels and planets, then set their plane aside like another toy, wipe their hands and say, 'What's next?' They are not even worthy of my hatred.

"The air, space, is pure. All offal drops down; the

ground draws at it. Some souls defy that force of mortality and transcend to a higher thing. The greatest thing I know is flight. It is a glimpse of God.

"There is a reason why when people say heaven they look up."

He turned back to me, his face impassioned. "Do you follow that, Anton?" he said hopefully.

I wax purple on the subject of flight, so this sounded poetic to me. "Yes, I follow that. Where were you in the last part of the war, Reid?"

"Anton, you sound suspicious."

I shrugged my head to the side. The Manta had to be *some*one, and Reid had owned half of Erdetechnik. Some diabolical developments came out of Erdetechnik. From its labs came the deflector system that diverted enemy beam fire to another ship of the attacker's own make. And the Erdetechnik recognition system was without peer. Erden ships never ever fell to friendly fire. Not by accident, anyway.

Reid took my insinuation with a shrug. He was flattered, I think.

"They pulled my wings off, Anton."

"Who did? Griesmann?"

He wrinkled up his face. "God no. He couldn't. I can ignore his orders. A warkapten answers to the Autokrat."

No wonder Griesmann hated him. "But then why did they—did *he*—" the Autokrat himself—"take you out?"

Reid sat back on the couch, curled up tighter, and hugged his cushion. "When I get up there I have this overwhelming urge to shoot everything else out of the sky—fighters, freighters, theirs, ours, doesn't matter. You're in my air, you're a target. I'm a territorial bird. The whole sky isn't big enough. Did you know I shot down *Flag One* in simulation?"

The Autokrat's plane.

"He threw you out for that?"

"No. I shot down a passenger liner. A real one."

"Accident?"

"No."

I stumbled over this, plowed ahead. "Well, I guess that's hardly commendable, even reprehensible, but I don't see why he didn't reconsider in the end. We were desperate—"

"Ours, Anton."

Not a Tannian liner. An Erden liner.

I stared at the gentle little man in disbelief.

He gave a weak half-shrug.

It was some time before I could speak again. I needed to reconsider whether or not to press my offer.

Sidetracking, I asked who the authorities thought owned this house. It was rather conspicuous for a hideaway. And I think it was one of Reid's estates before the occupation.

"I. T. Kern," Reid answered.

"I. T. Kern is a *Tannian* businessman."

Reid smiled, proud of himself. "He's a persona I made up before the war was over. I just slid him into the Tannian infonet, shoveled some money into his bank accounts, bought him some stock, paid some taxes. Nobody suspects him because he was doing business before war's end—so he couldn't possibly be a Kralle in hiding." The hunters take a hard look at people who appeared only after the war. Kern was clear. "Kern bought this place at auction when the Tannians confiscated it from Reid. The hunters never thought to look for me in my own house."

"You did this before war's end? Reid, you were counting on us losing?"

"No. I was hedging against disaster. What did you want me to do on the ground, Anton? I saw everything falling apart. They wouldn't let me fight."

"Do you want to fight now?"

"I can't." He shuddered, couldn't look at me, couldn't look at the sky.

"Okay, can you put me in contact with anyone from ESRA?"

"You don't want to find ESRA. Those people are nuts, Anton. Please stay away from them."

I got up.

"Anton—" he started as if about to ask a favor. It had a wounded sound to it. He stopped, waved the idea on unspoken, so I let it go too.

I had a rendezvous to keep. The eclipse was near. I

had to be on the other side of the world in two hours—Erden hours; they are quite long. I could be there with time to spare.

I knew some of the Tannians were expecting me not to show, waiting to gloat at the naive ones who had trusted me. I pictured the MP doll with his broad shoulders, cleft chin, and snap-on blue-black hair. Well, he wasn't going to collect any bets on *me,* I could assure him. Keeping my appointment would be worth it just to dash the smug off his face.

I was coming back empty-handed, but at least I was coming back.

I didn't make it.

VI.

The eclipse would be visible in its totality in the city of my appointed rendezvous. I was outside when it started. At the first real dimming of the light I knew the eclipse was about a fifth underway. I was in good time.

I don't know why I was walking. I had gotten used to it, living on the Tannian base, and got to missing it while I was in prison. At any rate, I was walking. I turned a corner, found the street blocked.

I was squeezing between the vehicles barring my path when I was yanked into one, a hood was jammed over my head, and I felt the auto commence.

I didn't know who had me, what they intended. It could have been murder, but all I could think was that I was going to miss my rendezvous and that damn plastic MP would be sneering.

My abductors did not take me far. When my head was uncovered I saw through the high windows of a basement room the eclipse was yet in progress, so I was still within the city. It was the moment before totality, when the shadow bands march across the faces of buildings with the fading of the light. My time was up.

The Tannians were not going to understand.

Who had me? There were the two generic street types in plain dress who held me, and a third man in uniform, the design of which I had never seen. The uniformed one was a thin omro of a youth with dead-straight white-blond hair limp upon his low brow. Eyes like palest blue ice were so clear you'd swear you could see through them, and I was surprised he didn't cut himself on those cheekbones. He had a gaunt face with a tic under his eye.

I was strip-searched, then they did not give me back my clothes. Two prison terms takes a lot of dignity out of you and I hadn't recovered entirely from the last stint, so I was not as humiliated by this as I might have been. I was more irritated. The fear I felt was at seeing the light brighten through the high windows—the eclipse was passed. I was officially late.

"Let me know when you're done snickering," I said. "I am cold."

My clothes landed on my head in a pile. My hands were bound so I could not put them on.

I waited, not to seem too impatient. People were gathering, murmuring among themselves but saying nothing to me. Then, at last annoyed, I said, "All right."

"The defendant will wait until he is addressed."

"Oh for God's sake."

"Silence!"

I knew who had me. With sinking feeling I realized Reid was right: *You don't want to find those people.*

This was the melodramatic posturing of the self-appointed liberators of the planet wielding their small power.

I had hoped ESRA would be more than this.

I was informed that De Hoge Raad was now in session. De Hoge Raad—the old name for the Erden Supreme Court in the time of the Autokrat. The Tannians had dissolved it. ESRA resurrected it.

I was quickly tried—rather, they waived trial and proceeded straight from statement of the charge, collusion with the enemy, to the sentencing.

The execution was to be an old-fashioned lynching. My shirt was hooded over my head and tied with a wire, and I perched standing on an unsteady chair. I heard the other end of the wire being laced over the pipe that ran along the cellar's ceiling.

The chair rocked under my feet. I lurched from side to side to keep my balance as the chair canted one way, then thumped on four legs, and listed far over the other way, my captors jeering and cackling. Why I bothered, I don't know. They controlled the chair. I was simply prolonging their fun, but it was hardly a conscious decision. The chair leaned, I felt the wire at my throat, the passing of center, my insides tightened, and I leaned the other way. The same way a drowning man can't keep from thrashing. You just do it.

Suddenly the chair pitched too far over, too fast, my foot slipped off the steep surface, reached, missed, it was gone from under my feet.

I hit the floor, hard.

The wire twanged, cement impacting my legs, knees, hip, elbow. Chair legs in the ribs.

The ESRAns howled.

This was very funny.

Spread on the floor, I tried to keep from showing how I was shaking, I don't know if in rage or delayed terror. But I was naked and could not hide anything.

I should have known. The tip-off was when they covered my head. Had this been for real they would have wanted a good view of my face and neck. I should have known. But I didn't. I fell for it. (No, I truly did not mean for that to be funny. I was not laughing.) I had believed them. The unexpected result did not cause relief, only anger, and that was what they wanted, and I could not help but give it to them. Tears sprang to my eyes. That was great.

Is there anything more pathetic than impotent rage, the kind that yells, "I'll get you for this!" because all it can do is threaten and yell? I didn't threaten. I knew I would never get them for this. They did not only have all the high cards, they had the whole deck.

They did it again, executed me. Firing squad this time, only I wasn't fun anymore. I did not believe them. They insisted this was it. I shrugged, retreating into an apathetic torpor, which served the dual purpose of insulating me and taking the fun away from them.

"You don't believe you are about to die? What if this is real this time?"

"I don't care," I said. And I didn't. I was so mad after the first one that they could not affect me, and unlike the pitching chair there was nothing here for my instincts to betray me. I just watched them ready, aim, fire. I don't think I even flinched as the blanks roared. So fucking what?

A new person came down to the cellar. My shirt was

pulled over my head again. Some muttered discussions followed and then I was informed that someone powerful had bought me a temporary reprieve.

Footsteps approached. The newcomer stopped in front of me, paused as if looking me over. I didn't know the voice, female, but I knew the disparaging tone: "So that's why she married you."

"Kit!" I said. "Kit?"

The shirt was pulled off my head. I could see her.

I didn't know the face and she'd had her larynx worked on too, but some people you know in any guise. Kitty Hawke.

She still wasn't pretty. She was defiantly *not* pretty. Far be it from Kit to give a damn how anyone judged her from the outside. She'd gotten the bargain-rate overhaul, shortened the nose, added to the chin, the usual disguises without regard to how it all fit together. But I recognized her walk, a brusque commanding march. "Kit," I said again, sure this time, and not exactly happy about it. Kit had always hated me.

As a person I never liked her either. But air/space and ground are two different worlds, and you can be a different person in each. We judge each other by who we are in the air. We had a certain regard for each other as pilots.

Kit was wearing a black ESRAn uniform, of higher rank than the others to judge by the elaborate insignia. All the buttons were stamped with the image of a phoenix where Erden uniforms had borne eagles.

Kit indicated her companions with a backhand wave of her hand and said to me, "The kids missed the war. They don't understand."

I swore at her.

"No gratitude? Well, maybe you shouldn't. You aren't clear yet, Nordveldt. Or should I say Northfield? You're a Tannian these days, aren't you? I have only convinced them to try you. I can't get you an outright pardon."

"Pardon" was a word that struck instant ire in me. "And who the hell are you and your strutting snot-nosed *varks* to *pardon* me!"

"They wish they had been in the war," said Kit. "They

are jealous of you because you were. And they hate you because you lost it for them."

"I did that on purpose," I snapped.

"I told you they don't understand."

I should not have been yelling at her. She was all that stood between me and a pack of monomaniacal little boys playing with guns.

"They seem to have forgiven *you* all right," I said.

"That is because I conceived the idea for ESRA. *I* am trying to make good. You sold out, Northfield."

"You founded Erde Shall Rise Again? Of course you did," I said ironically. "It's so like you."

"I don't think I like your tone of voice."

"I wasn't being complimentary."

"Behave. I might have leverage to win you a pardon on a condition."

I didn't want to hear it.

Kit continued, "If you belonged to me I don't think they could hurt you."

"If I *belonged* to you?"

"Marry me."

Kit was my first wife's best friend. Kit had never forgiven me for marrying Israela.

Kit did not want me, then or now. She wanted to prevent me from inflicting matrimony on anyone else. She did not believe in the institution. She said marriage was an archaic system of male subjugation of women. The nuclear family was as relevant to anything as the roles of a baboon troop. I hope that sums up her argument accurately. She is no longer around to defend it.

In some other circumstance I would have laughed.

I was furious. I had just been kidnapped and executed twice, I had come here on a mission of planetary defense, and Kit chose this moment to pick at an old wound which I had little sympathy for in the first place. Marry her? I wanted to drop-kick her into orbit and go explain to the Tannians why I hadn't made my appointed rendezvous.

"Kit, I am tired of being jerked around here, and I couldn't take you up on that idiotic offer even if I wanted to. I remarried."

"Since when?" she challenged. "You've been in prison."

Evidently she had been keeping an eye on me, but my marriage was too recent to be in her file yet.

"The day I came to Erde."

One eyebrow lowered over a narrowed eye to tell me this sounded highly unlikely.

She checked the public records, certain she was going to catch me perjuring myself before De Hoge Raad. She was not pleased to find me truthful.

"I'll shoot her down," said Kit. "I'll shoot down your Tannian puppy."

Puppy? Where had I heard Maggie called a puppy before?

The Occon. So Kit knew about that encounter.

Kit's intelligence network was better than I thought—better than Tannia knew. I was more than angry now. I blew up. "If you know that, then you know why I am here! God damn you! God damn you! Give me your goddam answer and let me go!"

"Oh no no no, Northfield. You think this is a charade? I assure you they are serious." She nodded toward the ESRAns.

"I don't understand you. You know what has been happening! If you don't help, there won't be any Erde to rise again!"

They laughed. Kit said, "Is that what the Tannians told you?"

"It's true. You know. You saw the attacks."

"Attacks? On *Tannia.*" To the ESRAns she said, "He isn't treacherous. He's stupid." Then back to me, *"Occons have never laid a finger on anything Erden!"*

I blanked. For a moment I considered this, unable to respond, because what she said was entirely true. I thought she might actually have a point. Then I realized I was not the naive one here. "Kit, the Occons have never hit Erde because *there is nothing to hit.* We have no military installations." *We* I had said—Erde. "Why in hell would they bother? It's out of practicality, not out of *love.* God, Kit, you think they're on our *side?* The Occons are coming across on a crusade to liberate Erde from Tannian subjugation, is that what you think? They are coming to take over the double planet while one planet still has its military teeth pulled!"

After the War of 174 the Tannian victors had thought they ought to have bases on Erde, but they rethought this, reasoning that, besides fomenting hatred, the bases would, in event of rebellion, be the first places hit. The first sign of rebellion would inevitably be the capture of the bases, and *then* where would the Tannians be? The advice taken was: don't put weapons on Erde unless you are absolutely sure they cannot be used against Tannia. And thus there were no military bases on Erde. No wonder Occo was leaving Erde alone!

"What a novel interpretation," said Kit, unimpressed. "You know you even think like a Tannian now?"

"Kit, will you consider that for a minute? That I might be right?"

"You know what I'm considering? That if Tannia is in such critical need that they are crawling to us for help, they must be very very very weak. *Let's go get them now!* Erde shall rise again!"

The others joined her battle cry. "Erde shall rise again!"

As Kit turned to me the yellow flecks within her eyes appeared to ignite. "And *you* are wrong, by the way. Erde does have a military installation."

Someone hissed at her, "We have to kill him now!"

"Trial first," said Kit firmly.

"Trial," said the thin one. "Then kill him." The ESRAns hustled me down another corridor.

I said we judge each other by who we are in the air/space. This is not what I meant. They dragged me to a flight simulator.

"This one has an added feature," Kit explained. "A whole new level of accuracy."

"Weightlessness?" I said hopefully-doubtfully.

"Death," said Kit. "It convincingly simulates a crash'n'burn. Any way there is to die in a cockpit—fire, suffocation, vacuum—this can handle it."

"Who is my opponent?"

Kitty Hawke smiled with half her face. "Oh no, you don't get to take pot shots at me, Northfield. You'll be opposing a program. That's all you need to know."

Rather that was all they were telling me. A program

means infinite potential opponents. I would be fighting a machine which knew all the rules.

The only thing I knew was that I was flying a KR-22. That I gathered from the configuration of the cockpit. Kit would not tell me what I would encounter, how many, where, in air or space—nothing. My objective was to live through the program and get out of this thing.

They pushed me into the cockpit still naked. Oxygen mask I had, and a helmet, which I put on at once and netted myself in. I didn't know when the program was to begin. I was as ready as I could be in this situation.

Stars appeared in my viewports. It had begun. Begun in space. So much for my idea of just opening the hatch and jumping out. Were I to loosen the seals now, the program would vacuum me all over the cockpit. The ESRAns would be hosing my insides out of here for a week.

I took a quick scan of the vicinity, found it vacant, but I immediately moved on a random vector of my own choosing, not the computer's. Not that it wouldn't know how to find me.

I could not help but wonder if there was any way to win.

I located the nearest planet. It was Erde at 5000 klicks. I had an impulse to make a straight line for it.

I swept for mines. Antimatter mines are easy to spot, but only if you look for them. I found a zone of them between me and the planet. Their energy casings gave them away.

Without a spacesuit, I could not afford a ruptured hull, so I steered wide of the mines.

First contact with another craft came in the form of a radio hail in an old war code. It should have been easy to trace back to its sender, but nothing was registering on my scanner. Now this really is cheating, I thought. The program really ought to have my enemy obey the laws of physics.

Since I had little choice, I answered the hail. A computerized voice bade me give my controls over to its radio signal. I tried again to trace the signal back to its origin, but it was coming from nowhere. I asked, "Who are you and where?"

It said it was not in the program. It was coming from

outside the simulator, now hand over the controls. It wanted to read the program and pilot me through it.

"Who are you?" I sent.

"Manta," it said.

I hesitated. I searched the space which the simulator presented me. Nothing was there.

It could be a genuine outside voice.

It could be the program baiting me.

I had heard that the Manta was a member of ESRA. I'd also heard that no one knew *which* member.

I remembered seeing the *Manta* during the war, those tremendous flapping midnight wings.

I wavered at the switch. This could be yet another trick.

Then again, the whole thing was a colossal game. There were no good decisions.

I gave over the controls.

Abruptly my stomach was in my throat, a lunge too great to be compensated, my body pulling at the restraints, then squashed into the seat with a change of direction. *Oh God, I let them get me again!*

A jolt, a heave to one side, the other. I opened my eyes, looked at the instruments to see what my puppeteer was doing to me.

Fighter craft had appeared on all sides, and my pilot was wheeling me through the gauntlet of them, antimatter bombs detonating in every space I vacated, my ship reacting so fast it could only be another computer at the helm.

And I realized I was being pulled through a nearly impossible maze, like Theseus in his labyrinth. All heroes have a god cribbing for them. I got the Manta.

It took me on a roller-coaster ride down to a landing in a wind barrel.

When the simulated winds died down, the ship's hatches popped open.

I unharnessed and leaped out of the simulator before anything else could happen.

I had been inside barely minutes, and the ESRAns were still standing around the simulator, except Kit. They gawked at me. "What did you do?"

"He short-circuited the program!" said the white-blond youth. "He cheated!"

''Is the Manta in your program?'' I croaked. I sniffed, wiped my nose with the side of my hand. It was bleeding.

All the ESRAns were blank-faced.

Finally one breathed, ''Oh my God.''

I sensed the speaker might even have been invoking the Manta there. The Manta's name had divinity to it in this group.

But my white-blond paranoid came through again, shrieking, ''Tannians! There's a Tannian monitor on him!''

Kitty Hawke returned, attracted by the noise. ''What is going on in here?'' Then she saw me. ''Who let him out?''

''Claims the Manta did.''

''The *what* did *what?*''

''That's what I say!'' said the blond, his eyes colorless in his zeal. ''It's Tannians! They're watching us!''

I said tiredly, ''If Tannians are monitoring you, why aren't all of you under arrest?''

''They're fixing our position!''

''So they know where to send your mail, I suppose?''

Kit told me to shut up. ''You're a cat, Anton. And of your nine lives you just hit number twelve.''

Since I had passed their infernal trial, I thought I might carry on with my task, and I repeated Tannia's offer of pardon for all past offenses and commission in the fleet.

''Answer him,'' said Kit.

I was hit from behind and all was instantly black.

I woke to pounding. It was on a door. My door. Disoriented. Head hurt. Dried blood under my nose. Stirred. I was in a stifling little room of a seedy flat. Alone, except for the people breaking down my door.

I sat up as the door crashed inward.

Tannians jumped in. Guns, many guns pointed at me.

In the rear of the team, an MP—the MP with the blue-black hair—speaking into a com: ''Tip was good. We caught him.'' To me, with an electric stunner close to my face and enjoying it: ''I knew they never should've let you out. Now everyone knows you like I know you. End of the line, Kralle.''

VII.

The horse is an apt national symbol for Tannia—the left side does not know what the right side is doing; no corpus callosum in this beast.

I was taken into custody and tossed into a holding cell. I did not even try to explain. It would be a waste of breath.

My Tannian jailers came to me with a message. "We intercepted this. You want to tell us what this says, or do we run it through the computer?"

It was in code, but I was quite willing to tell them what it said. It was a simple cipher made for them to intercept anyway. "It says, 'I see how good is Tannia's offer of amnesty. I know you believed what you said, Anton, but remember who you're speaking for.' "

"What does it mean?"

I thought it was rather obvious what it meant. "It means I did my job and you just undid it."

"Who sent it?"

"I don't know. It wasn't signed."

"You mean you have no idea?"

"Of course I have an idea. It was one of the people I contacted," I said irritably. These Tannians were so stupid.

"Who did you contact and where are they?"

"Go to hell! *I* see how good Tannia's amnesty offer is!"

I was feeling like an imbecile for ever carrying such a message to my old comrades. I was every bit as gullible and misled as ESRA said I was.

Then Admiral Thomasina Wright showed up on Erde.

None of these little toadstools had ever seen a full admiral, and they trembled in the face of Lady Thom. Then, upon learning the whole picture, she became angry, and all the cowering underlings (who gave a whole new meaning to the term "petty officer") nearly vaporized under her gaze.

She was livid. A very cultured, very proper old gentlewoman, she, in her marvelous round tones, called them all assholes.

She freed me from confinement one more time and groaned, "Good Lord, wasn't that a wasted effort! The whole recruitment operation down the tube, just down the tube!"

"Well, not entirely."

That was not I who said that. We both turned to see who had spoken.

The doorway was dark, and he wore a dark oversized shirt, so he seemed to be little more than a pair of large eyes peering from within deep sockets. Reid.

"Did I shock you?"

"I should say so!"

He had been adamant about not coming.

A little sheepish, he shrugged. "There's an old saying—Erders don't know how to say yes." And to Lady Thom he said, "Be nice to me. There's someone else waiting to see how I fare. We drew lots. I lost, so I got thrown into the lion's den first."

And as soon as Reid's record was cleared, Gerhardt Recht came forward to volunteer. Sense of duty got the best of him. His new life and hard-built reputation were taking it on the chin, but the Gerhardt I knew could not walk away from responsibility. I wondered how he had broken the truth to his wife. Even as I thought it, he turned to me and said, "You're right, the three-eyed look was not terminal."

Back on Tannia, I and my own young wife were reunited. We were stationed at the same base and even got to see each other sometimes between flight maneuvers.

Leaving details alone, suffice it to say we were newly wed, and though I had trouble expressing myself in words, I think she could tell I loved her.

I was still not communicative, but it was a joy to hear Maggie's bubbly chatter.

She asked about my odyssey on Erde. When I came to the part about my trial by ESRA, she said, "The Manta bailed you out but didn't come forward to volunteer. Isn't that odd?"

"I don't know," I said. "Maybe he did."

And as it turned out, all the volunteers were not done coming forward.

Admiral Wright informed me another conditional volunteer had expressed interest. "Manta?" I said.

"The whole of ESRA."

"What!"

Admiral Wright showed me the offer. It was worded in such a way I knew Kitty Hawke had composed it. The Erde Shall Rise Again fleet was offering aid to Tannia against Occo on several conditions. In addition to the offered amnesty for all alleged crimes, ESRA demanded that after the crisis was over, Erde be allowed to have its own constitution of Erden authorship, and be allowed to maintain a standing army.

"There is no way I can accept this," said the admiral. Nevertheless she sent it upstairs to the Tannian legislature.

The response was violent. No. Never. Absolutely not.

But the demand inspired a surge of national feeling in me. As much as I detested the ESRAns, I agreed theirs was a valid demand, and I almost walked out to hear it refused so flatly.

But I had a Tannian bride (a pregnant Tannian bride!), and you have to be alive to defend a principle. If we did not repulse the Occons, the question of a free Erden constitution could be permanently moot.

And there came yet one final surprise of a volunteer. Admiral Pieter Griesmann. He said he'd had a change of heart.

"A change of what?" Reid muttered.

I could not recall extending the offer to *him.* I had only asked him where I could find the others. And he had been no help.

Griesmann did not look like the Griesmann I had seen in his subterranean Center City den. He had slimmed down, had his muscles toned, and he dressed like a human being. He looked like the admiral of the Erden fleet again.

He still did not have a throat. Even without the multiple chins, the skin still dropped straight from his jaw to the base of his neck without indentation. He was not trying to look attractive, only distinguished. And he succeeded.

The man was a chameleon. I recalled referring to the Manta as a Zorro. Zorro's alter ego had been a thorough bounder. But Griesmann went beyond the facade of a frivolous cad. He was a genuine *vark.*

But he had many resources, and I had underestimated him more than once.

A major problem facing Erde-Tannia besides our dearth of skilled pilots was our inappropriate equipment. All our fighters—Erde's and Tannia's—were designed to travel between Tannia and Erde—a 750,000-kilometer hop—not to Occo.

"Just how many megaklicks is that?"

"On what given day?"

Over 190 years after the first landing, we were still not skipping between planets in our solar system. The only other planets we frequented were the next one out, Iris, for the iridium mines, and the one beyond that, Augea, the garbage planet. The most fuel-economical route is a time-consuming transfer orbit, and for those two trips, Iris and Augea, we have time. Robot ships embark and return about once a month. Once the conga train was set in motion, there was no need for haste. So what if it takes two years to get there, if the next delivery is in one month?

The need for better, faster travel between planets outside our double world simply has not been there. Occo is the only other habitable world, and the Occons have forbidden us access for the last one hundred years. They called it securing their border against outer-planet encroachment.

The journey to Occo is neither quick nor always convenient.

Our ships can get to anywhere on inertia. In space, give a ship a push and it goes. But can its passengers live to see the destination is another matter entirely. For that we were dependent on launch windows.

We had the wherewithal to get to Occo and even get back without stopping to refuel. What we could *not* do was pause and fight, let alone enter their atmosphere.

We could design a ship to do that. The Tannian labs had designed several. The gap remained between the possible and the practical. First we had to decide exactly what we wanted, then get the funds for it.

Which meant deciding what we needed, and that we did not know because we did not know what Occo had. It's like a card game—all hands but one are beatable. It's having the right cards at the right time to beat the other player's hand that decides the game.

So even if our ships were designed to fly to Occo, what weapons did we take with us, prepared to combat what?

They had come at us last time with low-tech bombs. That did not mean Occo was low-tech. It meant Tannia was well defended against higher-tech and the Occons knew what would get through its defenses.

We (we, Erde-Tannia) have the technical know-how to combat all kinds of weapons—if we have the proper equipment built, fueled up, maintained, placed, manned, turned on, ready. All those ifs are how we (we, Erde) lost the first war. We had all the equipment. We did not use it properly.

And, especially because Erde the aggressor lost the war of 174, some people did not believe we needed to go to Occo now. They said Tannians were not aggressors. If Occo wanted war, we would fight it here in Erde-Tannian space.

But anyone knows if you have an infestation of cardits you have to hit the hive or they keep coming, mutated to hardier strains every time.

However, the fight-'em-here party did have a point: a supply line stretches kind of thin over twenty-seven million plus miles.

We were still carrying fuel on our ships. Even if we could bag enough to achieve acceleration sufficient to thrust a small fighter to Occo in decent time, the g force of the requisite acceleration would kill the pilot. Slower, and you face the fact that comfort facilities on a small fighter are abysmal. A pilot cannot sit in one for days, then expect to fight a battle.

A spacecraft carrier would solve a lot of problems. Of course, the carrier would need to be designed so the fighters could get in and out of it in negatively numbered time—I mean fast fast fast. You know the satisfaction you get from crushing a blattoid's egg case? Picture an Occon hitting a loaded Tannian spacecraft carrier. Precisely why opponents of the idea opposed it. It would put all our eggs in one basket.

But how else do you propose to transport the eggs without the basket? Pitch the eggs one by one?

I was pushing the carrier concept myself. All that was needed to make the carrier workable was to cut down the time it took to get in and out of it. My father was a racecar driver, his crew the masters of the six-second pit stop. My father was a champion. The pit time is everything.

And there was one more problem with equipment. The Tannians call it the widow factor, a not-quite-acronym for What If It Don't Work? No machine is 100 percent, and the sober fact is most of them are far short of it. It was something to keep in mind.

The next Occon invasion was expected in four months, precious little time to organize our defense.

Before we could even start, a boom rattled the windows and alarms were blaring.

No time at all. The Occons had come early.

VIII.

The Occons could not be here. And yet here they were.

Suddenly the base received the order to scramble, scramble everything.

I was caught behind a log jam of fighters on the launch rails. The base was well insulated under a defensive shield dome which had activated automatically at the Occon approach, so we were spared the sight of our fighting ships being crushed on the ground while they waited in line. But Occon fighters were ready to pick us off as our ships rose outside the protective umbrella.

Our base lit up like a radiant star, defensive beams spraying into the air/space. Our ships' computer pilots guided them up through the shifting cluster of beams like symbiotic fish within the poison tentacles of an anemone.

Reid, Gerhardt, Griesmann, and I were last in the launch order. We waited in our cockpits for the galling bottleneck to clear. Tannia boasted that it could have its entire force in the air in three minutes, which sounds fast, but it is a deathly long time to watch the ships in front of you get shot. But it also gave those of us in the rear time to watch the Occons' tactics before jumping into the ring ourselves.

Gerhardt's voice sounded in my ear over the B com, coolly analytical, pointing out strategies and comparative weaponry. He pointed out that the Occon hardware was not exotically different from ours, not so far, but they handled it expertly.

Reid, a little less instructively, said, "They're *rude!*" He was impressed.

I barely heard them, my heart in my throat. I was watching Maggie take to the sky.

I didn't think she should go up at all. I know next to nothing on the subject but I didn't think weightlessness was a good idea in the first weeks of pregnancy. Maggie said she would be sure to mention it to the Occons while she was up there.

My first wife claimed that the moment I married her I turned into her mother. Excuse me for being terrified while watching the woman I love fly into mortal danger.

Nothing would keep Maggie on the ground. She was a puppy with a score to settle. She wanted to get that Occon who had so condescendingly let her live in her first encounter. She went up barking.

I watched her make it out of atmosphere alive before I remembered to breathe again.

Then she sent a Dogfighter missile into an Occon's prow.

"You don't use a Dogfighter in *space!*" I blurted over the com.

"She just did," said Reid.

It was the last thing the Occon expected, I imagine. The very last.

Now that Maggie had some maneuvering room I was able to consider what Gerhardt had been saying about the Occon ships. They were not long-range vessels. They were just fighters like ours. So how had they gotten here? The time factor, the launch windows, were all wrong.

On a wide scan of surrounding space—the widest scan possible in my ship—I detected a persistent beam generated from Occo which bypassed Erde-Tannia by several thousand kilometers. It seemed significant of nothing, but there had to be a reason for it. I asked someone. The controller said it had been there for days. It was a laser, nothing more.

I was about to ask further when Reid sent, "Check out zone double beta, Anton."

In double beta the Occons were *stealing* two orbital platforms. I mean they hooked tugs on them and blasted them out of orbit. These were civilian platforms. One was a greenhouse and one was a service station. The

Occons *took* them, people and all, and ran with them. And there was little our fighters could do to stop them.

Finally came our time to go join a losing battle.

"I'm so embarrassed," said Reid. "C'mon, Anton, let's show 'em how it's done."

The four of us Erders launched and climbed to the perimeter of the defensive dome, then our computer pilots wove us along shifting defensive beams through a blizzard of enemy fire.

Griesmann went up with a show of bravado, broadcasting all the way, "Prepare to meet Admiral"—he wasn't, not with this fleet—"Pieter Wilhelminazoon Griesmann!" As if that should strike terror into the Occon hearts.

We were still in the atmosphere when Gerhardt was hit.

For a minute I felt nothing but denial and disbelief. No. It had not happened. Couldn't.

Then I felt sick. I had brought him here. Just for that. I had dragged him away from everything he loved just to die like a slapped bug in the first seconds of combat, without enough time to become a hero. I had done this.

I tried not to think that way. Erders believe in a modified predetermination. Your time here is fixed. When your number is up, it's up. Your karma, moira, nemesis, allotment, destiny, whatever, will find you wherever you are, hiding in a cellar or facing battle, so go into the teeth of the dragon without fear.

I learned to take this to heart early. My father was a racecar driver. He was fast and clever—where I get it. The Tannians have since outlawed automobile racing as blood sport, but my father did not die in a race. He wasn't even doing anything dangerous. It was a freak accident. We were in the stands, *watching* a race, when a piece came off a collided car like an armor-piercing bullet, flew into the stands, and drove straight into his brain.

When your number is up, it's up; when it's not, it's not. When I think of all the times I should have died and didn't, it convinces me this is true.

I tried to hold on to that belief as I watched Gerhardt's ship disintegrate, but I couldn't. He hadn't even gotten off a single shot.

What had I done?

"Wake up, Anton!" That was Reid. He knew.

"I'm here," I said.

Reid and I made it into space. I didn't see where Griesmann went.

We tried to shoot the Occon bombers, but their fighters were all over us, so we had to face those. They were hard to hit. I felt like a clumsy cadet. It was all I could do to stay alive.

I had a score of exactly zero when a fleet arrived from Erde, blazoned with symbols of Erde Shall Rise Again. It was true what Kitty Hawke claimed, ESRA had a base. It had a fleet.

And they were coming out to help. They were coming out to help *the Occons.*

The ESRAn flagship transmitted an offer of alliance to the invaders.

The Occons kept a far distance from the new fleet but sent back a message capsule encased in a protective sphere of energy. Rather that is what ESRA assumed it was, because the ESRAn flagship took it in.

Reid and I must have had the same thought at the same time, because we both turned tail, flank speed. There is a panic button in every cockpit you hit when you realize you are in an ambush. We weren't the ones in the ambush, but I hit it and Reid screamed over the com, "Trojan horse!"

The protective energy sphere around the "message capsule" disengaged. Antimatter met matter and the ESRAn fleet ripped apart. Part of the flagship was gone, absolutely gone, in an instant, while gamma rays and exploding parts of the rest of it tore through the others with the force of a million bombs.

At our distance our computer pilots were barely able to avoid the radioactive shards that came hurtling outward faster than missiles.

I thought of my father in the stands, saw another possible death speed past.

When the path was clear, Reid and I started back to battle, but we saw some Occon fighters and bombers splinter off and head for Erde. Of course we were Erders and we had to get them. We abandoned the defense of Tannia and ran to defend our home.

The Occon fighters turned to engage us. I got my first and only kill of the battle—but not before the bombers found their target. They made one localized hit on the planet surface, then veered off.

They had hit ESRA's secret base. We knew it was a base by the way it blew up. It had not blown up as a hydroponic farm, as it was labeled on map, should have. The chain reaction of explosions was apocalyptic.

Reid's voice sounded in my headset. "Anton, does anything strike you at all odd in this?"

"In this *what,* Reid? The whole thing is bloody odd!"

"That all ESRA's force was taken out so neatly, one, two, I mean like a tumor."

"Should it be odd?"

"The Occons knew exactly how to get Erde's forces, knew ESRA would swallow that prettily wrapped antimatter bomb. The Occons brought that Trojan horse with them. It had to be prearranged, which means they knew ESRA would offer alliance, and they knew exactly where ESRA's base was when Tannia didn't even know Erde *had* a base."

"Occo's intelligence net is obviously better than ours," I said.

"They bombed an empty Tannian prison! What fucking intelligence?"

This struck home. "Almost empty, Reid," I said thickly.

"We were sold out, Anton." We, he said, ESRA.

"But how is that possible?" I said. "It would have to be by someone within ESRA." And that was inconceivable to me—that a member of ESRA would turn traitor. As much as I hated them I had to admit they were fanatic loyalists. They would die for Erde. Such people do not sell out. "I can't believe anyone in ESRA would do that."

"No one actually in ESRA," said Reid.

"But who else knew?"

"Did you see the base, Anton?"

It took me a moment to catch the innuendo. "Fuck you, Reid, I did not!" And then I countered, "How about *you,* Reid?"

"Ten o'clock high, Anton!"

My ship had already seen the Occon and evaded. "Ten o'clock" is twelve o'clock on an Earth face—Erde's is a decimal clock—and "high" in space is a direction in relation to your ship's prow.

The Occon ship was a bomber. Reid took it out.

Reid and I were about to follow the other Occon bombers back to the battle around Tannia when Reid sent, "Anton, I have another thought."

"Do I want to hear it?"

"That laser coming from Occo. The one that has been firing for days. I think I know what it means."

"What?"

"Laser sails. That beam pushed the Occon carrier near enough to Erde-Tannia for it to launch all these fighters and bombers. We didn't detect the presence of the carrier because it's got no powerplant. It's a sailing ship."

This made sense. Fifteen years in hiding hadn't blunted Reid's battle sense. If what he said was true, we knew where the Occon carrier was.

"Let's go get it."

Reid is also crazy.

"Just us?" I said.

"I'm going to hit that sow, Anton. You can stay or you can come." And Reid took off, rocket blazing like no return.

On my life count catwise, Kit had said I was on number twelve, which would be up to thirteen now. I always considered it a bad number. Pilots are superstitious, so that should have told me something. But of all ways to skin a cat I thought I'd been flayed all there were.

I was spectacularly wrong.

I don't know who won the battle. I did not see the end of it.

I lost.

Reid was already out of visual range. I was about to follow his trail when I was hit.

I don't know who hit me or even if it was an intentional shot. There was no enemy ship registering in that direction for thousands of kilometers.

I think it was a random wild-ass hit from the battle around Tannia. My number, I thought, was up.

The auto-squelches dampened the blast, but my rocket and my Chrysalis engines and life support were out.

I had a suit on this time, so I wasn't dead yet, but I was drifting toward the planet. Erde's cloud swirls looked closer. Definitely closer. If I did not find power soon I was doomed to burn up.

Had I not lived so long I would have pulled my air right there. I had seen enough unexpected things in my time to wait and see if another was coming. It didn't look like it.

I had an idea. If I could rig a power supply to activate the controls to one of my small directional rockets it might afford enough thrust to kick me into a parking orbit around Erde.

After the battle someone could come and pick me up, but I had to live that long.

I had a computer still functional. One directional rocket seemed to be aligned properly, and the computer said its small thrust could achieve a parking orbit but only within the next ten minutes. Once I was within a hundred kilometers of Erde the gravitational pull would be too great for my little directional to save me.

I was at one hundred plus one kilometers and falling.

Finding a live power supply. My emergency transceiver.

Now to get it to the rocket control.

I hate space walking.

It wasn't really space walking, it was space *reaching*. I had to lean out and connect a cable.

But first I had to convince the computer to let go of the hatch. One hundred plus 0.5 kilometers and it refused to open up, saying I would compromise the atmospheric integrity of the cockpit. The only thing that functioned on board this craft and it wouldn't let me out. I had to break it to its bubble mind that all the atmosphere that had been in this cockpit had already vacated—which is to say I threw the manual override. I wouldn't be needing the computer again anyway if I didn't get the hatch open right now.

Leaning out into infinity, trying not to look down, as downness was just coming back into real being, I jerry-rigged my ship. The looming clouds made me dizzy, and for a moment I thought I would slide out and fall into them.

One hundred plus 0.1 kilometers.

I pulled myself in and sealed the hatch again.

No time left. This was it. I threw the switch.

One hundred kilometers. Nothing happened.

Seconds ticking past. I beat on the switch.

A flash. The ship lurched.

The wrong way.

Between the time I hit the switch and it engaged, my ship had turned slightly. The directional rocket's blast drove me into the atmosphere, and my ship with me in it was burning up.

IX.

Another shock, a thump. I thought it was an explosion.

Rising. Clouds smaller. I was moving away from the planet.

I've been picked up, I thought. A Harpy had come from a civilian airport on Erde and snatched me up. Thank God.

I was about to signal thanks. Then I glimpsed a wing at the very edge of my glowing port.

The wing of an Occon bomber.

I was being shanghaied, like the orbital platforms. I was taken, ship and all, to the Occon carrier, which was as Reid deduced an enormous rotating torus of a ship propelled by a titanic laser sail.

Spacesuited people pried me from the wreck of my ship. I was afraid it would be only my ship they wanted, and me they would jettison. But they threw me into a hexagonal cell and sealed it.

Another person was in the cell, wearing a pilot's jacket but not a spacesuit, so I had to suppose the atmosphere was safe. My fellow prisoner was sitting on the floor of the bare cell, his head between his knees. He looked up. Reid.

I took off my helmet. My suit was almost out of oxygen anyway. The air was breathable, the pressure not great, the gravity only enough to keep us on the deck.

Reid, like a gradually fraying rope, clasped and unclasped his hands jerkily, said quietly, "I hate cages, Anton."

"I know you do, Reid."

He beckoned me down on the deck with him, whispered in my ear, "I have another ship, if I can get to it."

I squeaked back, "How did you get *two?*"

"I brought my own along."

I tend to forget how rich Reid is. He used to own half of Erdetechnik. "Where is it?"

He twitched suspiciously, seemed to change his mind about confiding in me. "I parked it."

"In space? The Occons probably picked it up."

"Not bloody likely. They have to find it first."

And he clammed up for a while.

I paced the cell. It was tight, seamless, disconcertingly like the cell of a bee hive. I could not even tell how the air was circulating.

If it was at all.

"Anton."

Reid was clawing at his legs. My name spoken was a plea for help, and I couldn't. He turned his great dark eyes up to me like the little dog who begs you in the storm to make the thunder and lightning stop.

He began to bounce, literally, off the six walls. Blood spots marked where he hit.

Till he went catatonic. Poor Reid. I left him there. I did not try to draw him out, not that I know the first thing of how one goes about attempting that. It was better for him inside.

My skin blistered. Funny thing about burns—they show up later.

My arms were suddenly red. I could swear they'd been white last time I looked. Now they were red and bubbled.

A door appeared in our cell, and I got my first look at an unsuited Occon.

He was dark, as if in the sun too long, with an ill-proportioned face. He stuck his very long nose in to look at his catch.

We made a real prize, one catatonic and one boiled lobster. I hoped the Occon did not decide to toss us back.

Another Occon came in shortly, inspected Reid. What I mistook for concern was no such thing. They were considering throwing him off board. I don't know what clued me in, but I intervened. I told them Reid was fine. I made myself understood, I think. They left Reid with me and resealed the cell.

They gave me nothing for my burns. They were definitely not concerned for our well-being.

I wondered what we were being preserved for.

Time crawled. Surely the battle had been decided. The longer we remained in the cell, the worse the outlook. I had time to run through all scenarios from best to worst: from Occo had lost and was using us as leverage for terms to both planets were in Occon hands.

And where was my wife? Did she know where I was? Did she know I was alive?

I conceived a sudden urgent need to talk to her, to tell her I could not imagine life without her.

Maggie, should you ever see this, know that I love you.

Time dragged on. What must have been more than a day passed. I had nothing to gauge by. No cycle of light and dark. Once the lights went out. I thought the carrier had been hit. The lights came on again later without comment from our seldom-seen captors.

A horrible suspicion stole upon me. Suspicion that we were moving. I had a horror that we were going to Occo.

We needed to escape. I realized if we did not get off this ship there was an awful probability that we would end up on Occo. And once there we could not see home for months—and that only if we were lucky enough to get our hands on a ship at the right time. We would be dependent on launch windows, for we could not exactly hijack this sailing ship while Occo controlled the winds.

For the moment, however, we saw nothing to do, stuck in our cell. I was sick to my stomach most of the time, perhaps from my burns. My whole body was outraged with me.

Our captors fed us by injection what seemed once a day. I knew the injection was nourishment by the rush of energy I felt course through my blood, a feeling like drinking sugared soda when very very hungry. It did not keep the gnawing from my stomach. Injections were designed for short-term use—here to minimize elimination, I guessed. But we still had to drink. The water we were given tasted flat and many times recycled. We were moved once from our cage to clean it. Without being indelicate let's say that after the length of time (days?) we had been confined, it needed it.

I had to carry Reid out.

The rest of the ship, what little I saw, was as dismal as our cell, gray, stripped-down, closed-in, hexagonal.

From that time on we were allowed out to use the facilities. Our captors let me know that if Reid was not housebroken he was going out. I took care of Reid. I would not let them eject him.

The head was in a small compartment at the end of a cramped corridor, so I was able to see but little more of the carrier's layout.

All the Occons I saw were peculiar. Unsettling. I could not say they were unattractive and I could not say they all looked alike, but they were all out of proportion. If an artist were to draw a person's face, he would make the distance from the bridge of the nose down to the tip of the nose measure only the width of an eye.

All these Occons had too-long noses. Not just the nose, which did not protrude overmuch, it was the whole middle of the face which was too long, giving them a vaguely beastial, equine or canine quality.

But if I thought anything of it—and it took me a while even to pinpoint what was different—I thought, Oh, these are Occons. The Earth colonists who went to Occo must have been a different race than the colonists of Erde-Tannia. I knew they had come from a different part of the world than had the founders of either Erde or Tannia.

But that measure, an eye for a nose, goes for all people. It is surprisingly uniform. I had never heard of a race with such elongated faces.

And the Occons' fingernails were horny and black where they extended past the fingertips. And if I thought anything it was that most of these people were in need of a good clipping and what ugly nails they have. Maybe it had to do with the Occon climate or diet.

And they had boringly even teeth. Even their canines were blunt, squared off like incisors. I only marked this because my own canines are worn down to flat evenness; otherwise I should hardly have noticed.

Each observation was really nothing.

But all these nothings were adding up to a progressively stronger sense of unease.

The colonists of Occo had come originally from the Indian subcontinent and from Southeast Asia and the Pacific islands, representing five different language *families,* and God knows how many languages—I heard that it was triple digits. Sounds implausible to me that one world should spawn that many tongues, but I did not live on a naturally evolved world. If that number was anywhere near true, it might help to explain what happened on Occo: the Occons scrapped all their native tongues and made up a new one. (This explanation, as I was to discover shortly, was dead wrong, but it was the best I could devise at the moment.)

Occon, the language, has nothing in common with any Earth language.

The languages of Tannia and Erde are far removed from their Earth mother tongues, but you can recognize their roots. Tannian used to be English; in fact, it is still called English. English was the lingua franca of Earth at the time of the exodus. Erders came from Europe. The Erden language is a mélange of Dutch, German, Frisian, Afrikaans, and English.

"Erde" means Earth. "Tannia" . . . I've forgotten the derivation but I remember it was something sensible with roots and meaning. "Occo" is cacophonous nonsense.

The Occon language is like nothing anyone has ever heard. When Occons deign to communicate with us on interplanetary radio it is usually in Erden or English.

When the original colonists came to this system, the ones who became known as Occons veered off for the innermost habitable planet. They thought they had inside information not privy to the other two groups. But something was wrong. The theory is that Occo was hit by a large comet between the time of the robot ship's survey and the subsequent human settlement, and the colonists did not find what they expected. Occo's climate is hostile.

But the Occons never let on that anything was amiss on their world. They told Erde-Tannia that our readings were faulty and that everything was fine on Occo. We of the double planet could only guess that a fierce national pride kept them from facing up to a colossal mistake, and what was holding them together was mistrust of Erde-Tannia. They called us "the get of Earth's most imperialist nations."

I knew our readings were accurate, and I knew I did not want to go to Occo.

I sat down next to the compact tangle that was Reid. "Reid, if you can hear me in there, you've got to come out." And I explained the situation. I was fairly sure he could hear me, and I had the idea that if he had some goal to work toward he would be able to function. He would not notice the cage quite so much if he was actively plotting to get out of it. "Can you hear me?"

After a long pause, Reid gave a slow blink which I interpreted as affirmative.

"They let us out together to go to the head because they think you can't move by yourself. That looks like our only shot."

He blinked.

So next time we were let out to use the head, I dropped Reid and started to run the wrong way.

The guards followed me. No one gave any attention to Reid, because they knew he was helpless. By the time my guards corralled me, Reid was gone like an omro in the woodwork. I was thrown back into the cell. I rued that I hadn't sprung my plot after going to the head, but I can't think of everything.

Waiting again. Agonizing now. No one opened the door. I had not realized how much company there was in a zombie until he was gone. Just me in the cell.

My blisters shriveled, itched, scabbed, and peeled. My hair was an oily mat. I was glad I could not see myself. I was also glad I'd had my beard growth stopped when I was a teenager, so at least I did not have to deal with that.

A thud. Gravity went and I drifted off the deck. My heart seized. We are still in Tannian space, I thought. There is still a fight! The carrier is under attack!

Or Reid had done it. He had gotten control of the ship and knocked out part of the crew, and now the atmospheric controls had gone haywire, for I was drawn to the wall as if magnetized and became stuck there. Sense of downness pinned me to the wall. Cabin pressure increased, heat increased.

Fear creeping over me. Something was drastically wrong. Pressure increased past anything normal. I thought I was to be crushed. The wall had most certainly taken on the character of a floor. Gravitation increased past one g and kept increasing.

Reid, what are you doing?

Sound. A roaring rushing sound. I thought the hull had been breached and part of the atmosphere was roaring out. Buffeted, rocking.

A shock like an impact. Rushing sound ceased, engine sounds wound down. (Engines? On a sailing ship?) But the pressure, the pull, remained high to unbearable.

An opening appeared in my cell. I pulled myself off the wall/floor to stand. Guards marched me out, through the corridor (walking on the walls). I saw a bright light and was pushed toward it. I stood in a hatchway and blinked.

Ground. We were on the ground.

The sun looked swollen. Huge. But it had not grown. I was twenty-seven million miles closer to it.

We were prisoners of Occo.

The crushing pressure was Occo's. The leaden gravity was Occo's. I swallowed hard, blinked rapidly against the heat and light. I felt as if I weighed over two hundred pounds. I did.

I took a few tottering steps in the red dust, toward an enclosure. There were other prisoners, guards, and Reid in a little box.

Sorry, I'm so sorry.

He was peacefully catatonic, rigid and glassy-eyed as you please.

I looked back at the craft that had brought us down. It was a bulky carbon-streaked shuttle, designed to fit into the carrier as a segment of that immense torus.

I looked at the ship so I would not have to look at the Occons—Occons with their black-tipped narrow fingernails, their long faces, their neat squared-off teeth. Subliminal sense of wrongness about them culminated all of a sudden into revelation as clear and blinding as the sun in the Occon sky. I saw a man with what I thought was a headdress. No, those are real. Not a headdress. Not a man. Those are antlers, and none of these beings are human.

"Antlers! The man's got fucking antlers!" I could hear someone saying over and over.

My thoughts were absurd. Antlers, yes, and I didn't know about the adjective, but the man part was wrong.

I wanted to believe this was bioengineering. I wanted our captors to be human. To think otherwise was to wonder what in God's name had happened to the colonists and what in hell these were.

If it had been just the antlers I could have made myself believe that. But the nails, the faces, the teeth, the language defied my attempt at blissful ignorance. These were not human and they never had been. And not descendants thereof.

My knees hit the ground. I did not feel like bearing up.

It might have helped even had they been *odder*. They were so very close to human that the sense of vertigo was sickening.

The Occons started to herd the several hundred of us to a ground vehicle and prod us in like cattle. Most of the prisoners were civilians in work dress that marked them as inhabitants of the stolen orbital platforms, greenhouse workers and service station mechanics. Reid and I were the only pilots I saw. Except for Griesmann.

I sighted Griesmann, standing apart, talking to one of the aliens. "Chatting" might be a more accurate word.

Guards commanded several prisoners to pick up Reid's box and load him onto the transport with the others. Someone pushed me with a foot, bade me in an alien tongue to get up. I think that is what he said.

Despair of the marooned took all the strength from my limbs. Even if I had had a T-15 right at that moment, the next launch window would not occur for months.

Red soil and swollen fireball. Alien poking at my back until I lugged myself upright and shuffled to the waiting truck. Looking out of a dark crowded stinking compartment at this hell where I must stay.

Right about then is when I cried.

PART THREE:

OCCO

I.

I could not move. Could not breathe. Like being underwater and trying to inhale through a snorkel; a crushing pressure closes on the chest and it's a labor just to pull air into the lungs. It was a labor just to lie still and support my own weight in the dark hot transport as it jolted along.

I moved through the press of groaning cursing prisoners to Reid and dragged him out of his box. Once free of the confines, he stayed folded up. I tried to unbend him, and he passed out. Reid was accustomed to living in the Erden highlands. Occo's pressure would be even harder on him than it was on me. I was at least buffered by twenty years of living under the greater pressure of Tannia. Ambient pressure on Occo was four times that, so for Reid it was almost six times that of his mountain home. I thought he was dead.

For all I know he is dead. I have not seen Reid since we were unloaded from the transport. The Occons dragged him away like a corpse.

I held on to him during the long torturous ride, and kept his head from banging on the floor. Some of the workers from the space platforms, where the pressure is also considerably diminished from that of a planet surface, went into nitrogen narcosis. I was feeling a little drunk myself. I closed my eyes.

At least there were no tides on Occo—not as an Erder or Tannian would speak of tides. Occo's moons are grandiose boulders, so the solar influence was the only tide Occo had to contend with.

When the transport ground to a stop I had been dreaming. I dreamed I was in my own bed in my house on Tannia. I was about to get up and eat bacon and eggs and take a drink of water so cold that droplets of condensation beaded and trickled down the side of the glass. I was so disappointed upon waking that I almost cried again, but I was rather done with that. It's not something I do often or for long.

We spilled out of the cattle car into another enclosure much like the first one, except bigger, with a double perimeter fence and a few low bleak limestone block buildings inside.

The bloated sun was going down by then. Its enormous red disk wallowed in the rolling dust which obliterated any distinct line of a horizon.

The Occon soldiers were separating their captives into two groups, male and female, but they had some trouble differentiating. One pointed to the crumpled knot of Reid at his feet and said to me, "Male or female?"

"Male, you ass," I said.

I thought it obvious. The indistinguishable ones were the *Occons.* Except for the one with the antlers, who was not here at this end of the line, and a few deep-voiced ones giving orders, the rest of the Occons were so androgynous that I could not tell what sex was what. There was a reason for my confusion, but I discovered it only later.

For now the low-ranking ambiguous ones were sifting through our numbers. Flat-chested women and beardless men threw the aliens into total stupefaction. They took to poking between our legs, which only sent us all into crouches.

"Neuter?" one asked me.

I stared up from my crouch at the stupid thing. Before I could sputter some kind of answer, a deep-voiced officer pushed the androgynous soldier roughly and said—all in Occon but for the word *human*—"There is no such thing as a *ufin/i* human, you stupid *ufin/i.*" And he shoved me into the male group.

When finally the Occons had us segregated, they loaded the women back onto the transport and took them away. The men were at the end of our road.

The Occons herded us into a fenced enclosure within

the greater compound, where squatted a few dismal buildings at the edge of a wide field of waste scrub and rock. Rags of plants the colors of dust and stone fluttered under a sere wind.

Most of the higher-ranking Occons stayed outside this inner barrier.

The sun sank below the weltering horizon. A bloody-red haze lingered yet. In the blackening sky a single star shone brighter than all the others with a steady light. Not a star, I realized. It was home. From here Erde-Tannia appeared as one.

Through the prism of tears the light expanded and glowed, diffused. I blinked the image clear, back to a distant steady beacon.

Anger penetrated my misery. I remembered what Reid had said during the battle: we had been betrayed.

He was right.

And I knew who had done it.

I saw him here, the traitor, standing apart in his flight-suit, his nose in the air, arms akimbo, as he surveyed the lay of the land.

I stalked over to him and asked him why.

He reacted as if the question of loyalty were an absurd one.

"I should have fought for Tannia? For what they offered me?" His small mean porcine eyes became merry crescents. He roared laughter. "Tannia offered nothing! Immunity? I already had it! And ESRA? Kitty Hawke did not even want me in her puny fleet. Is that a laugh or what? Me. Admiral Pieter Wilhelminazoon Griesmann. Colonel Hawke had no position for me! I showed her what her puny fleet was to me." He made the motion of stepping on a bug. "You know me, Anton. I am a leader, not a grubber. The Occons are giving me a position in their hierarchy."

I eyed him steadily, wordless through all of this. How can anyone be so easily led by his great nose?

He must have read my gaze, for the wattle under his chin joggled. "You think they're using me."

I said nothing. He protested at length, to which I finally said, "Then why are you on this side of the gate?"

True. The gate had shut and he was locked in.

No sooner had I spoken than the gate opened again and a commanding Occon asked which was the informant. The guards singled Griesmann out and admitted him through the gate. Griesmann tossed a triumphant look back at me as he went.

The guards brought Griesmann face to face with the Occon commander, who took out a gun and shot him.

Griesmann had time to register shock before he died.

The civilian prisoners who had no idea what was going on were horrified. I watched impassively. I hurt too much even to feel very much vindicated.

The Occon commander turned to all of us and said, "Now, which is senior officer?"

I was pushed forward. I didn't look back to see who pushed.

The Occon commander entered the inner pen and approached me. He was young and ugly, with a very long face, a pointy nose, sharply sloping brow, and receding chin, which gave him the look of a ferret. His voice was rough and raspy, I think on purpose to sound more masculine.

I stood fast where I had been pushed out from the cluster. The commander looked me up and down, scowled at this offering. With my peeling scabbing burns I must have appeared diseased.

The commander spoke aside to a compatriot. I caught a few words of it, for I had, anciently, learned a little Occon. I knew the word which indicated a question, and I recognized the word *sick* as they discussed my sad condition.

I corrected, in Occon, *"Burn."*

The two of them leaped back as if a stone had spoken. Then they broke into a flurried exchange too fast for me to pull out a single word. At the end of it the ferrety commander, no longer dubious that I was the ranking human, said in Erden, "Tell your people this many." He held up eight black-nailed fingers.

"Eight," I offered.

"Eight in a room." He pointed to the limestone buildings, which were to be our barracks. He instructed us each to take a cot and to wait.

The cots were metal-framed, embossed with Occon

numbers. Once each prisoner was allotted a place, guards came around, room by room, heated the metal bosses, and branded the backs of our hand with our cot numbers.

I'm sure the last men were in a terror of waiting, hearing the progression of screams, not knowing what was advancing on them.

After the branding party passed through my room, one of my cellmates turned on me and snarled that it was the last time he would listen to me and he ought to break my neck. I told him I'd only relayed the order and he could take his objections to the source.

"No, Kralle. Since you're translating, translate this." And he came at me with a light stylus he'd had in his pocket, and stabbed at my face.

Even on Occo I was still faster than most people. I spun out of his path and punched him. We were struggling on the floor when the Occons came in and kicked us apart.

The Occons assembled everyone together in the yard, and instructed me to say, "This is what happens to prisoners caught fighting."

I relayed it and was promptly beaten until I passed out. Luckily that did not take long.

It was called a work farm. Not that we did much farming. *We* were the farm part—domestic animals. I ought to say up front that the Occons did not eat us. In fact it was as an insult that they called us "carnivores," a term which was roughly equivalent to "savages" in their lexicon, only more derogatory.

Occons did not eat meat, and neither did they feed it to us. Some of the prisoners would supplement their diet by catching rodents and cooking them over a fire, which was a spectacle of curiosity, disgust, and amazement to the androgynous guards who giggled and squirmed like teenagers at a horror show.

The guard dogs were fed meat. The dogs were well treated. They were Earth breeds, something descended from shepherds, mastiffs, and Rottweilers, big dogs, obedient, territorial, and fiercely loyal—to Occons. Man's best friend had become Occon's best friend.

At night the perimeter fences activated, and we could

hear the forcefield humming, while dogs patrolled beyond the boundaries.

On the morning of the first day we were instructed to clear the land of brush, the yellow tatters of grass and brown dried husks of last season's thorny vines, but we were warned to have a care of the red ones. The guards told us in Occon, in Erden, and in Tannian not to touch the fuzzy red weed because "it feels like fire."

Naturally someone had to try it. The Occons hadn't lied. The man's hand turned red, blistered, and blew up twice its normal size. The Occons gave him nothing for it, though there was a veterinarian in the compound. The vet was there for the dogs, not for us animals of lesser value.

The wounded man had to continue working one-handed with the rest of us, clearing the scrub growth from the sprawling rocky field.

None of us lasted past noon.

This close to the sun, eight-tenths of an astronomical unit, the irradiation is nearly double what reaches Erde-Tannia; and Occo's orbiting solar reflectors, which gleamed so brightly as seen from Erde-Tannia, only drove back a thin percentage of this onslaught. I thought we would be cooked inside of a single day, but Occo's thick atmosphere cuts the irradiation, so that what reaches sea level is not what is hitting the upper atmosphere. Which is not to say it was endurable. It was like moving in simmering soup. Even the native guards had cooled shelters from which to watch us, but by midday the temperature in the field soared past anything ever recorded on Erde-Tannia, and there was no one left standing for the guards to watch.

I had been beaten the night before, so I was one of the first to fall flat on my face under the blazing sun. The guards hit me to get up. A lot of good that did. I told them to go ahead and kill me. They didn't, but I think they considered it.

Others fell. The guards beat them at first, then just left them. The officers stood up one prisoner and made sport of him. An officer held branches to his own head as if they were antlers, while the others laughed and egged him on. One said in Occon what I guessed meant "Gore him, gore him,'' because the one with the ersatz antlers charged the prisoner and would have gored him except that the flimsy branches broke.

When all the humans were reduced to inert baking lumps on the ground, the guards piled us back into our barracks, which were like ovens but at least were dark, and we did not need to move.

The commander was furious. He came to me and told me to make everyone get up and back to work. I said from my cot, in Occon, ''We cannot.''

He said he would kill me. I said, ''Fine.''

When inevitably two of our number did die of heat exhaustion, no one expected concern from our captors, but they were in fact alarmed. Sulky guards made excuses, and the consternation it caused among the officers caused me to suspect there could be some repercussions from someone higher still.

The officers came into the barracks of the dead men and muttered over the numbers on the cots, and I gathered they were trying to fudge the gaps in the numerical sequence of brands which the deaths created.

This is interesting, I thought. We were not supposed to die.

I thought it was our weasel of a commander they all feared, but he stormed in and inspected the barracks, rubbed his palms nervously against his thighs, and poked his sharp nose every which way in search of somewhere to set the blame. He pointed his finger at everyone else, but no one was willing to take this fall alone.

They came up with a story they could all agree on—that the two prisoners had been sick when they first came here. The men had been wounded in battle and no one had expected them to live anyway.

This satisfied the Occons, but I interjected that the dead men had not been soldiers. They told me to shut up. The story was settled. The deaths were no one's fault.

I had to wonder who this story was meant for.

I should insert here some explanation which I only learned later, not to let you stew in the dark as I did until I finally met someone who could sort things out:

Adult Occons come in four genders.

All juvenile Occons are sexless. Most of them remain

neuters, *ufin/i,* into adulthood. Our androgynous guards were *ufin/i,* and they are at the bottom of the Occon social scale. *Ufin/i* might develop a sex later, and each one fervently hoped that it would.

Some neuters, juvenile or adult, develop into females, which are all fertile. There were none here at the work farm. Socially, females are on a level with dominant males at the top of the strata.

Dominant males are the antlered ones. Dominant males—*ashai* in Occon, doms as I got to calling them—were the rarest of the four genders. What sets them apart from other males, besides the damn antlers, is that they are fertile.

An intermediate stage between neuter and dominant male is the subdominant male, *g/ari.* All of our officers, including our weak-chinned louring commander, were subdoms. The *g/ari* have some sexual characteristics of a male. Their voices are deeper, and some develop male organs, but they are inoperative and infertile. And *g/ari* don't have antlers. Subdominance is a transitional stage, but it is often an end in itself. Every dominant male was once a subdominant male, but every subdominant male does not necessarily become a dominant male. *G/ari* are an anxious, evil-tempered lot, with all the aggressiveness but none of the status of a true male. (If you want to get the shit beaten out of you, use the term "true male" in front of a subdom!)

So Occon development goes like this:

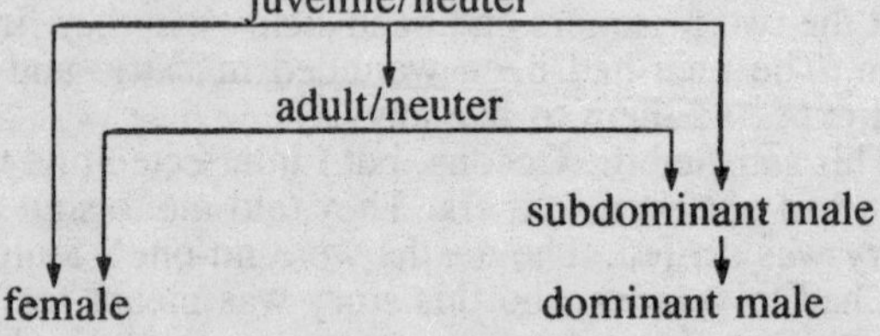

That's how they develop *if* they develop. An adult Occon need not develop a sex at all but may spend the rest of its life as a neuter.

For the first days in the work farm we saw only a preponderance of *ufin/i*, the neuters, who served as guards—and also as workers when we humans fell short—and a lesser number of *g/ari*, the subdoms who were giving the orders.

Where we fit into this scheme was below the bottom. Humans ranked below the dogs.

The Occons kept trying to squeeze work out of us. Everyone was sick. I was bleeding through my nose from the dryness. But dryness was why I suppose I wasn't dead. We did not feel ourselves sweat, but we must have been losing liters in the heat. The guards forced us to drink even when we did not want to, but we didn't see the equivalent coming out.

The subdom commander screeched about our lack of progress and came out regularly to kick us.

Lack of progress in what? I still wasn't sure what we were supposed to be doing.

When I did discover our purpose here I wanted to take off my work hat, wander out under the midday sun, and die.

We were digging. Then someone unearthed a big blue rock. It was rather dull-looking, soft, so it did not hold a polish well, but on one abraded side it shone a brilliant blue flecked with golden lights. It was lapis. We were sitting on a lode of lapis lazuli. That was what we were here for.

Not even diamonds, which have industrial use, but lapis, which as far as I know is good for nothing but being beautiful blue and making a specific pigment of paint.

Some of the prisoners were relieved that our work was unconnected with the Occon war effort and that we were not being forced to work against our own people. But I could not get past the squandering of human life on blue rocks, which, had the Occons wished to make a somewhat bigger capital investment, could have been collected entirely by automation.

More trivial still, some of us were detached from the mining group and given the task of improving the looks of the headquarters. HQ was a low cheerless structure like our barracks but set outside the work enclosure. We built an attractive facade on the limestone face of it with xyloid beams (oh hell, call them wood—close enough), with a verandah of imported saffron wood. We planted spiky little native flowers borne on leathery stalks around the building, arranged in a parody of a human flower garden with tough ornamental shrubs which grew neither leaves not needles but scaly bracts around succulent tubers, the only color on this drab landscape.

All this was done in anticipation of a new arrival of high rank.

I had been rotated onto the planting crew and was troweling in the rear garden when the limousine arrived, a long, smooth-riding, shining black vehicle with opaque windows. I could see subdoms cower and mutter among themselves while curious neuters stole glances out from the work field. I could only guess we had a new commandant.

I did not see who got out of the limousine, because I was at the back of the building, but through an open window I heard footsteps inside moving across a xylem floor at a crisp gait.

And I overheard an exchange, in Occon, most of which I'm afraid I understood. It began with an abrupt skidding of a chair dragged away from a table or desk, and someone standing up in haste. The first speaker I recognized from his raspy voice as our commanding subdom. "Greetings," he said, followed by a word I did not catch. (A name?) "So pleased to see you this season."

Then a voice, smooth, clear, and decidedly male, said, "Do you know what it feels like to be gored?"

A nervous raspy laugh, then a scream, which I interpreted as a sudden affirmative.

I dropped my garden trowel. The neuter guard overseeing my work inhaled audibly and rushed me back to the inner enclosure and into my barracks, where I told the other prisoners thickly, "I think a set of antlers has arrived."

We stood on our cots and peered through the high small windows to see a body bag being carried out of HQ.

Someone whispered a shriek: "Who is that in the bag?"

"I think it's our old commander," I said.

"Hallelujah!"

"Good! Good riddance, son of a bitch!"

From a cot, a weak voice asked, "Did he die slow, Nordveldt? Please say he died slow."

"I think he died in agony," I offered.

And we all muttered that we were well rid of that one. We hoped the new one was not worse.

The guards posted outside our barracks spent a lot of time talking to each other, and from overheard gossip I pieced together that our new commandant—or *asha!a'* as they called him—was in the doghouse here. He was a demoted field officer sent to this awful place as warden to slave labor very much against his will. The work farm was not a choice assignment for an officer of his standing. He was, after all, one of the *ashai*, the dominant class.

The *asha!a'* had taken no part in the space battle, for a reason I could not decipher, but that had not been by choice either. He was not happy about it. I was missing too many strategic words in my knowledge of Occon to glean the full story.

For a few days after the *asha!a's* arrival, nothing changed. We prisoners were still driven out to toil and fall in the heat, and be slapped and poked by impatient guards. Beyond the inner fence we saw all kinds of rich trappings being unloaded from trucks into the HQ, carpets and chests, curtains and furnishings all disturbingly human in design. The rumor went around that the new commandant was human. I could not refute this because I had not actually seen him, but I know what I heard.

We did not see the new *asha!a'* for days on end, and I began to think that we weren't ever to, then one evening someone—it was a neuter guard—gazed across the grounds and said in awe, "Look at him!"

So seldom did we hear any sentiment in an Occon voice that everyone within hearing range stopped what he was doing, followed the guard's gaze, and turned to look at *him*.

He—absolutely *he*, no doubt about it—stood on the verandah of his headquarters. A crowned head. Dominant. A taut, small dogfox of a man in black uniform, his hands clasped behind his back. The sharp-tined rack on his head gleamed like black coral.

Near me someone jabbed a shovel into the dirt, leaned on the handle, and whistled low. "We got ourselves a twelve-point buck."

And that's what the antlers looked like in silhouette, a whitetail deer's beginning at the base of the skull and arcing over and around the head like a spiked crown. The texture is not the same at all. Occon antlers are very smooth, lustrous, and black, sharp as a talon.

And I already knew he could be lethal.

His skin was a light bronze that seemed lighter in sunlight and darker in shadow. Whether that was a real change or trick of the light I never quite distinguished.

His hair was very dark, his eyes perfectly black and unreadable as a wild thing's, I can't say either cruel or kind. I sensed, or read into his expression, a retreat, a stoic bearing in the face of desolation. Picturesque as a wild animal, not as you would say a man is attractive, he had a beauty of a kind. When he moved it was with the unconscious economy of an animal, a regal naturalness without the human clutter that makes men look awkward.

The neuter guards gazed from the work field with admiration, longing, and wistful envy. The *g/ari* officers looked on with all that plus malevolent envy.

I overheard the androgynous guards whispering wishes to be called into his personal service as an orderly. This had to do with sex, but not in the way I assumed. Later I learned that a neuter in the absence of other females might easily develop a sex in the prolonged presence of a dominant male. As females were not menials, such an assignment was very likely a quick ticket up and out of here, so no wonder all of them wanted to get close to the *asha!a'*.

The *asha!a'* stiffened as he viewed his new domain, paled, so tightly strung I expected him to shake. He was embarrassed, I think, like nobility with mud on his face but maintaining stance. *Behold me in my exile.* He was going to be severe. He did not want to be here and he was going to take it out on us; we just knew it.

Echoing in my mind was the sound of our former commander being gored.

* * *

The day came—soon, but it felt like a very long time—when work choked to a standstill. No one could move.

A subdom officer clutching a bleeding hand stomped into my stifling barracks and kicked me. "Get up, carnivore. The *asha!a'* wants to see you." He licked the blood off his hand and exited, snarling, "And you are welcome to him!"

II.

Going to face the *asha!a'* I could not even pronounce the word. (You think you can do better? Here: ! is a palatal click, ' is a glottal stop. Go strangle yourself.)

To know a language is to know its speakers. As I trudged through the gate I tried to remember all I'd ever known of Occon. It had been a long long time since I'd tried to learn the Occon language, a long time since I'd said to hell with it.

At the time the language struck me as absurd. I was under the impression that Occon was an artificial language created by humans, and as such it was the most illogical system ever conceived. But knowing it to be a naturally evolved tongue of alien beings put it in a new perspective entirely, so I felt I ought to try again. Since I was here.

Occon is difficult to speak because it is smattered with three different clicks—nine if you count each as voiced, voiceless, or nasalized. I've put / for a dental, ≠ for an alveolar, and ! for the palatal. I can't really describe these and I'm fairly rotten in my own pronunciation. Listen to a recording of Bushmen speaking if you want to hear how it's really done.

There is also a glottal stop, for which I'm using an apostrophe. Just close your throat before you're quite done.

To add to the confusion, the Occons borrow English auxiliary verbs for expressions of time. Occon in its pure form had an ill-developed sense of time, as if Occons had little use for time referents until the coming of humans. Future, perfect, and pluperfect were alien concepts to them. To the Occon view, things were either happening presently or done happening.

Or else they were in question, which is indicated at the beginning of the inquiry by the word *tel'*.

Vocal expression counts for little. The Occons use only two tones of voice, as far as I can discern—anger/irritation and statement. Much of the time they sound like very bad actors reading lines cold.

To this limited repertoire the *asha!a'* added a third voice, the dangerous whisper. Not quite a whisper but a very soft gentle sound you need to lean forward to hear, almost sweet, but counter to intent. Imagine a very soft, congenial "I'm going to kill you." That's the dangerous whisper. I don't know if it is exclusive to doms, but the *asha!a'* is the only one I've ever heard use it. It's a threat. I did not recognize it as such at first. I don't know how many red flags I flapped in the bull's face before I learned the signs of mortal peril.

I mounted the steps to the headquarters and shuffled across the fragrant saffron wood verandah we had just built. I glimpsed my reflection in a window. Had I the energy I would have recoiled. Scarecrow. Gaunt reflection with scorched straw hair and clothed in rags.

I suddenly did not want to be seen, but the office doors parted to admit me.

I walked into cool air, felt instantly more alert.

No guards followed me in. The door seals sucked shut.

Black crown lifted, black eyes looked up. The *asha!a'*.

At the foot of his chair sat an enormous black dog with a wide muzzle and wolfish ruff. It stood up as I entered and it growled. The *asha!a'* barked, in English, "Sit!"

The dog settled on great haunches.

Between the antlers and the dog, not to mention the sidearm, I saw why the *asha!a'* did not feel the need for guards in here with us. And I had seen in the window that I was not a formidable sight.

The dog was another mutt mixture of big breeds. We got to calling them all "Occon Guarddogs." Occons had turned man's best friend against him. You don't know how betrayed you can feel till you've seen a dog fawn at the feet of an alien.

The *asha!a*'s expression was impenetrable. The dog's was transparent; it was slavish adoration.

Aside from the dog, everything else in the office was unsettlingly Earthly. The uniform was human-style, and it did not look right for something with antlers to be wearing it, from the square-shouldered military jacket down to the black boots like a horseman or a storm trooper. The *asha!a'* was seated in a chair behind a desk, and *that* looked strange.

He was small, my size, on the limbus between man and animal. I sensed from him power and intelligence and great strain.

His face might have been human, with swollen sinuses perhaps. The plane of the Occon face comes forward; the nose does not project in such a sharp ridge as in humans. His hands were smooth, with the same finely textured alizarin skin as his face. His nails were kept short and neat, with a bare crescent of black grown out.

On the corner of his desk rested a set of gauges in a carved wooden case, the work of human hands or a close copy, a barometer reading 3,978 millibars, a thermometer reading 28 degrees centigrade, and a hygrometer reading 30 percent.

Next to that, the model of a spaceplane caught my eye, a black ship bearing the markings 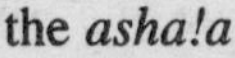 (Occon for 2734), which I assumed was its series type, because I had seen those markings before on that kind of ship. The model was carved from black hard stone—no, from *antler,* the pieces joined smoothly as if fashioned from a solid block.

I looked from the ship model to the *asha!a'* behind the desk, the reluctant warden, and it came to me all at once:

He's a pilot!

A sudden flood of sympathy overcame me, and I knew I would never be able to regard him objectively again. The irritation in his manner, the tremor, the beaten look were too familiar. He had missed the battle, I'd heard said. Another grounded bird.

He observed me critically. "You are Erden," he said at last, a statement awaiting confirmation.

"Yes."

"You speak Tannian."

"Yes."

"They say you speak the language."

The language. Occon. "A very few words only."

"Enough. I know these others. You will hand down my instructions. Accurately." I guessed there had been some problem with this in the past. "You will not say you understand when you do not. You will tell the workers my orders. They will obey. Understand?"

"I'm sure I do," I said.

"*Tel'*, why do the humans not work?"

I stared a moment. He could not be serious. An impulse seized me to cry out, "You stupid alien! If you stepped out of this air-conditioned office and looked, you would know the answer to that!" Why I refrained I don't know, because what I did instead was even more rash. I snatched his gauges from his desk, beat them on the floor, stepped on them, set them back on the desk, and said in my best bewilderment, "They don't work."

I saw something writhe within his sleeves at the forearms. A muscle stood out along a clenched jaw, and he rose. His dog growled. That *asha!a'* stepped out from behind his desk.

I thought, This is it. I will know what it feels like to be gored.

He said softly, dangerously, "My *g/ari* say you refuse to work. They say you are not tired. You sit to avoid work."

"Oh. That's true. We like to bake in the sun and be beaten."

His dark brows drew together slightly in a human look of confusion and suspicion, then he said, "This is not true. This is, what is the word?"

"Sarcasm."

"Sarcasm. You will not use it. Understanding is difficult enough."

I said. "How can I argue with what your guards say? If you believe them, why do you need me to say anything?"

"Who told you I believed them?"

I faltered, realizing I had been on a bad approach. "I assumed—"

"Then stop. You will not assume. You will tell me why you do not work."

I told him we couldn't. It was too hot, the gravity was too great, the pressure was too great, the sun was too intense, the guards were beating the last strength out of us.

"No," he said. "Other humans work on this world. *Tel'*, you think I will believe everything you say now?"

Other humans. The colonists! Some descendants must yet live!

And work. As slaves like us.

I asked the *asha!a'* if he knew what snow was. He said no, and I explained it to him.

"I know what ice is," he said testily. "It is made in a freezer."

"It falls from the sky," I said, and if he didn't believe me he could explain what was the white stuff on Erde's and Tannia's poles.

"So there is snow at the poles. What means this to me?"

"We come from a cold place. The humans you are familiar with came from equatorial Earth. They don't know snow either. And where are they, anyway?"

He ignored my question. "You mean this whole lot of humans is useless?"

The way he said it made me afraid to say yes. I said, "It will take some time to adapt—time without being beaten."

"Then adapt. And do not take too much time. If you do not become cost-effective you will not be maintained."

That was what I was afraid of.

I said, "We would do better with better care. We have a doctor with us, if you will let him practice."

The doctor was the only one of the prisoners who was anything like a friend to me. (We called him—what else?—Doc.) The other prisoners loathed me because Occon orders often came through me. Doc, on the other hand, was trying to get a message back in the other direction, and I took this chance to recite to the *asha!a'* what the doctor had said: that humans must keep a core temperature of 37 degrees centigrade to survive. Even with the low humidity we could not dissipate metabolic heat when the temperature was as high as it was, and we were doing heavy labor. We also needed to keep an electrolyte balance, which was being thrown off because of the way we were sweating.

The *asha!a'* did not interrupt me, but neither did he acknowledge that I had spoken. He told me to leave.

"Erder," he detained me as I reached the door. I looked back. "What will your kind do when summer comes?"

Summer? "What season is this?"

"Winter."

"We'll all die." Simple as that.

I scuffed back to the barracks. We were not driven out to work that day. The men were relieved. I worried that the Occons had resolved to cut their losses, shoot us and call it a bad debt.

All through the daylight hours we sweltered in the barracks. From time to time I slept. I told Doc that I'd delivered his message to the *asha!a'*. Doc thought this was great.

I tempered his enthusiasm. "I may have just told him we were more trouble than we're worth."

And come nightfall guards roused us and gave us shovels with which to dig wide circular pits. I thought we were digging our graves.

Turns out we were digging our summer quarters.

Then we received a delivery, a gargantuan expanse of featherweight material, the kind used to make solar sails for satellites, acres of it, which we erected like an umbrella over the entire work farm. It doubled as a sunshield and a solar collector to power the cooling units which we installed in our new underground barracks.

The voluminous tarp blotted out the direct sun, blotted out the stars at night. I could not see Erde-Tannia's steady light anymore. We lived in perpetual shadow. Work became merely agonizing instead of fatal. Those of us who fell were not beaten but taken to see the vet.

I wondered about the other humans whom the *asha!a'* had mentioned in the present tense, humans who survived the heat better than we did, who worked. So all the descendants of the original colonists were not dead. But what had happened to them that there should be such a shortage of humans on Occo that the Occons needed to shanghai *us?* The populations of Erde and Tannia numbered now in the millions. It would seem the human colonists of this ill-fated planet had not been so prolific.

"Well," said Doc. "One reason ought to be self evident."

The other prisoners regarded him blankly. Nothing was evident.

"How many women do you have handy to you?" I filled in, and Doc nodded.

"Precisely."

I wanted to think that segregation was the worst that had befallen the colonists. But from the way we had been treated before the coming of the *asha!a'*, I did not believe this.

The *asha!a'* was treating us with forbearance under stress. I could tell he would love to torch this whole work farm and us with it. I cannot say he was clement, but there was an absence of atrocity.

His relative lenience made me bold enough to venture to request an audience with him to ask for a few more things that he might not think of but would be easily accommodated.

I asked the *ufin/i* to carry my request, and they laughed and did nothing. I went over their heads and asked a *g/ari*, and he laughed and did nothing.

I was just asking them to ask, dammit.

There was a human parallel to this situation. It is in the Book of Esther: whosoever goes to the inner court of the Great King uncalled is put to death immediately unless the King holds out his golden scepter granting mercy. And this is why no one was taking my message to the *asha!a'*.

I didn't know this.

I saw him one day on the verandah, where he was playing with his dog. He held the dog's muzzle shut with his hand. It growled and squirmed free, snapped at the *asha!a'*s hand. He ruffled its mane, grabbed its tail, and wagged it in its face. The dog writhed and snapped, yarred, wagged its whole body.

Strange watching an antlered alien act like a man, sitting on his heels and playing with a dog.

The inner gate was open. I saw my chance. I put down my shovel, climbed out of my pit, trotted to the verandah, and asked if I could talk to him.

The guards who had let me get this close gasped and grabbed their guns, about to shoot me, but the *asha!a'* stayed them. He stared at me.

Finally he said, very slowly, "Do you know what you are doing?"

I hesitated, glanced at the guns. "Perhaps not," I admitted. "Have I done something?"

The *asha!a'* seemed satisfied that I acted in ignorance. "Come inside."

I presented my requests. Things like being allowed to cook the rodents we killed. The guards had put an end to this practice as soon as the *asha!a'* had arrived. I also asked for heat-dispersing clothes such as the guards wore, and work gloves and bandages.

The *asha!a'* sat behind his desk with his hands clasped, and when I had finished he said, "Is that all?" He let me know he already thought it a great deal.

"No," I said. The cooling systems in our new quarters only brought the temperature down to 100 degrees Fahrenheit and quit working when the temperature outside was less than that. I asked permission to leave the barracks doors wide open for circulation on nights like those.

He granted half my requests. Those he did not grant were the ones I had little hope of anyway, things that cost money and he hadn't the budget for.

It was as I had begun to suspect—he was treating us as well as he could afford to.

The greatest disappointment was that he would not—or could not—send word back to Erde-Tannia to our families that we were alive. He seemed regretful, though how I gathered that from his lack of expression I could not say. Maybe I just wanted to see regret. He told me the request was impossible.

On the subject of doors, he said, "Make them as wide as you like. Knock out the ceiling if you like. But. One man, just one, at any time, for any reason short of fire, climbs out without leave, the barracks will be bricked up solid. All of them. Yes?"

I was hesitant, not sure if I ought to commit to this

deal. Rather than get air circulation I might suffocate us all, for I really could not swear that one idiot would not go over a wall without permission. But I could not back down now. The *asha!a'* was watching me with narrowed eyes and lowered head, his circlet of tines pointed toward me.

"Yes," I said.

"It is your responsibility."

"Yes."

His antlers tilted to the side. As he sent me out he said, "Count in this list of favors that you are alive. You will never come again to me unbidden."

III.

I was summoned into the presence rather often after that, whenever the *asha!a'* had a directive to hand down, or a question to pose. The questions I hated. He would ask me why the men did as they did, and, as I and the men did not see eye to eye, it was difficult for me to provide answers. Had they a choice, the prisoners would have picked another spokesman, but the *asha!a'* chose me, so I was it.

For one thing, the other prisoners were civilians. They had come from orbital platforms and were by trade greenhouse workers and mechanics. For another thing, most of them were Tannian. Our ways are not identical. Erders do certain things out of habit, because it is always done. Taking a bath, for example.

When cleansing booths were made available to us, the Occons expected us to use them. The few Erders among us did so readily. But the booths were dry baths, not pleasant water showers, and they did not appeal to the Tannians.

Tannians, as a group, won't do anything if they don't see an immediate clear purpose (this I discovered trying to teach literature to student pilots). Bathing seemed a lost cause in a place like this, so the Tannian prisoners just wallowed and stank and accumulated parasites.

Occons, it turns out, have noses like bloodhounds, and our guards were complaining. There was also some threat of disease, I surmised, because I was called into the *asha!a'*s office, where he handed me a piece of fruit.

"This is fifteen days off the vine. Do you know how it stays fresh?"

"I assume it's radiated."

He nodded, human-style, then threatened to preserve *us* the same way.

I passed this information on. Suddenly the Tannians found purpose in bathing.

The *asha!a'* also summoned me several times to issue warnings against breaking lapis.

The men were smashing good stones out of spite. Lapis bashing was our major sport. When we were caught we were beaten, but the Occons suspected that we were getting away with a lot more than they observed. The suspicion was well founded. I broke a few big ones myself. It was our only way of getting back at our slave drivers. You find a great precious stone, give it an Occon name, and then bludgeon it to little blue bits. An unspoken code existed: Thou shalt not turn in a big stone intact if you can possibly get away with it.

I relayed ever more severe threats from the *asha!a'*, to no avail. Finally I said, "If I can suggest, I think you would get a better result if you gave a reward for big stones."

The *asha!a'* was vexed. "You suggest."

"Yes."

"Why should you help me get better results?"

"I wouldn't, except it happens to work both ways this time. I withdraw the suggestion if you are offended. Do what you will."

"I will do as I will!" he shouted. "And you will stop making decisions for me, and what makes you think you can withdraw something spoken? How stupid are you? Spoken is spoken! It cannot be unspoken." Then matter-of-factly he said, "Since you know why humans do this stupid thing and how to make them not do this stupid thing, you will tell me of your suggestion."

I advised that the offer of something like a few extra hours' sleep or better food or a light shift to anyone who turned in big gemstones might discourage some of the damage. It would come down to a simple decision of who was robbed more by smashing a big gem, the finder or the Occons. As it stood now, we had nothing to lose so long as we escaped notice, and the guards could not watch all of us at every moment.

The *asha!a'* bridled. "As I see it, the prisoners create the problem. Why should I give them something in order to make it stop? This is blackmail."

"The *problem,*" I said, trying to contain my own anger, "is that we are prisoners. What would *you* do?"

"Did you ever break stones?"

"Yes."

"Why?"

"Because I hate you."

First ripple of emotion I saw actually touch his black eyes, and he looked hurt. It was probably something else. Sometimes I think we forgot what we were to each other. He dismissed me curtly.

But he took the suggestion.

Though the covert stone breaking did not stop—it was still our only way of expressing rage—more big gems surfaced. I think the guards were disappointed. They hated rewarding us, and their failure to disguise it was a joy in itself.

There came an unforeseen bad result of the lessened abuse. When you're no longer three-quarters dead all the time, the sex drive returns. In the beginning all I dreamed of was water, food, rest, and cold. Now I was dreaming of Maggie and missing her.

Prisoners began to harass each other. Younger, beardless, smaller ones took the brunt of it. I was not young but I looked it, and I fit the other two counts, but everyone left me alone in that regard. I suppose they thought I would tell the *asha!a'*.

Then the rapes began. We did not know it was at first, because the first victims did not admit it until they discovered they were not alone. But no one could say who was doing it. No one got a good look at him. The attacker didn't care who he took, what he looked like. He lurked in the dark cleansing booths and grabbed whoever came in. Everyone assumed it was an Occon, but I had learned by then from gossiping *ufin/i* that Occons *can't,* with the exception of the *asha!a'*, and it could hardly be he. "I think you'd have noticed the antlers."

Then someone saw his attacker and told everyone else. No one told me. Conversations stopped when I walked into the group. But I gathered that everyone else knew who it was, but could do nothing. Nothing got us into worse trouble with the Occons than fighting. My first lesson. And the penalty had become more severe since then. Beatings had become routine, so the penalty for fighting was a sweatbox at the edge of the field where the sun slants under the tarp. And if you're afraid of dogs they let a dog snap at the airholes.

Eventually the *asha!a'* got wind of the problem, and called me into the headquarters.

"What is going on?"

I hedged, but had to tell him all I knew.

"Who?" he said.

"I don't know."

He told me to make it stop. Actually he told me a little story.

"I had a pet once. It ate its tail. Every time I looked, it had taken off the splint and was gnawing at the scabbed end.

"I killed it. It was not a wholesome creature, something that gnaws itself. Death was where it was heading anyway, so I hastened it along. I was not going to sit and watch it die slowly. Do you understand?"

I was afraid I did. We, as a whole creature, were an unsound organism. I had no doubt he would exterminate us with no more compunction than he had his pet.

"Why don't your guards stop it?" I said.

"They do not know who it is. They have not caught him, and no one tells. You keep this among yourselves; you may fix it yourselves."

"And what if we get caught taking matters into our own hands? You'll beat the hell out of us."

"I would put much less effort into tracking down a murderer than I would an animal such as this. If a prisoner turns up dead in the next five hours and the disturbances subsequently stop, the investigation would be cursory."

"Cursory?"

"Nonexistent."

I took this message back to the barracks. It was greeted with mistrust, but someone was willing to gamble that the *asha!a'* was sincere, because a man turned up dead next morning.

As promised, the killer was never hunted down. *Promised.* He states a fact and that is a promise. He never used the word; that would be overly insistent. He was brutally honest—or brutal and honest. He never lied.

I began to wonder if Occons lied, but of course they do. The charade of sending idyllic pictures to Erde-Tannia was a world-scale lie. And the *asha!a's* mistrust of his own underlings indicated duplicity. It was characteristic of the *asha!a'*, not of the species, that he was honest.

We had a break, some of us, in our mining labor when a flatbed rolled an Erden spaceplane into camp. Where the ship came from I didn't know, then I had a thought—Reid!

The craft was brought to our work farm because half of our prisoners were mechanics, and the Occons wanted to know everything about how the spaceplane functioned.

The *asha!a'* asked me first if I had ever flown one.

I said no. The vehicle was a freight shuttle, not a fighter.

He started to ask me something, stopped, took a hard look at me, decided not to ask, then asked anyway. "Were you in the war between Erde and Tannia?"

"Yes."

He seemed surprised. "How old are you?"

"Thirty-six, Erde-Tannian."

"Occon?"

"I have to think."

He pushed a stylus and light pad at me. He must need to write out figures too. "Fifty-seven," I calculated.

And the *asha!a'?* Yes, I asked. He was thirty-six Occon, twenty-six Earth standard, twenty-two Erde-Tannian.

I had thought he was much older. He had thought me much younger.

"What did you fly?" he asked.

"A KR-22."

"Which?"

"The *Storm Petrel.*"

"I know you," he said, nothing else. He did not say what he knew of me or what he thought of it. And not just "I know who you are," but "I know you." I was not sure the phrasing was a language problem either.

I asked, "Where is Reid?"

"What is Reid?"

"A prisoner."

"Which is he? You think I know prisoners by name?"

"The one brought here cataleptic. He was never among the miners. He's a pilot."

"Oh. That one," he said.

I waited for more. When nothing came I pressed, "Is he alive?"

"He has something we want. Until then he is alive."

His ship. I guess the one in the yard was not it. Of course not. Reid would not have brought a freight shuttle.

"Please don't kill him. He's a friend of mine." Why I bothered to say that I don't know. As if that should be a valid criterion in his eyes for sparing a life.

"Your friend? He is too ill to be anyone's friend." He was not talking physically ill. "That man is an unexploded warhead."

When speaking in Erden the *asha!a'* did not differentiate between them and us. We were all "men." I suppose that is because Erden has no word for them besides "Occon," which we thought referred to humans.

He lowered his head at me. "Do you know where his second ship is?"

"No."

Something twisted within his sleeves.

I quickly finished, "He told me he 'parked' it. He wouldn't tell me where it was—I suppose so I couldn't betray him." And under torture I would have. I'm an idiot in the face of torture. If you want me to talk, don't bother to clutter my mind with drugs, just hold a meat cleaver over my wrist and ask your questions.

The *asha!a'* glared at me with onyx eyes, deciding, I think, whether to test my answer.

I must've turned white enough that he believed me. "No," he said at length. "I suppose he would not confide in his 'friends.' "

* * *

Someone tried to escape in the Erden ship. We all heard the engines engage. Guards dashed toward the freighter, but it was too late. The craft rose a few meters off the ground, skimmed low, bumbled over the fence, cleared from under the umbrella into sunlight, bobbled in the air, and then fell back with a crash. The pilot writhed out the hatchway, doubled over and rattling.

We all ran, but the fence was between us so no one could help him—had there been anything we could have done.

"What's wrong with him?"

He lay beyond our reach, twisted in agony.

Doc said, "He's bent."

I and the mechanics understood at once. It was something which, in my visions of escape, I had failed to consider. The prisoners who had been greenhouse workers—we called them greenies—were still confused. "What happened? The Occons rigged the ship!"

"They didn't do anything to the ship," I said emptily. They hadn't needed to.

I let the mechanics explain.

The ship was an Erden spacecraft. First thing that happens when you seal the cabin, the atmospheric controls activate to simulate Erden at sea level, or 13 psi. The ship was never meant to function on Occo. When the man was decompressed so swiftly, his blood had bubbled like an uncorked champagne bottle.

Some *g/ari* went outside and carried him to the veterinarian. The guards let the rest of us stand helplessly at the fence in futile vigil over the wrinkled spaceship for a while. Let that be a lesson.

I was an abject workbeast. What ship could ever carry me home? I could never escape here. Never.

I stared through the fence links, spirit crushed, my dreams of escape a smoking bale of creased metal on the parched Occon ground.

IV.

After the first devastation passed, hope bounced back. Rather, denial kicked in. I refused to believe I would not see home again. I still refuse.

Funny what the mind will do to cope with the unbearable.

And soon afterward came a chance to get out, out of the work farm and maybe off Occo. I thought: God has not forsaken me. Here I go.

Half of our number were to be taken out of the mines and, after *slow* decompression, sent up in space for a construction job. Needless to say, the half sent would be those of us with the background for the work, i.e., the mechanics, and, I thought, me. The greenies would stay behind in the lapis mines.

In preparation, the Occons taught us a little about reading Occon technical directions, simple things like on/off, danger, and units of measure. It was not difficult once you got past the alien symbols, which I already knew. I just needed to know what the units of measurement were, and, as Occon instruments were based on Earth technology, the units turned out to be all the same. Reading the controls was a matter of transliteration.

This, I thought, would be easy. Maggie, I'm coming home.

At the last minute, as we were boarding the transport that would take us to a spaceport, I was yanked out of the group by a subdom. "Not you."

Insides constricted, mouth soured, heart wobbling in my throat. I was so close. Two steps forward and one up and I would be on that transport.

"Who said?" My voice sounded shrill to my own ears.

"The *asha!a'*."

My heart sank.

He must have read my mind.

I'm a pilot. Put me near a ship and I'll run for it.

You think you're on the bottom and one more thing happens. On board the transport my only friend, Doc, waved ruefully goodbye as the door shut between us.

The transport's caterpillar treads kicked up dust as it lumbered through the outer gate.

Someone was at my side. I heard his voice before I was aware he was there. "It had to be, you know."

"No. No, I don't."

"No matter," he said.

"No matter," I said.

I was in the *asha!a*'s office later. He had no orders for me. I don't know why I was there, but I didn't question it at the time. I was numb from disappointment. Maybe he was only keeping an eye on me. Or maybe misery wanted company. I picked up the drift that *he* had hoped to get out of here too. But we were stranded here together.

A chunk of lapis lazuli lay on his desk, the day's prize find. I let slip a comment, a sigh, a complaint: "It's not even as if we were doing something vital."

Something writhed within his sleeves. I'd seen the motion before but not the cause. This time he pulled his sleeves up to free what was constricted, a long claw on either forearm. What to call them? Spurs? Dewclaws? They curved at his wrists like billhooks.

The *asha!a*'s spurs twisted outward, at me I thought. But though it was at what I said, the wrath was not directed at me. Suddenly he was on his feet and slashing, hitting things, black drops spurting from the dewclaws. He threw the lapis chunk and it shattered against the wall. He stabbed into the wall, pulled downward, slicing long gashes through wood veneer and scoring the limestone block underneath.

Finally he stopped. His chest heaved, his bronze skin was overlain with a haze of perspiration. He steadied himself against a wall, taking long breaths, the wildness leaving his face. He said in his dangerous whisper, meeting my stare, "That is the name of it, isn't it."

The spurs on his arms turned slowly in toward his wrists to a rest position. He assayed the wreckage soberly, looked again to me. "Did I hurt you?"

"No, sir," I said. *Sir,* as if he were my commanding officer. It just slid out. The Occons never demanded bows, salutes, or recognition from us. I don't think my slip escaped notice. He didn't miss much.

He pulled his sleeves down, embarrassed that I had witnessed that.

"Leave now."

Without the mechanics, we had only half a work force, but someone in authority above even the *asha!a'* expected the same output as before. I was in the office when the *asha!a'* took the call. I understood more of what was said than I think he suspected. Or maybe he knew and allowed me hear it. As he signed off he muttered a word of Occon which I translate as *"jerk."*

He reminded me of no one so much as Reid, talented, slightly mad, and grounded.

I told him the technology on Occo was much more backward than anyone thought.

"Not backward. Uneven," he said. "You have seen nothing of Occo."

"Machines could do this much more efficiently, and neither of us would have to be here," I said.

He did not anger yet. In the early days I would not have dared talk to him like that. I was getting an idea what would set him off and what wouldn't.

And, gazing out the window as he was, he could not argue in the face of the mercy-forsaken, sunbaked wasteland. He merely said, "It is very difficult. There would not be war if it were not difficult."

I asked what the Occons wanted.

"Erde-Tannia. The worlds." He turned to me. "Where it snows."

"What of us?"

"Some might be useful. As you are here."

"As slaves."

"I think that is the word." He spoke Erden so fluently

it surprised me when a simple word tripped him. "Workers?"

" 'Slave' is the word you want."

"Not the millions. We cannot have millions." Then he said faintly, to himself, in Occon, "How have we come to this?"

"Some openness and cooperation would have averted the entire war. No one would've faulted you—"

His fist came down on the desk. Movement in his sleeves, which I knew now were claws turning, backed me away. He shouted, inflamed, "How dare you criticize Occon policy!"

"You were."

"And should I choose to open my heart to my *dog* I will, and expect it not to talk back to me!"

"I was agreeing—"

"It is not your place to agree! Agreement is a judgment! 'No one would fault us—' No, they would not!"

And he ordered me out.

Nothing intensifies patriotic feeling faster than a challenge from outside. A people may be critical of themselves, but let an outsider shoot down a ship or kidnap a citizen, and out come the patriots waving flags. The same way a police officer breaking up a domestic quarrel can expect the combatants to turn on him. Occons are just like humans in that respect. The idea of such a primitive childish feeling driving national policy is scary.

I paused in the doorway, risked, "Do you know how small you sound when you do that?"

And I held my breath.

I must have gotten through to him, because I did not end up in a sweatbox. He simply repeated, "Get out."

Time approached when a launch window ought to be opening. I hadn't kept an accurate track of time, but summer had come, which meant I had been on Occo half a local year.

About that time an eerie hiss erupted from the sky. We were accustomed to weird noises, animal cries, insects that squalled like alarms, and the wind soughing through the vents in the expansive sunshield. This sound was like none of those.

We all moved to the perimeter fence, where we could see past the edge of our shading umbrella to the open sky. The whole of heaven had become one massive aurora, snaking violet and electric blue, to the accompaniment of that horrible hiss.

A barrage of hard rays rained from Erde-Tannia. I overheard Occons say what it was and that we were safe enough down here on the planet surface, insulated by Occo's thick atmosphere and substantial magnetosphere, but no ship could fly against that storm.

Looking at the phosphorescent sky, I did not feel safe.

We stood at the fence, watching the horrible dispiriting light show. The guards did not try to make us go in.

Our people did not care that we were here. They were trying to kill all life on the planet, us with it.

It had to mean the Occons were winning the war.

All through the day the electric hum and sizzling hiss tormented us. When night fell, an eerie angry carmine afterglow reflected under the edges of our shield, and we glimpsed on the horizon the ghastly colors and darting streaks mapped out vividly against the black sky.

The worst sound was of men sobbing at night. We had thought we were out of tears.

The Occons cleverly said nothing. If they tried to disparage our home planets' tactics we would be honor-bound to defend their actions. But since no criticism came, we had nothing to rebel against and we could only wonder why our countries thought so little of us that they were shooting at us. It was hard to dream about home when home did not care if it killed you.

We were expendable.

V.

Next time I was summoned to the *asha!a*'s office no one was there. On the desk was a note addressed to me—actually addressed to the *Storm Petrel.* He never used my name. I don't think he knew my name. I was beginning to forget it myself.

The note listed my instructions for the day. It said a "shipment" of human workers was being transferred from another site. I was to show them to their barracks and instruct them on the normal routine.

Other humans! I was anxious to talk to a descendant of the unfortunate colonists of this planet. Then it occurred to me: talk to them *how?* Did these people speak a language I knew? How was I to pass on the *asha!a*'s instructions?

I needed to see the *asha!a'.* This problem might not have occurred to him.

I thought he must be in his headquarters, though sometimes he did leave. There was a town at some distance. (It was thirty kilometers away. I stole a look at the limo's odometer before and after one of his trips.) Maybe he had a lady friend there, or maybe there was nothing for him in town and he was just getting out of *here.*

But this day his limo was here and I was sure he was too.

I nudged open a door from the office to an inner chamber where I had never gone. It was dark within. *"Asha!a'?"*

"What do you want!"

I blinked in the hot gloom. I had thought the chamber empty till he growled.

Then I saw a bed and him in it. Oh shit, I have walked in on him and a lover, I thought. But another blink resolved my view; he was alone but for the dog lying at the foot of the bed. The dog lifted its broad head.

"I have a question," I said apologetically.

"Ask and get out." His voice was ragged.

"Are you ill?"

"That is your question?"

"It is now."

"I am well," he said and sneezed.

My eyes adjusted to the dimness. The *asha!a'* was miserable, bloodshot eyes drawn into a squint. His nose was red, his face painful just to look at. He tried to sniff, couldn't.

One bare arm rested above the sheet, giving me a good look at the dewclaw turned dormantly inward. Since it wasn't in attack position I ventured to ask, "Is there anything I can do for you?"

"Why would you?"

"I don't like the people who were in command before you got here."

"I am not dying," he said, resenting the implication. He rolled over, mashed his face into the pillow, and with a rather limp arm beckoned me nearer.

When I stood at the bedside he looked up with watery black eyes. "It's a human plague."

"It looks like a cold," I said.

"That is its name."

I bit the inside of my mouth so I wouldn't laugh. I said, "It is not fatal to us."

"Nor to us," he said. "You are not to tell anyone."

"No."

"I could go into battle right now if I had to."

I assured him I believed this. Bullshit.

It's a pilot's malady, not to seek help or admit weakness. We admire stupid shows of courage. We are children that way. It's why our kind withers in peacetime.

Listen to me—our kind, me and an Occo dom. The heat and the pressure have dulled my brain.

He hunched over the pillow, gave a juicy cough. I had never seen him not looking sleek. His dark hair was disheveled and needed washing; marks of sheet folds were pressed into his skin. He breathed through his mouth.

"Is it cold in here?"

"No. Those are the chills."

He blinked tears from his eyes, rolled onto his back. "What was your question?"

"The humans who are coming. Will I be able to speak to them? I mean, what language do they speak?"

"Tannian."

"Tannian! Are these—? Where are they from?"

"From Tannia. They have been here. They invaded last year."

The invasion force that had been lost while I was in prison! I had thought they were all dead.

This was joyful news to me. Not just that they lived. Tannia thought they were dead; well, so too maybe home thought all of *us* were dead that they should see clear to shoot hard rays at Occo. It wasn't that they didn't care if we lived or died; they did not know we were here!

"Thank you," I said.

"For what?"

For restoring my dreams of home.

As we waited for the transfer prisoners, I overheard a pair of subdoms talking about them. I was getting better at eavesdropping on Occon conversations. One said, "I heard they are very lazy."

This should have struck me with horror, knowing subdoms as I did and what they called lazy. But I did not put one and one together.

The transfers arrived in a cattle car such as had brought us. The prisoners stumbled off the truck.

Dante was right. Hell is in levels. We were at the top ring.

These men had come from one of the lower rings.

They looked about as if they had arrived at the promised land. They squinted up at the wondrous sunshield. Most of them could not see well. None of them had teeth. They appeared to be eighty years old, but I knew they were pilots and so in the prime of life.

Some of them had cancer lesions on their skin; some were missing limbs. They could barely stand.

Lazy.

I could not greet them. Words clotted in my throat. I coughed and in brusque numbness instructed them to follow me.

They were afraid to touch the cots I assigned them. "Ours? These are ours? We get to sleep in these?"

I nodded, mute.

One of them found a vent, looked to me in alarm. "What's this?"

"The cooling system. Keeps it down to a hundred Fahrenheit in here."

This so delighted them I had to look away.

I pointed out the cleansing booths to them. One asked, "We get to use those?"

"It's required," I said.

"Don't tell me you have toilets."

"No. There's a garden of big cabbages at the downwind point of the enclosure." I waved my arm in the direction of the open latrine we called the "rose garden," then I had to run out of the barracks.

I jumped into the mines and pulverized every blue rock I found.

The new inmates were not forced to work for a few days. ("You see?" said the *g/ari* to each other. "I told you they were lazy.") The newcomers dubbed our work farm the Country Club.

By nightfall I had recovered from my panic, so I was able to talk with them. They were all Tannians, but they were pilots, so there was common ground between us. They recognized my name.

"You're the Kralle who shot Brute Burke in the back."

"He did what?" one of greenhouse workers cried. When the greenies learned my past they were not surprised, though they were shocked, if that makes any sense.

"I'd've thought you'd still be in prison," said a Tannian pilot named Zulu. "How did you get out so quick?"

"And just who do you think is left defending the planet with you here?" I said.

"My God, is it that bad?"

"It is."

"Who won the last battle?"

"I don't know. I think we lost."

"Of course you did," said Zulu, reasoning that if they lost, naturally a Kralle understudy could not do better.

"Any of you other guys pilots?" asked a newcomer named Brace.

The greenies shook their heads. "Just him." They indicated me.

I said, "There's Reid if he's still alive."

"Who's Reid?"

"De Falke," I said, then added dryly, "Another Kralle."

One looked up toward the hissing sky, sighed. "At least there's still a fight."

A line from an old earth anthem runs: *And the rockets red glare, the bombs bursting in air, gave proof through the night that our flag was still there.*

The sizzle was no longer a sound of despair to me. The death rain scorching the Occon sky meant Erde-Tannia was still holding its border. *For the love of God keep shooting.*

I told the pilots why half the barracks had been empty, that our mechanics had been shipped out to a space construction project. "I was supposed to go too," I said, dejected.

"Don't feel too bad, Nordveldt," said Zulu. "If it were a good job they'd've trained Occons for it. As it is, there's *that* to contend with." He pointed up at the hiss of the hard rays. "Those mechanics probably got three eyes and no balls by now—"

He stopped himself, saw me staring.

"Oh shit. I hope they weren't friends of yours."

"One was," I said. I tried to visualize Doc, couldn't. Could only feel loss.

Among the new prisoners was someone who could explain the world to me. I didn't catch his name; everyone called him Dogger, a slight man (what am I saying? They were all slight!) with one arm, and a bobbed nose where the vet had taken off a skin cancer and done a lousy job of it. Dogger had conceived a fascination approaching an obsession with the Occons. He could speak Occon fluently, and he corrected my pronunciations.

From Dogger was the first I ever heard the term "subdominant." He was the one who explained the whole alien system of neuters, subdominant males, dominant males, and females.

I thought it a peculiar natural arrangement. "Doesn't the small number of breeding males give the Occons a limited gene pool?"

"Yes and no," said Dogger. "The selection is still there in the neuters; supposedly what develops fully is the 'best' gene pool. Only the strongest, healthiest, genetically 'best' develop the ability to reproduce. Less than 'perfect' ones stay neuter or only develop halfway and stay sterile and uncrowned. It's a real kick in the ass to reach *g/ari* and go no further. It's what makes the *g/ari* so mean. They're genetic also-rans. It's why the neuters and subdoms enjoy beating us. Breeding equates with rank on Occo. Here's a chance for a half-caste to kick a breeding male around and get away with it."

"We had a real son of a bitch of a *g/ari* in command before the *asha!a'* got here," I said.

"Well yes, your *asha!a* was late coming out of hibernation this year—"

"He was late coming out of *what?*" I said amid a minor uproar of the greenies.

"Hibernation?"

"You don't know much, do you?" said Dogger.

"Explain it to him, expert," said Zulu.

Dogger began, "Once a year Occon doms shed their antlers—"

At this the greenies started laughing so hard it was some time before I could get Dogger to continue. I think some of them hurt themselves. They screamed as if this were the funniest thing they'd ever heard in their lives, falling on the floor, kicking and gasping. Tears streamed down their faces, and they were still breaking out in sporadic fits of giggles when Dogger resumed.

"Without their antlers the doms fear for their lives. They are absolutely vulnerable. Their metabolism slows down, and they go into hibernation in hiding. If they're found, they're dragged out of their burrows, brutally humiliated, and tortured to death."

"Who does this?"

"The *g/ari*, the subdoms."

"So who is in charge while the doms are hibernating?"

"The subdoms."

"Isn't that a cheerful thought."

"Once upon a time it was the females. But the legal system has upset the natural order of things, so the *g/ari* can be viceroys now. By law the *g/ari* aren't supposed to go hunting up hibernating doms, but you know law only curbs a natural impulse so far."

"It's natural for a *g/ari* to dig up and torture a defenseless dom?"

"Subdoms are vicious. How do you face yourself when your genes are less than right? If they kill the doms, it's more likely a *g/ari* will develop into a full male to fill the void."

I told Dogger the incident of our *asha!a*'s first arrival. "All the *g/ari* said to him was: 'So pleased to see you again this season.' And the *asha!a'* gored him."

Dogger was not surprised. "That subdom was lying through his teeth. Little doubt he was *not* pleased to see the *asha!a'* this season. He might have been trying to kill the *asha!a'* in his burrow. The *asha!a'* made it out alive and got him for it."

"That would make more sense," I agreed. The killing had seemed so unprovoked. And while the *asha!a'* was violent-natured, he usually had some kind of reason for what he did.

"Your *asha!a'* is probably feeling pretty testy. I hear he missed this last battle—the one you were in. He came out of hibernation late. Normally he's a pilot."

"I know."

"*Hell* of a pilot," Zulu inserted. "He was in the force that brought *us* down."

Brace added, "He's already got the horns; give him wings and he's Satan himself."

"He's not flying anywhere now," said Dogger. "Being in charge of a work farm is the bottom of the birdcage for doms. That's why you don't see him out here. Your dom never comes out to see what's going on. He knows only what the subdoms tell him. He pretends he's not here while subdoms skim off your supplies. Doms never talk to humans."

"Hello?" someone said to accompanying cackles from the greenies.

Some of the greenies pointed at me.

Dogger was confused. "You're not a subdom, are you?"

I looked left and right, realized he was talking to me. *"No!"*

"Sorry. You could almost pass. With that nose. Look at those teeth."

"My, what Occon teeth you have," said Zulu, and I shut my mouth.

"What'd you do to your canine teeth, Nordveldt?"

"I don't know," I said, irritated. "They just wore down."

"Black your nails and you could pass for a *g/ari.*"

"Just what I always wanted," said I.

"We always knew he was one of them," said a greenie.

"Are you?" said Dogger. "Really?"

"He's not an Occon, he's a Kralle," said someone.

"Same difference," said someone else.

"The commandant talks to him. I think they're sleeping together myself."

"Why do all the guard bitches back away when they see you coming?" I shot back.

"A dom talks to you?" said Dogger, astounded. I think he was actually jealous.

I said, "He talks to me because he doesn't trust his *g/ari.*"

"Did he tell you that?"

"Yes."

G/ari *are treacherous and not a little stupid. I want my messages intact. The more mouths that handle it, the more garbled it becomes. And fact is, it is less garbled through you than through my own* g/ari. G/ari *are given to free interpretation.*

Dogger nodded. "Subdoms didn't always have this much power, and they weren't always this mutinous. Their natural inferiority kept them in place, and they did all their challenging on the sly, while the doms were sleeping. But in a technocratic age, physical prowess ensures nothing. The gun is a great leveler. With a gun a *g!ari*—hell, a *ufin!i*—can kill a dom. It's only their laws that keep them from destroying each other.''

''What about dom versus dom?'' I said.

''That is in the natural order of things. But that's all controlled by law now too. That's why the *asha!a'* sits still for this shit when he'd rather be just about anywhere else.

''Put two doms in a room and they'd like to kill each other but they don't because they are also thinking beings. Just as if you put a man and a woman in a room—instinct might be to start conjugating more than your verbs, but you don't necessarily do that because society has rules.''

''Wouldn't stop me,'' said a greenie.

''So,'' I started slowly. ''Just how recent was this technological revolution?''

''You don't know?'' Dogger grinned.

The pilots chuckled fiendishly.

''I'm having suspicions.''

''Real recent,'' said Dogger.

''Like one hundred and ninety years recent?''

''Give that man a ticket home!''

''Oh my God.''

''The Occons learned technology, civilization, everything from humans. They were in the *stone age* when humans came. The Occons lived in nomadic tribes—can't even call 'em tribes. They lived in *packs* like wolves. Within a single lifetime they absorbed everything the humans brought to them. They have the learning capacity of children, but it's lifelong. They're sponges. They advanced seven thousand years in fifty. And not only did the Occons manage to assimilate it all, they used what they learned to turn around and conquer their teachers.''

''But why? Why did they turn on humans?''

''Ah! You see, it was a very paranoid society that came to Occo. The Occons learned everything from the colonists, even their paranoia.

''You notice the colonists *never told* the colonists of Erde or Tannia that anything was wrong? The colonists of the third world came from a part of Earth condescendingly known as the third world. They had a long tradition of being used and downtrodden. They were religious minorities of India. They were from islands which other nations used as military bases, or atomic test zones.

"The colonists of Erde and Tannia were from America and England and Germany and South Africa, nations not known for their meekness. The third-world colonists did not call them for help, as their 'help' tended to be overwhelming, demeaning, or not helpful at all. And they were afraid if it became known that a native intelligence existed on Occo, they would be made to give the planet up—and to move to one of the other planets where children of imperialists already had a head start and they would become second-class citizens all over again. So they decided to assimilate the natives to their own society.

"The native Occons read the Earth histories, found out what usually happens to aborigines when colonists move in, and decided it was not going to happen to them."

"This is incredible," I said. "And yet the humans never called for help?"

"By the time they admitted to themselves that they were in over their heads it was too late. Who'd have thought? You just said it: it's incredible. These creatures were *stone-age.*"

"Where are the descendants of the colonists now?"

"In work farms. Doing the hazardous, dull, toxic labor. The Occons keep them stupid. The Occons control the information flow now, and they don't want a double turnabout."

"How many humans are there?"

"Not many, I think. Thousands maybe. Takes too long to breed 'em and raise 'em into workers, and you might have noticed subdoms aren't patient. Easier to snatch new ones while we were in the neighborhood."

"That's horrifying."

"That it is, mate."

"They're still animals for all that," said Zulu.

Dogger nodded. "I thought the antlers were for show. Saw our dom grab a man, bow his head to the side, slash sideways, and take his face off. Just hung down in a flap.

Filleted. Sharp, sharp, sharp. Then there's the dewclaws. Have you seen those?'' he asked me.

I nodded. ''Those things.'' I pointed at my forearms.

''What? What?'' said a greenie.

The claws generally stayed in the sleeves, so the greenies didn't know what we were talking about. And I knew less than I thought I did.

''I call it a dewclaw, but it's too high-set and too long to be a real dewclaw,'' said Dogger. ''Looks like another antler tine. It comes out of the inner side of the dom's forearm and curves in at his wrist in a point. Looks like he'll prick himself, but he doesn't. In anger the thing twists around so it hooks outward and drips venom.''

''That's *venom?*'' I said. I remembered black droplets spurting.

''The venom doesn't flow when the claw curves in. The muscles cross and block the venom sac. When he's mad, out they come. Each dom's venom is unique. They can't poison themselves. The antidote is in their blood. But they can poison another dom, and they can poison you. Any Occon sees the dewclaws turn and he runs like hell. Guards with *guns* run. If you know what's good for you, you run.''

I started laughing.

''You've seen 'em turn, Nordveldt?''

''All the time!'' I laughed. The longer I thought of it the harder I laughed. They must have thought me insane. I don't think I had ever been with the *asha!a'* when he *hadn't* turned his claws. ''I get him so *pissed!*''

''*You* are living a charmed life,'' said Dogger.

Instantly I sobered. I looked at the circle of broken men around me in the crushing air cooled to 100 degrees, looked away out the tiny window of our cell to the livid horizon where it was raining cobalt and crimson fire.

''Could've fooled me.''

VI.

It was an odd day when the *asha!a'* came outside to do anything other than get into his limousine and leave. This day he descended from his HQ, came right out to the prisoners' enclosure, and barked for one of his subdoms by name.

The subdom approached diffidently, and the *asha!a'* told him to take off his shirt.

I was watching from a pit. Dogger came scrambling into the pit with me and pointed. "Watch this, Nordveldt. Here's something you don't see every day."

"What am I seeing?"

"Just watch."

The guards did not make us get back to work, because they were all watching too.

The subdom undressed. Underneath his clothes, his chest and abdomen were covered with a pelt of short hair, or maybe it was even fur.

Someone in the pit asked me if the *asha!a'* was that furry. I know when I'm being baited. He just wanted to know if I had seen the *asha!a'* with his clothes off. I said I didn't know.

The *asha!a'* made the subdom turn around.

Down the subdom's back, along his spine, was a darkened stripe.

The *asha!a'* made him turn around again and seized his arms, bringing to light two dark spots like bruises on the *g/ari*'s forearms, as if he had given blood in an emergency situation with an old-fashioned needle. Or was growing spurs.

"He's turning into a dom," I said.

Dogger nodded. "Lucky bastard."

I glanced at all the other Occons on the grounds. They were watching with unbridled envy.

The *asha!a'* grabbed the new dom by the hair, drew him into a rough embrace with the *asha!a'*s chin resting on the younger one's head.

"See that move?" said Dogger. "That means, 'I have antlers and you don't yet.' He does that because he *can.* If the kid had antlers, that gesture would take the *asha!a'*s chin off, so he does it now before they grow. Doms do that to their wives and their children too. Then it means protection—he puts his antlers over their heads, lending strength, you see. It's an expression of fondness."

"And here it means?"

"Dominance."

"Not friendship?"

"The crowned ones have no friends. Especially not another dom. Watch. Next thing, he's going to send him away before he has to kill him."

The very next thing. The *asha!a'* took the young dom's wrist, led him to the limo, threw him inside, slammed the door, and sent him away from the lapis mines.

Nothing lapis decorated the *asha!a'*s office, not because he could not afford it. The *asha!a'*, as I'd come to know, was personally wealthy. He had no lapis because he had learned to loathe it.

I ventured to ask what was the most valuable substance on Occo.

He flicked a finger off his antlers.

That I should have guessed. I would be interested to know what the Mohs' scale hardness was. I'd seen him score limestone with his antlers.

He picked up the spaceplane model which had been fashioned from antler—his own, presumably. Dogger said the doms lost their antlers every year.

"Your ship?" I said.

From the pensive, loving way he handled it I did not actually need to ask that. I was trying to make conversation—foolishly, because I always get in trouble when I try to speak of anything past the necessary to him.

This time I did not get in trouble. He talked about his

ship, bragged a little. He asked about mine, not like an intelligence officer, but like a pilot talking to a pilot.

One of those all-too-human, can-you-top-this conversations that runs along the lines of "My ship can . . ."

"Well, *my* ship can . . ."

He balanced his model on his fingertips. "Have you ever seen one of these move?"

I told him I had. It was the kind of ship that took a shot at my wife. The Occon pilot had told Maggie to come back, puppy, when she was a dog.

And I grew long-winded on the subject of Maggie. It somehow brought her closer to talk of her. I even told him she was expecting a child and I was worried about her.

"Give me your hand," he demanded.

Hesitantly I did. He pushed up my sleeve and rubbed my forearm with his thumb as if probing for a bruise such as the changing subdom had shown. As if I were about to sprout dewclaws. "You've bred?" he said.

"Any human can breed," I said.

He dropped my hand, moved to the window. "I want children. They haven't let me breed. I think that's obscene."

I said it didn't sound fair.

He rambled a little, more than he'd ever spoken to me, or to anyone within my earshot, longing for a simpler life, in the open without walls or roofs. Eight wives. He wanted eight wives.

I had to smile. "Why eight?"

He said he thought he could keep that many happy. "How many do you have?"

"One," I said. "One at a time."

"Of course one at a time," he said, irritated, then, concerned, "You do only have one—?"

I had to supply the Erden word and assured him that yes, human males only had one. "I meant married to one at a time, not mate with. My first wife was killed in the Erde-Tannian war. She was a pilot too."

The *asha!a'* was highly critical of letting women fight in front-line combat.

"They do what they want," I said.

"They do," he agreed.

As I was going out he asked if I wanted quarters of my own.

The offer surprised me. I could just imagine how that would go over with the other prisoners! I said I had better stay with my men in the common barracks, that I didn't think they would like the idea much.

He said to hell with them. He thought I would want my own *burrow.*

From the first I had the impression that the *asha!a'* was secretly averse to killing us. His efficiency was as much a desire not to have to exterminate us as it was being a good Occon administrator. He hated us, or, more accurately, hated having us on his hands, but wholesale slaughter was not in his makeup. Not from human compassion, but from the same revulsion anyone might feel given a herd of warm-blooded creatures either to use or to put to death, he did his best to keep us alive.

As time went by I think some sense of our common "humanity" overtook him. And that was when he really seemed to be cracking.

He reminded me of Reid, and I had always liked Reid. Maybe I have an affinity for madmen. But I liked the *asha!a'* for the very reason that he was going mad.

He never succeeded in that psychic numbness, the sublimation of moral feeling to duty, that was required to be a good slave master. To do things repulsive to conscience on the excuse that it is one's duty is to relinquish responsibility for one's actions. One retreats into the moral neutrality of pursuing a job. The *asha!a'* never abdicated either self-sovereignty or "humanity," and, protest as he would, I don't think he succeeded in denying his prisoners' "humanity," and it was tearing him apart.

The *asha!a'* became wound tighter and tighter. He would shake, visibly shake. I thought he was sick again. I reached toward him. He snapped, "Do not touch me."

I withdrew, but the impulse came again. He was shaking. I forgot. On reflex I touched his arm by the incurved spur.

Suddenly it was curved out as he jerked it away from me. And in a blink he had seized up a stylus and stabbed my hand, the point driven through to the desktop, pinning my hand to the desk.

Something caught in my throat, or I would have shrieked. As it was I made no sound, and I think that won me some respect. It wasn't courage. My throat closed. Pain. Sweat slicked my sides. Trembling. He yanked the stylus out, and I started bleeding freely. "Get out."

I moved to the door, clutching my wounded hand with my other hand, red drops spilling between my fingers.

He snarled at me, "I was not meant to keep cages. I am a pilot."

"I know."

"You know nothing."

My hand throbbed, and I was feeling belligerent in pain. "Is that what they tell you? It is. They tell you we are animals, so the beatings, the cages, are OK. But you got trapped playing zookeeper only to find out that we are in fact as *Occon* as you, our blood as red." I quirked a smile at that.

He looked angry, then anguished. Then he said, "Come here."

And he wrapped my hand, with a self-conscious, light touch.

He'd missed the bones and tendons, perhaps on purpose, but it had been fast as a snakebite, so I don't know how studied a shot it could have been. Then again, a pilot has to make hypersonic decisions.

"You are wrong," he said when my hand was bandaged. "That is not what I have learned at all. Most of your compatriots *are* animals. You. You are a pilot."

And he grabbed me by the shoulders, drew me in, and placed his chin on my head.

I returned to the barracks, found Dogger drawing a calendar on the wall with a soft stone, an Occon calendar with Tannian correlations. Dogger could tell specifically what the date was. From that I could calculate the next launch window. I picked up a stone and started helping him.

He glanced at my bandaged hand. "What happened?"

"I pissed him off again. He stabbed me."

"What'd you *do?*"

"I touched him."

"Oh, that was dumb. Where'd you touch him?"

"Where? Just on his arm."

"Forearm?"

I paused. "Yeah."

"Ho, bad move." Dogger chuckled. "I don't know how you get away with it. You're lucky that's all he did to you."

"What did I do?"

He informed me that to touch a dom under the antlers or under the spurs was a dominance move when it was male to male, sexual when it was female to male. I had intended neither. I'm fairly sure the *asha!a'* knew that, but he got mad anyway.

"You might have warned me, Dogger."

"Warned you, hell. Where do you get off trying to touch him, asshole?"

I did not feel like telling him what the *asha!a'* had done to me next. I busied myself figuring when the next launch window occurred, and I marked it in the calendar.

"Coincides with the end of hibernation," said Dogger, circling those days.

"When does hibernation begin?" I asked.

" 'Bout in here." He circled a date thirty Occon days away. "I'll sure hate to see it. Damn subdoms go power-mad without the doms around. Sadist pigs they are." He lifted the severed stump of his right arm. "There goes the Country Club."

I was figuring how long it would take to get back to Erde at the next launch window. "As if I'll be near a ship that can decompress me," I muttered over my figures.

"As if you'll live that long," said Dogger.

I looked at him queerly. "Why did you say that?"

"Subdoms are going to get you, pal," said Dogger factually, with no doubt in the world. "You want warnings? Here's a warning. Since they can't get at the *asha!a'* direct, they're going to take it out of you. You've been speaking for the *asha!a';* you're going to do a lot more for the *asha!a'*. Anything they'd like to do to a dom dragged out of his burrow—they've got you. And who's going to stop them then?''

Some greenies around us were beginning to grin.

Even Dogger seemed eager—like a subdom who hopes to advance with the removal of the resident dom. Obsession glowed on his face. Dogger wanted my position in the *asha!a*'s favor. There was no regret in his prediction.

I couldn't argue. He could only be right.

I remembered what he said about doms pulled from their burrows out of time.

''I wouldn't give two cabbages for your chances, Nordveldt.'' He tapped at the date thirty days hence, underlined it. ''You're dogmeat.''

VII.

There was another escape attempt. I never learned the details. It wasn't anyone from my barracks. I thought for certain if anyone ever tried it, it would be our newcomers. Fighter pilots are not easily domesticated, and I thought as soon as they regained their strength, one of them would make a break for it. But the would-be escapees were a trio of greenies tunneling through the "rose garden," where the sensitive-nosed Occon guards and guard dogs did not inspect closely. And the greenies might have gotten away with it had they been better engineers, but the tunnel collapsed, leaving a sink hole—a stink hole, said the man who fell into it—in the vegetable garden/latrine. The tunnel was discovered, and by hindsight it was not difficult to figure who had dug it.

The *asha!a'* came out to the work field in person and called the three tunnelers by name. He deactivated the current in the fence and told them to run for it. They bolted for the fence, and the *asha!a'* pinned the three of them to it with three quick blasts of his sidearm—just hung them up there, shot in the back, fused by the middle to the fence like bugs smashed on a windshield. He made the rest of us bury them and clean off the fence. He left the field in a vibrating rage.

The crackdown was on after that. All the concessions I'd gotten out of him were gone instantly. The *asha!a'* thought he'd been conned. This attempt angered him the way the abortive ship theft had not, because this one reeked of complicity. The incident with the stolen ship had been an impulsive solo grasp at an opportunity. This one left suspicion like fox's spray over the entire prisoner compound. Who else was in on it? The *asha!a'* imagined everyone was.

And if we didn't like the way he was running the work farm, he would go back to the subdom way.

We moved back into our aboveground, uncooled barracks—with the doors shut. The height of summer had passed, but it was still not unusual for the man in the next bunk not to wake up in the morning.

I was thrown into a sweatbox and kept in. I was not let out even to work. I was not let out at all. I was given a pot to piss in. I peered out my tiny window in the mornings to try to see who was being buried this day.

I record this quite coldly. I think if I am ever in a safe comfortable place again and look back on this I shall start screaming.

I passed my birthday in there. The *asha!a'* came to see me, asked me what I wanted for my birthday.

I was surprised he knew it was my birthday, but birthdays are important on Occo. I said, "A return to the way things were."

"That is a very big request."

No, it wasn't. What I really wanted was for him to let us all go.

"You asked," I said. And I am not sure to this day why he did ask. I think he wanted me to make that request, to have an excuse to lighten up again. Productivity had gone straight down the stink hole with the dead men.

"Done," he said. Then sharply, "Except regarding you. You stay." He paused for me to reconsider a different request.

I did consider. I did not like these men. I thought of choosing something for myself, but what the hell. I expected to be dying by slow torture soon anyway, according to Dogger's prediction.

I did not change my mind, and the *asha!a'* left.

He came back at night after everyone else had been moved back to the underground quarters. It was a hot night. They were all hot.

Strange to see the *asha!a'* in this surrounding. My cage was barely two meters by one and a half and not high enough for the *asha!a'* to stand up straight. Even bowed, his antlers scraped the top.

He crouched, balanced on the balls of his feet, with his back to the wall.

I sat propped in one corner on a scatter of straw on the floor, wilted. My hair, long and stringy, hung in my eyes.

The *asha!a'* was well-groomed as a cat.

"Used to be a man chose his pack," he said. Pack. He used the wolf word; I didn't supply it. "I loathe this pack. See what humans have done to us?"

"You did it to yourselves," I said.

"We did not have to contort ourselves to your ways? You think? And what would your kind have done to us primitive savages then?"

"I'm sure the point is well taken, but wasn't there another way?"

"I was not here, and neither were you." As if we would have done differently. "They that were did what they could, and you have no right to judge."

"Is there no way up from here?"

He made a sound I think was an Occon curse or obscenity. The dewclaws were twisting. In such close quarters I drew my feet in and tried to be small. But he was not looking my way. "I cannot get myself out of this morass! That man with the crown, the seventeen points, in a fair fight—" He snapped his fingers, puffed air between his lips and teeth. He was talking about his commanding officer. "I salute that topheavy tottering fossil and he wears that crown as if he earned it. He is so feeble. What strength has he?" He gripped his sidearm in its holster. "What kind of claw is *this?*"

He radiated dark brooding strength and youth, attractiveness that translates across species lines, as a man can say a horse is beautiful, or a big cat, or an antlered deer, but still close enough to humanity to disturb.

"And what kind of children will we breed—when things like that procreate while the stronger are stuck in sterile holes because they offend an alien system of authority?"

"It won't work anymore," I said.

His head jerked. He looked as if startled to see me. He'd been talking to himself. "What won't?'

"The whole system. It won't work. If it ever did. What of compromise and cooperation?"

"Even if I agreed with you—and I don't—we do not make policy. There is nothing to be settled here. So you may shut up."

"Every time I agree with you, you turn on me. I guess that's what happened to compromise and cooperation."

"We are perfectly capable of compromise. *This* is a compromise." He pointed at himself. "We are capable of putting savage instinct aside for a purpose, but not with humans, because humans don't know how to do that."

"All right. Take this as a microcosm. Under the present system you and I should be at each other's throat. If you and I can come to some kind of balance under extreme conditions, why not on a larger scale?"

"Because this is not a microcosm. It is a stupid accident, and as for you and me getting along, never think that we do. Do not mistake my forbearance at any given moment as anything more significant than whim."

"But I do."

"Your mistake."

"Your bluff."

"I ought to shoot you now."

"Do."

I was not sure he wouldn't do it, just to prove he was not bluffing. But he knew me as a person by then, and he was not a psychopath, though others will swear he was, so cold-blooded killing at this close range would be a big leap.

If he was as human as I was gambling he was.

"No," he said. And to cover his retreat he said, "Your usefulness outweighs any need to prove anything to you, which carries no weight at all."

"Since you don't care, I'll consider this my round then."

"Why did I come here?"

"Why did you?"

"I don't know," he said—spoken softly with nothing for a long time to follow. Both of us stayed silent. I watched sweat bead on his smooth bronze skin.

It was an odd tense little scene. Sweat and heat and his presence too strong for this confined space. Quiet.

Onyx eyes moved, scanning the wall as if there were

something on it to see. Crouched in attitude of hiding, he did not want to leave, could not think of a reason to stay.

Finally he climbed out of the box and stood up just outside the door at his full height, facing aside, not looking at me. Softly accented voice that was never personal asked in Erden, "Do you want a woman?"

That took me by surprise. I didn't know how to answer. I attempted a joke. "Is that in the budget?"

"My gift to you." The *asha!a'* was a rich man. He was dead serious.

There are personal gifts, and then there are personal gifts. "No," I said.

He turned to go without a word.

Some things are sometimes stronger than pride. I was in this box and I was alone and it was night. I hadn't let myself admit how sick to the soul I was of this fucking place. I just about shrieked as the door was closing, *"Yes!"*

He stopped, still said nothing, then walked away.

Next was horrible. The *asha!a*'s offer wakened something I'd put to sleep and now it would not rest again. Heat is supposed to sap desire; it usually does. It was having no effect now. I wondered if this was some insidious torture, and I tried not to be too expectant.

What I wanted was Maggie. What I was getting, I had no idea. Or I had too many ideas.

I suffered in squirming doubt. What, if anything, would show—a toothless human slave dragged from a women's work farm? An Occon? I had never seen an Occon female, and I began envisioning horrid differences.

Dark.

All the lights in the barracks' high windows that peered above ground level were out. My light stayed on faintly always so a guard could look in on me.

At long last, footsteps neared my solitary cage. Images piled one on the other, fear at the forefront.

A guard opened the door. A woman stepped lightly inside, big, raven-haired, exuding sexuality, dressed in shimmering black, her lashes long, thick, and soft. She looked like what she was, a very expensive prostitute. Her nails were painted frosty rose and her nose was rather short, so I did not know for certain until she smiled with perfect even teeth that she was an Occon.

Close enough, I didn't care.

I stood up as if she were polite company, stammered something like "I can't offer you a seat."

She tilted her head at the pile of straw, said in Occon, "Is this your bed?"

I nodded, and she sat down there. "This is fine. Sit with me."

I sat down beside her. We talked a little.

She was pleasant company and made me believe she thought I was.

"You're not nervous," I said.

And she wasn't. She had a very easy manner. She gave a one-shoulder shrug, and her dress fell off her shoulder. "A man is a man."

I was staring at her bared shoulder, her dress draped so precariously I was waiting for—never mind. I stalled. "How do you feel about being given to an alien slave?"

"I do not think you can surprise me. I understand you look like a *g/ari* and act like an *ashai*. I have introduced many young *ashai* in transition."

"*I'm* nervous," I said.

"I am not your mate; you do not need to impress me. And if you want anything strange, it is paid for, so do not hesitate, whatever you desire."

Big of you, *asha!a'!* Just in case I turned out to be a pervert, hm? But that's OK, it's paid for. This was really accommodating. I started laughing.

My companion's name was N≠alika. I think. Transliterating names is hell. The woman's name begins with a nasalized alveolar click, and I'm not sure about that *k*, which might be a soft click too, but N≠ali!ka looks like a cat walked on a keyboard. So I shall say her name was N≠alika.

I shouldn't admit it, but I didn't know her name until we were talking later. I would have asked sooner, but she was running her tongue up my neck and I mumbled something about wishing I could have taken a bath before she got here. She said not to worry about her, and we quit talking for a while.

I was glad she didn't look like Maggie. I did not want

to have any flashbacks of this night when I was with Maggie again. I was certain I would see Maggie again.

A little later something N≠alika said came back to me. *I am not your mate; you do not need to impress me.*

I asked, "Occon doms have to impress their mates?"

"Well, yes," said N≠alika. "If a wife is not happy, she leaves."

And the *asha!a'* thought he could keep eight happy!

Bought women, on the other hand, don't need to be happy, just paid. Prostitution is not the oldest profession on Occo. It's a scant 190 years old. That's right—a human import. It had since become a legitimate profession among the Occons, and prostitutes came in grades, like cuts of meat. Occons have no qualms about using people, even their own. N≠alika was of the top level. I asked her how she felt about it. She said not to worry what a prostitute thinks; that's why they exist.

I tried to envision what human civilization had done to Occons to create a need for prostitutes. I pictured the *asha!a'*s seventeen-point commander, a tottering fossil who in natural circumstance would not hold the authority he did. I pictured all his wives recognizing him for a propped-up phony and walking out.

Women do what they like.

They do.

Artificially imposed authority might need to acquire companionship artificially.

And there was the *asha!a'*, forbidden by some authority that should not rightly exist to marry.

I asked N≠alika how well she knew the *asha!a'*.

She said they were acquainted. A nice vague word. I asked what he was like. She said, "He does not have me talk so much."

"Do you prefer that?" I was afraid I was annoying her with my questions.

"Keeps me from lying."

I took that to mean she was not going to answer any further questions regarding past clients with any accuracy.

"But you're not shaking anymore." She smiled. "So questions are good."

I said, "The *asha!a'* seems to think of me as a subdom."

"Oh no. Not at all," she said as if I'd insulted myself. "He sees you as a dom they have pried out of his burrow out of time, whom lesser beings abuse, and they have no right."

"An antlerless dom," I said. This was a new thought.

"Definitely a dom." She moved seductively on the straw. I wonder how much she was being paid to act as if I were not disgusting to her.

I asked if the *asha!a'* had any friends. She said, "The crowned ones have no friends."

"What am I?"

"You are lucky you have no antlers. If you were a rival he would have to kill you."

I was embarrassed to face the *asha!a'* again when at last he let me out of solitary. And he did let me out—professedly because he needed his go-between. He made no reference or inquiry on the subject of my birthday, as something that did not bear commenting on. It was effectively forgotten, I thought.

The other prisoners did not know about my visitor in solitary. Had they bothered to pick up the Occon language they would have known, because the guards gossiped furiously. One prisoner did pick it up. Dogger winked at me, but otherwise kept his mouth shut.

Dogger pointed out the current date on the calendar. It was later than I thought. My days, he said, were dwindling. More than ever he was convinced the subdoms were going to let me have it when the *asha!a'* left.

The *asha!a'* was leaving in two days.

"You have till day after tomorrow to live, mate."

I had light duty the last day. I was packing away the *asha!a*'s personal belongings into storage chests, making way for the interim commander. The *asha!a'* had me doing this because he could not stand to have his own kind near him.

I spied him making frequent trips to the mirror, surreptitiously touching the base of his antlers, worrying at them like loose teeth. He shied at sudden noises and kept one hand on his sidearm.

At the same time, the prospect of getting out of here had put him in a fair mood.

The hard rays from Erde-Tannia kept up a spitting storm in the Occon sky, yet the *asha!a'* talked optimistically of flying against the double planet when he came out of hibernation. With any luck he would not be coming back to the mines.

I asked the *asha!a'* how the Occons expected to survive on Erde-Tannia with our tides.

"Very simple. We intend to eliminate the tides."

"You would need to destroy one of the planets to do that."

It was barely out of my mouth—no, even as I spoke the cold leaked into my veins. I was talking to an Occon. What kind of argument was that to an Occon?

"Yes," he said. "The smaller one. Your planet. Erde. No one could breathe there."

There was plenty of oxygen, but the pressure was not high enough for the Occon lungs.

"Pity," he continued. "I like Erde. Its civilization is better than Tannia's. But we shall eliminate that too."

"Tannian civilization?" Why should that shock me when the man had just told me his people were going to blow up my world? What was the end of Tannian civilization after that? After all, I had been part of an attempt to rub out Tannian civilization myself at one time.

He closed his last packing case, turned to me as if he realistically expected to see me again. As if I had a prayer in this prison without him here. "Storm Petrel. If I ever meet you in the skies I will not hesitate to kill you."

"I know," I said. "Assuming I don't get you first."

"You are a braggart."

"I am very good."

"Someday when we are both free, God willing, I will challenge that."

VIII.

On the day the *asha!a'* left I made my move. It was a simple, obvious trick I used, and absurd enough to go unlooked-for. When the *asha!a'* left, I left with him in the trunk of his limo.

The trunk did not lock, and while I was loading in the few things the *asha!a'* was taking with him, I figured out how to open it from the inside. I squirreled away a day's worth of food and a guard's uniform—I wanted a *g/ari* officer's uniform but I could not get my hands on one. I stained my fingernails black with rust inhibitor, then climbed into the trunk when I hoped no one was looking. If I got caught, so be it. From what Dogger was saying, death would be much easier if the *asha!a'* rather than the subdoms caught me.

Inside the trunk was dark, hot, and cramped. My heart caromed off the walls of my chest; more thunderous than the telltale heart. I was doomed to failure, I was certain. I thought it inconceivable that the *asha!a'* would pull out without accounting for my presence first. But then he did not go checking my whereabouts or taking a head count every time he left the grounds, and this was just one more leaving. My guilt on this occasion was the difference.

I don't think I breathed until the limo began to move.

Once through the gates I waited as long as I could. In no time the heat rocketed within the confines of the trunk under the direct sun. I could think of no good plan to get me out of there, and I had no time to wait. I was going to pass out.

When the limo slowed, I bailed out and ran.

And kept running.

I did not look back to see if anyone saw me pop out of the trunk, if the robot pilot sounded some kind of warning or just reshut the trunk. I would be enlightened soon enough in the form of a shot in the back.

I crashed through wilderness. I did not even look at it before I had darted off the roadway and was running headlong through it, a dry jungle of twisted xylem stalks, thick, wild, fantastical, all brown, yellow, and desiccated green. I ran blindly, feeling like a bug skittering through someone's parched lawn. Trolls must live in here.

When I was too dizzy and too overheated to keep running, I staggered to a halt, sat on an elephantine blade of woody grass, and waited for my heart to stop hammering so I could hear if anyone was chasing me.

The dry jungle was absolutely quiet, then gradually began to hum and burr and sing, so I guessed I was quite alone.

The only thing that caught up with me was pain. All the blood rushed from my head, and I huddled in a fetal ball on the ground, retching.

Presently I recovered a few degrees, sipped some hot water, and eased myself upright.

I changed into the Occon uniform and bruised my forearms. Hurt like hell, but my bruises were works of art. *I* almost believed I was sprouting dewclaws.

I yanked some hairs out of the back of my head in two spots. I did not think I could survive hitting myself to gain some knots, but that proved unnecessary; the skin puffed up convincingly without it.

I worried about my untrimmed hair and the way I smelled. My lack of body fur could not be helped. Well, I was just beginning to change. Would anyone buy this?

I had picked up enough of the Occon language, or so I hoped, to be a believable if slightly reticent Occon dom. Disguise complete, I picked my way back to the road and started walking.

And stopped. Heat rolled off the baking pavement and stung my eyes. The sun sucked the strength from my limbs, forcing me to take shelter until evening.

I curled up under a gargantuan leathery leaf. It was amazingly cool underneath but already populated by two lizards, which I nearly evicted, but they were lapping up bugs, so I had to let them stay.

At dusk I started out again. By morning my food and water were gone, but I was in sight of a depressed outpost of a town, turned inward and half buried against the heat.

I had no money, but luckily certain things, like water and bread, are free to soldiers. And my bruises got me a cup of malted brew and a bowl of thick black soup from an old female innkeeper who took an instant liking to me.

The sight of women, odd after so long, sent me into a small panic. In some Earth languages the form of address, the verb suffixes, are different if you are talking to a female rather than to a male. I was in big trouble if Occon turned out to be one of those languages.

But Occon is a very simple tongue, and I dropped no bricks by talking to the women. And they thought I was adorable. They all smiled, mothered, said hello.

My innkeep was a bestial-looking matron, her arms thickly furred, so it appeared to be a clawed paw at the end of a dog's leg which handed me a cup of tea. I looked up into her benignly smiling horsy face.

My eyes are gray. Occons think all humans have dark brown or black eyes, so they didn't automatically think "alien!" when they saw my light eyes, but they did think them unusual and interesting.

I did not know how I was expected to react to all this female attention.

The sum total of my knowledge of Occon women stemmed from one night with an Occon prostitute. Until now, that prostitute had been the only Occon woman I had ever seen.

So when I looked across the cool shadowy room and met those velvet eyes, I died on the spot, or felt like it. What were the odds? What were the odds of meeting someone I knew here? I had seen *one* Occon woman and here she was.

And so was the *asha!a*'s dog, sitting at her feet, looking at me and thumping its heavy tail on the floor.

The *asha!a*'s woman. The *asha!a*'s dog.

Was *he* here?

I sat like a stone. The innkeep came over. Did I want

more soup, more brew, some baking, did I want baking? No, I could not eat another thing. I think my smile was kind of sick-looking.

I wondered if I ought to run.

Not with the dog. With the dog after me I would never make it. I stayed rooted.

Across the room I saw that N≠alika had turned to talk into a wrist phone. To whom about what I could only worry.

After some moments she sauntered to my table, slid into the chair next to mine, and crossed her forearms. She asked me, in Occon, if I was looking for something.

Everyone was looking at us, either directly or over mugs or news slates. The other people in the inn were a mixture of civilian *g/ari* and *ufin/i.* I was so accustomed to seeing them in uniform I hadn't been aware they were detachable.

I answered N≠alika weakly, "I can't afford you."

"If you need to find a burrow this season," N≠alika said, pressing a key crystal into my hand, printing my ID into the lock. She left the inn, making eyes and inviting me along with her walk. The room was subtly oh-ho-hoing at me. I think I turned red and hid my face behind my mug.

Trying to keep composure, I did not immediately run out after her. I forced myself to sit there and finish the dregs of my cup of brew. If the *g/ari* military police should come, so be it. If N≠alika wanted to turn me in, I was done.

She had taken the dog. The *asha!a'* was not here after all.

I stood up at last. Legs wobbled under me in a quiet panic.

I left with the innkeep's motherly admonition that expensive women could ruin a young dom. She warned that a bought woman could be in the pay of another dom.

I realized that and almost asked this woman to shelter me.

And what would happen when I didn't go into hibernation? It wouldn't work. I would have to take my chances with N≠alika.

Outside, the hot glare was a relief after the cool darkness of the underground inn, which had taken on all the dimensions of a death pit to me. I did not run. I walked. I met no eyes. I turned corners casually and got myself lost in the streets, which had an eerily human plan.

I did not look at the key until I was well away from the inn. I withdrew my tight-clenched hand from my pocket. When I uncurled my fingers the key's perfect print was embedded in my palm, and only then did I see that it was not a room key.

It was a key to a transport.

I inhaled a dizzy breath and pushed the call sequence. The transport arrived unoccupied, without military escort. The transport was at my disposal.

I could go anywhere on Occo.

The most habitable places were located beneath the solar reflectors. But given the choice between the natives and the sun, I would take my chances with the sun.

I went far away from everything, from any settlement, to a desert, and set up camp, a place where my bruises could heal and my nails grow out.

And here is where I am.

I'd had survival training twenty-plus years before. In the transport was a survival kit with a cooling tent. Even though it is winter, in the desert the days go to 121 Fahrenheit in the shade. I stay in the tent and let meals come to me—sand eels attracted by the scent of moisture. They don't taste bad, but I'm sick of them.

This place used to be a lake, I think, then a mud flat. The clay has dried and cracked into warped plates, curled up at the edges, baked so hot some have been fired on the surface as in a kiln, making them hard, bright, and glassy orange-brown.

My ceramic wasteland. Things slither along the cracks, and I eat them.

The yellow sun turns red on the horizon, the air cools but glows with the sanguineous light like the inside of a kiln, the sky marled with blue-violet jets of the hard rays, curtains of ions, snaky jagged darts of serpent tongues, all red. Medusa's head sliced open and bleeding and writhing across the sky.

I am incoherent much of the time.

No police have come, but I woke one morning and found a spaceplane parked outside my tent. I had heard the powerplant in my sleep and had thought it was N≠alika taking her transport back. But the transport is still there. And so is this plane.

Smooth, flat black, bent-winged, it looks just like the model on the *asha!a*'s desk, but it has different markings. It appears to be the same make.'¬⌈⌈V 04556 instead of ⊽⋀═ ¬2734. I don't know what accounts for the different designation. To all appearances, it is a twin.

And I thought my escape so clever. This machine did not come from N≠alika.

I thought: He has given me a burrow.

Then: Ha! No! He gave me *antlers!*

And now he has to kill me.

I know what this means. When the time comes, Storm Petrel, come out and fight. Equal this time, instead of one of us stripped.

Equal? He anticipates my moves. He anticipated my needs. He knew what I was going to do when I hadn't known myself. Who planned my escape, anyway?

I know this gift is a trap, in a way. It stands here in the desert inviting me. Silent, I can hear it: take me, take me. And oh do I want to.

Of course, there is nowhere to go. The storm of hard rays from Erde-Tannia keeps everything grounded. Under the open sky again I can see the bombardment. They've painted the sky like a drugged hallucination. Electric blues, hissing violet. Red burns. Outer space is deadly. Even the open sky scares me. I stay inside my tent. I don't turn on the radiation counters. I don't want to know. And if it read safe, I would not believe it anyway. I can only wait for the siege to lift. Maddening beckoning of the shadow-black spaceplane. It sleeps. Bent wings feel nothing but desert wind. I run out in the middle of the night, dreaming it is gone, but it is always here.

I sit inside it going through the motions. It's all familiar. The in-atmosphere powerplants are Chrysalis turboram/scramjets! This is stolen technology! Not just from the human colonists of Occo, this powerplant design was stolen from *us!* (Us, Tannia!)

It's a marvelously designed ship. The position of everything makes perfect sense, once you get used to reaching high for the overhead controls—the added space up there is for your antlers.

I know how to fly this ship. I want to take her home.

I am OK as long as I exist moment to moment. When I think of home, patience shreds, I become erratic. I want to fly.

I saw a primitive pack of nomads wandering the wasteland like Bedouin. The tribe was led by a big female, heavy-breasted as an ancient mother goddess. She walked in front. All of them were swathed in robes, with gauze veils covering their heads, shielding their eyes from grit and glare. They looked like pictures of Moslem women from old Earth, and I could tell them apart only by the color of their robes. White was for the women—at least, anyone with a distinctly feminine form was robed in white. All the children wore bright red; they were hard to lose. Blue I think were subdoms. And the ones whose undyed garments blended in with the dusty surroundings had to be *ufin/i*.

The ones I guessed were subdoms lifted their blue veils and sniffed toward my camp, perhaps thinking it a dom's burrow they wanted to raid. The female slapped them back with angry gestures, and the whole troupe vanished hastily into the desert haze.

I guess when a planet advances seven thousand years in fifty someone gets left behind.

I come out only at night. I search for the bright steady light of home in the phantasmagorical sky, locate it, and go back inside.

The date has passed when the baby was due. If I stay here much longer it's going to have "Mama" down pat and we're going to have to catch up and learn "Dada."

I hope someone is helping Maggie. An Erden nanny maybe. I wonder how hard it was on her. Maggie is such a little girl. Did she call out for me? Do I have a son or daughter? What is its name?

I hurt. I want to go home.

The air boils, presses down. I cannot breathe.

I've begun this chronicle not knowing if I can finish. I

was hoping to be interrupted before I recorded to this point. I've run out of events and I am still here and I still hurt. What do I do now?

I am running out of time. The launch window advances. Once Occo's orbit completes another 5 degrees of arc I can kiss Erde-Tannia goodbye for another five months; I and all the other small ships will be out of range.

I have been in prison. I have been uprooted and adapted to a strange world before. Being stranded would be nothing new. But the end date looms like a horror. I do not want to spend another five months here. I cannot. I ardently want to see Maggie again. I have to go home. Have to. Mad single-minded obsession nearly drives me to take that spaceplane up and fly into the face of the radiation storm. I have resolved to do that rather than stay here. If I have three eyes and no balls by the time I get there I am going home. If I crash-land already dead into a blue Erden mountain, I am going home. When time runs out, and the window is shutting, that is what I will do.

It has stopped! Oh my God. The hard rays. Even as I record. Now! The sky is pure blue. It stopped!

And there are silvery glints and flashes in the sky that have to be spaceplanes. They have come on the heels of the storm, an Erde-Tannian invasion fleet.

I have made a dash for my spaceplane and sit here depressurizing.

My long-range scanners are on. I watch. The attack is on.

Good God, what have they brought! Carriers. Two of them, spitting out fighters like guppies hosing out their young. I have never seen ships like these. Are these ours? The way these ships move, the way they accelerate and turn, can only mean one thing: there is such a thing as antigravity and they have it. They! We! Erde-Tannia!

The Occon defense fleet rises. Is mowed down. The first wave falls to a steady enfilade.

Groundfire spatters the heavens. I gasp and clutch at

my restraints. But the Erde-Tannian ships flit out of harm's way like playful sprites, too fast to measure.

A second wave of Occons mounts more cautiously. Some of them make it into space to fight.

And I'm on the ground. Decompression is agonizingly slow. I have no charts with which to plot this, and I don't have the process memorized—especially not for pressures like these. Temptation becomes irresistible just to bolt. But I will need my senses alert, so I wait a bit longer.

A little less pressure. I feel I am coming back to life. I don't know where I've been, but I haven't been alive till now. My head clears. I can breathe. I am home. Not Erde. A cockpit.

Cabin pressure is three Tannian atmospheres, down from four. Good enough. To take it all the way down would take hours. I don't have hours. And maybe I can't even tolerate normal pressure anymore.

I'm going. Now.

Powerplants come to life. I rise.

Immediately I have a shadow. I was looking for him. I want him. I turn over the desert to face off with the *asha!a'*.

Spaceplane pilots are a bit demented. This is better than sex. The worthy opponent.

We feint, circle, climb.

Waitwaitwait someone has a sight on me and it's not the *asha!a'*—

"Don't shoot! I'm a friendly!"

I'm screaming into the com on all frequencies. Erde-Tannia has brought a juggernaut and I'm wearing enemy colors.

A woman's voice, one I know well: *"Anthony!* Where are you?"

"Maggie! I'm in an Occon fighter!"

"Which?"

"This one! Down here!" I roll. I'm in the atmosphere. The ship strains.

Another sight fixes on me. Maggie screams, "Don't shoot, Marty, that's my husband!"

The sight goes off.

The *asha!a'* is running, low to the ground. Maggie takes a shot at him. Good one. It is deflected, hits a rock formation. Infrared sees a shape blitzing through the dust and falling debris. I am, of all things, relieved.

"Damn!" Maggie cries. Then, "Anthony, get up here and into the carrier. Get out of that ship!"

I rise from the atmosphere, shoot at an Occon which does not evade at my approach. He is surprised.

I can't go back to the carrier. I had thought all I wanted was to go home. That was before I got up here. I am alive again. I have a ship. I have heard Maggie's voice.

And I have an assignation. But already the *asha!a'* is gone.

A police ship comes to me and splats my hull glowing interplanetary orange like a ship in distress. The directive goes out: Don't hit the orange Occon; it's one of ours.

Someone else orders me to get out of the way.

I transmit: "I'm going. I have a conversation to finish with an Occon."

Maggie sends: "I'll get him. That's my date, Anthony."

It comes to me in an instant. 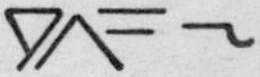2734 is not a series type. It's a name. That is why my markings are different. The *asha!a'*s ship is the only 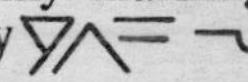2734 up here.

Come back, puppy, come back when you are a dog.

He is the pilot who let Maggie go.

He knows she's my wife. And he didn't tell me he knew.

There was a lot he never said.

"Sorry, Mag, he's mine."

And Maggie is part of a squadron. She is not free to chase a personal vendetta.

I am.

This is a new breed of fleet Erde-Tannia has brought. My ship and the *asha!a'*s ship are nothing next to these new fighters. I am worse than a spare part in this battle, and the *asha!a'* is outclassed.

I shall get out of the way. I and the *asha!a'* will go off by ourselves and butt heads.

I know where he is. There's a message pulse in my receiver. It contains only coordinates. I know who sent it as he ran.

* * *

Am over the equator, sunside. No spaceplanes, no shooting. There are no targets here. Except me.

I check the message pulse inserted in my com. The coordinates are an invitation to continue our private war.

This could be either a rendezvous or an ambush. Which is it?

I go.

I am ready for a blast on the way, too early, in case this is an ambush.

But he is there, waiting like a gunslinger in a deserted street.

Am careful not to feel fortunate.

People who give breaks are very sure of themselves. I remember my duel with Burke. I could have killed him on the launch rail, but I let him get in the air. I gave him a break. And I won.

The *asha!a'* knows what I will do before I think of it myself.

The *asha!a'* sends an Occon equivalent of *en garde.*

I: *Ready.*

IX.

Obviously I lived.

I had meant to keep recording through the duel, but I guess I forgot to talk, because the bubble is blank from the moment I said "Ready" to the *asha!a*'s last words as he was going down in the atmosphere. The conscious mind shut off and reflexes and conditioning took over.

I'm not sure I could even recount the fight. It's a blur now, though it was crystalline while it happened. It was short—like the gunslingers' showdown in the street. I timed the gap in my recording. Ninety seconds between "Ready" and "One thing I have that you will not. A good death."

The prophecy will probably turn out true. The *asha!a'* and I could understand each other on this matter, because Occo, whether of itself or of human contamination, and Erde have a long tradition of the concept of a "good death." Tannians are slightly less likely to see what is so bloody wonderful about dying in action or any other kind of dying.

I gave the *asha!a'* a good death because he was shot down by the best. There's a circular logic here: I was the best by virtue of being able to shoot him down.

He transmitted once more, for he was several seconds in the going down: "Know who your friends are."

And that was it. I did not see him impact.

The parting words were unsettling. It was a sneaky divisive Occon thing to do, to turn me against my own kind, and I would have dismissed it coming from any other Occon, but coming from the *asha!a'* it preyed on my mind. It was a warning against a despicable end.

I reentered the battle. And though my machine was from another era than these new Erde-Tannian superships, I was able to give a few Occons a less than good death, for they, believing mine was a genuine Occon craft, showed to me their vulnerable sides.

I almost fell to friendly fire again. This . . . *thing* came around the planet. I hardly recognized it. That ugly duckling of a craft I called the lost golf ball. I take back everything I said.

Out of action the vehicle is as graceless as any dead thing. It is a *joke*. Here, however, it appeared the epiphany of War, all ports blazing. The engineers had refined the containment system of its M/AM powerplants, added a grav stabilizer to keep from crushing its crew, so now it could accelerate at any rate it cared to with its matter/antimatter propulsion, limited by nothing. It could also read a target nearly instantaneously, determine whether it was friend or foe, choose an effective weapon to combat it, aim, and fire.

As soon as that thing came around the planet, Occons as far as the instruments could read exploded under its fire. One of its weapons was not even conventional, some kind of disrupter which broke its targets apart.

In panic I realized I couldn't let it focus on *me*. I hid behind one of our ships and sent, "Does that thing know I'm friendly?"

A voice on the com transmitted, "Don't hit the orange ship. *Golf Ball*, do you have that in your program?"

Golf Ball. They kept the damn name.

"Negative," came from the killer ship. "Amending that now."

It hadn't known. I could have been gone in a moment. The machine just does not miss. Once it sights, that's *it*.

The voice of my intercessor sounded again: "Now somebody get this orange ship out of here before *I* shoot it. Captain Collier, do you outrank your husband?"

Captain Collier!

"Negative," Maggie sent. "He's a colonel."

She inflated my rank. I was lieutenant colonel. But there was a commodore on hand to order me finally back to the carriers whatever rank I was.

I was headed in when something appeared in my way,

flapping at me out of an old nightmare. From the dark side of a small Occon moon. Black terror.

Manta.

Startled transmissions from our ships crisscrossed my com. They were surprised to see this apparition too.

If Erde-Tannia had not brought it, where had it come from?

The only answer was that it had *been* here. No, it was not an Occon. It had been here. It had been *parked.*

A shot crossed my bow, warning me to halt. The black ship menaced.

I sent, "Get out of my way, Reid."

"I am never going back, Anton, and neither are you."

"Come on home, Reid."

"No!" Another bow shot, closer. "Next one's going in, Anton."

The bottom of my mouth prickled. I wanted to reason with him, but I did not think reason would work. I could not even think of a proper path of *un*reason to take. "What is this about?"

"I will never set foot on a planet again. A man who piloted a ship called *Storm Petrel* must understand that."

"I don't. I can't fight you."

"Tragic. Because I can fight you."

"Reid, don't."

I did not want to do this. This was not war. It was not even a personal feud as with Burke. What was this? Blood sport. And I did not want to play. I could not justify this to myself—and I could rationalize a lot.

He justified it for me. "How does self-defense sound? I'm going to kill you, Anton."

This was the man who'd shot down *Flag One* in simulation. Could he shoot down an old friend just for the hell of it? I didn't think so.

Laser sight on me, I rolled. Deflected a blast.

Yes he would.

A laser sight on *him* at the same time—from the carrier—prevented him from following me. Reid evaded. The *Manta* moved so fast it was as if he just vanished. My computer could not track him.

A transmission from the carrier: "Whose side is that *Manta* thing on, anyway?"

"He's a little crazy right now," I said thickly. As if what ailed him were something from which he could recover.

I put into a hangar on board the immense carrier, but I could not come out of my ship. I still had a few atmospheres' worth of depressurizing to do. The carrier's computer could at least tell me how fast I couldn't go.

"Hope you're comfortable, Nordveldt. You're going to be in there awhile."

They asked about my "friend" the Manta. I did not want to talk about him. I said only that we had been through hell and he might not be himself.

"Do you need medical attention?"

"Not immediately." I had a multitude of ailments, but I looked forward to recovering from them at *home*.

For now, shut up in my Occon ship, I had time to think and to ask questions.

I felt like Rip Van Winkle. I'd been gone from Erde-Tannia less than a standard year, but advances had accelerated a bit since Rip's day, and I think I missed more than Rip had in his twenty-year sleep.

In my absence, somebody had cracked the unified field theory. The result was these ships zinging around in apparent defiance of physical law. They have no fuel tanks! They move as if they have no mass, and they've never heard of inertia.

Actually, this advance was not as recent as I thought. A pair of theorists over at Erdetechnik had been sitting on the theories and attendant formulae for years now. Only under the general amnesty and Occon threat did they admit they had some machines in development and had worked with grav pulse once before—building the *Manta* for their boss and codeveloper, Reid.

When the theory was loosed on the Tannian laboratories, the inventors went wild. There hadn't been a discovery this profound since relativity.

A door opened. The world changed forever.

Erde-Tannia revolutionized its fleet in a matter of months.

And to make certain that Occo could not spy on what the labs were developing, or invade before the new war machines were ready, Erde-Tannia fired the steady barrage of hard rays at Occo, the death rain, to keep the Occon fleet grounded.

As soon as all was prepared, Erde-Tannia dropped its deadly screen and unleashed its new creations on Occo.

Now I wondered what could be keeping our ships out there so long. The Occons were like cavalrymen wielding sabers at tanks and helicopters.

Or like things with antlers versus things with starships.

The fleet at length returned to the carriers. I thought I would get to talk to Maggie on the journey home. But the journey home took no time. Because the carriers controlled gravitons, they could counteract the g crush and accelerate at will. We hopped home along another dimension.

In no time my hangar opened, freeing me into Tannian space.

The planets were beautiful, and they were right *here.* They were huge and immediate. Blue-white Erde shone lovingly.

I put down on Erde, counter to orders.

The Tannian fleet authority screamed threats after me. Erde welcomed me like a hero.

I spent a week in an Erden decompression chamber. I was right; I couldn't stand normal pressure anymore. I tried to walk outside and keeled over from "altitude sickness." So they pumped me back up and tried again. I had a whole team of distinguished Erden doctors instead of one surly Occon veterinarian looking after me.

I had a radio on constantly, for the political situation was changing at breakneck speed. We, Erde, dissolved our Tannian Congress and were in the process of holding elections for a free independent Erden Congress. Tannia kept telling us we were violating the law; all this was not permitted.

Tannia threatened to take action, but following through on that threat would be difficult, for I had inadvertently staged a mass mutiny. All the Erden fighters had followed me home instead of returning to a Tannian base, and now Erde refused to disarm.

Tannia told us that Erde was not permitted to keep a standing military force.

Too late. We had one. Much of it had been built here

at the revamped Erdetechnik and Weltraum factories, so there were even more where those came from.

I was automatically commissioned in the new Erden fleet. Tannia hailed threats on me, said I had committed an act of gross criminality. They told me to bring myself and the Occon ship back to the base from which I'd been commissioned and to persuade the other defectors to do likewise.

No. I won't go back to the old status. The ability to choose my own destiny had been recently returned to me, and I held it very dear, so I was not going to give up my planet's right to it. My nation was good enough to stand equal to Tannia in defense; it is good enough to stand beside Tannia in peace. The interim government let Tannia know that Erde's military was no longer under Tannian jurisdiction. We could renegotiate a treaty as soon as we elected a free Erden government.

This was not acceptable. Tannia told us to disarm first, then we would talk.

Tension escalated quickly to a prewar situation. By the time I got out of decompression, I, with the Erden fleet, was on standby alert.

Through all this, Maggie and I had been sending messages of our own back and forth between Tannia and Erde. As soon as I had set down I sent: "Maggie, I am home. Can you come to Erde? I love you. Anton."

She sent back: "Come home. Maggie."

I sent a message telling her a return to Tannia was impossible right now, but I desperately wanted to see her.

She told me I was being unreasonable. Come home.

I repeated that I couldn't.

She threatened divorce if I did not come home.

I called her bluff.

She divorced me.

I hadn't believed her. I felt breathless, kicked in the midriff, mouth opening and shutting like a fish. Bleeding all over like an amputated piece of something.

Shocked. Depressed. I thought I would be so relieved and grateful if I ever saw home again I would never have another complaint as long as I lived. But I was depressed and lonely. I had been holding on, just holding on, until I saw home again. Home, and I let go and I find I've been holding on for nothing. What I was holding on for was all ash, gone, false.

So when I was let out of my pressure chamber to rediscover my world, I felt, So what? What was it for? The color, familiar scenes, comfort, temperature controls, water, gentle breezes, Erden voices, pillows, music, flowers, political speeches, superconductor trains, blue mountains, meat, pastries, showers, wood floors, nice clothes, carpets, women, lots of women but not the one I loved. What was it all for?

Left alone to my own thoughts, I become a zombie, so I dove into the maelstrom of the state crisis headfirst. A side effect of Occon, I thought grimly; I only functioned under pressure. I was all right so long as I was in the thick of things. At night I was so lonely I would've fallen in bed with anyone whose name I knew. But all my old friends were dead or dead to me.

I almost considered going to Tannia, but I had come too far. Erde was on the brink of war and my name was being mentioned for a Kommissariat in the new regime. I could not leave now.

And I sensed in the speed of Maggie's decision an ulterior motive. She did not really love me anymore, I guessed. Or she had taken a lover in my absence and just needed an excuse to unload me.

Wounded heart and questions of war did not go together well. Anger is an easy avenue for hurt. But I could only hurt.

How had we come to this?

Just wars are dangerous, leave you with a taste for war, an idea that there is goodness and nobility in it. Here we were, victorious after an absolutely righteous war—invaded by nonhumans who committed atrocities upon our people. We had gone through hell in defense of our homes and loved ones. Now both of us, Erde and Tannia, were primed for a fight, the enemy was gone, and we were left facing each other.

I heard tough talk in the Erden streets: ''While we're at the business of throwing off slave masters, Tannia, you're up next.''

That threat was horrific, because what befell Occo was

an abomination. You see, we didn't just win that battle. We won the war in infamous style.

Those impossibly fast ships returned to Occo in search of human survivors. The refugees they picked up were in such pitiable condition that few people felt much guilt over the next stage of normalization.

The "normalization" of Occo meant returning the planet, as nearly as possible, to the condition in which humans discovered it.

Occo had advanced seven thousand years in fifty? Occo was sent back seven thousand years in fifty *days*.

Occo was leveled. The cities, the industry, all trace of civilization.

Spaceplanes buzzed over the Occon settlements in a warning pass, driving the inhabitants out, then returned in earnest to pound the deserted cities into the dust—the buildings, transports, everything of human design. They skimmed the land, blasted and strafed, sending it all up in a pillar of fire like the wrath of God, but God never did such a thing.

We left Occo to the Occons, the way we found it 192 years ago.

Some called it atrocity. Easy answers usually are, but it's an academic exercise to figure now what else we could have done then.

Anyway, it is done, for worse or for worse.

I wonder what the Occons think. Was it the greatest catastrophe ever to befall them, or a painful blessing? I thought of the *asha!a'*. I imagine sometimes he did not meet his good death but bailed out before impact.

The *asha!a'*, though born to human ways, never quite took to them. An old tribal instinct ruled many of his actions. He had let Maggie go because he could not bring himself to shoot a "puppy," a juvenile. And me, once he'd decided I was an equal, he gave me a ship so I could put up a fight. With a 190-year-old civilization, instinct had not caught up. For all that, the uniform and language and rank and order, he was still a wolf/buck with an old-fashioned sense of pack order.

If he survived the crash, I think he would survive the devastation well.

I like to think he made it, reverted to the ancient way,

found and took on the old seventeen-point fossil in fair combat, head to head, and was out in the wild somewhere collecting eight wives.

Just remember to keep them happy, *asha!a'*. If they're unhappy, they leave.

Thoughts circled always back to Maggie.

I was called before Congress for a hearing pending the election of seven Kommissars.

It was suggested that we, the new government, appropriate all Tannian-owned land on Erde and confine all Tannians currently residing on Erde. As a Kommissar, I was asked, would I put that idea into law? I said it was the most asinine and preposterous idea I'd ever heard in my life.

A congresswoman asked if I wanted to rethink that answer.

I said yes, I had understated my case.

I ended up walking out of the hearing. And for that I thought I could kiss the Kommissariat goodbye. Stupid, really.

I took to a spaceplane, an old-style KR-22. I don't know how to operate those new things. I think better in a cockpit. And I felt less powerless. I had a gnawing fear that only subsided when I had guns at my command.

One of my vague troubles circled around the fact that the *Manta* was still at large. Reid had never come home.

Nothing I could pinpoint, shifting like a phantom pain, something in that detail filled me with unreasoning—or prescient—dread.

If he never intended to land, what in God's name was he going to do?

Fighters wither in peacetime, and this was peacetime. But some conditions are subject to change with little effort.

The peace was shaky. Nothing really held it. Like a cartoon figure, it needed only to notice there was nothing beneath it and it would fall.

I would think the desirability of peace would be axiomatic, but that's not true. It must be reinvented in every age.

Some say there exists no good without evil, no joy

without pain—and you don't appreciate freedom until you've been in prison.

Erde was angry, and the only war Tannia knew was wonderful. That one-sided wrecking crew which effected the demolition on Occo gave a false portrait; there were few deaths in that, and those weren't even human, so who cared? There was a whole generation on Erde and Tannia who didn't know the meaning of true war, but they were eager to learn.

They say if you can only keep the romance from combat, people will avoid it. Show it to them in stark gritty horror. You know what? I don't think it will work. They *want* pain, something to kick them out of complacency and into joy. It validates the worth of peace.

Few there are who see the ship on the shoal and don't go there.

And on both sides was the universal motive, fear. Nothing pulls a trigger faster than fear. Each side thought the other was about to shoot first.

So I brooded on my moody patrol. I had come as far as the DMZ. The zone has not been established by treaty, only by threat. Each planet has drawn lines and dared the other to cross upon pain of armed retaliation.

A ghost crossed my scanner. I called up a picture.

The *Manta*, flapping into Tannian space.

I know what Dr. Frankenstein felt, the personal onus to stop the creature he'd awakened. But the *Manta* had gone where I was forbidden, and was fast disappearing from camera view. If I lost sight of him, my instruments might never locate him again. I could not afford to lose him.

Make a decision quickly. It's irreversible.

I crossed into Tannian space.

If I got caught here, it would begin. And suddenly I knew he was going to do it. I saw the hook as I closed my mouth on it. My despicable end. Reid was going to start the war and sign my name.

X.

I had been baited, hooked; I heard the reel buzzing, felt the yank on my mouth.

O Lord, I thought, I am going to be pinned with breaking the truce. I am about to ignite the Second Erden-Tannian War.

I tried to signal Tannia, to notify its defense that I was in Tannian space, in pursuit of a terrorist, and requesting armed, *modern* assistance. My transmission was jammed. Reid had thought of everything.

Soon my scanner detected another ship. This one was hard to miss—a great flying wedge, its silvery-white hull illuminated from stem to stern, its green and red running lights outlining the famous profile of the Life Ship. The ship is big as a space station, carrying a brood of tugs, shuttles, and ambulances tucked in its belly. It exists to save lives. The Life Ship rescues runaway spacecraft, picks stations out of decaying orbits, delivers emergency care and supplies, evacuates disaster areas. I had always wanted to pilot her. It is considered good luck just to cross her path.

Not this time. Fear clawed where there should have been joy.

The Life Ship had combat engines for speed, but no armament and minimal defenses, for no one in his right mind would take a shot at the Life Ship.

I was chasing a man who had shot down a passenger liner.

''Reid!''

I called to him, but he had no mind left. The Occons

had taken it. The only thing left of the Reid I knew was the impulse to shoot everything else out of the heavens.

And I knew who was piloting the Life Ship this tour of duty, because I'd been keeping track of her (I'm not the only man ever to have put a tag on his ex-wife): Captain Mary Magdalene Collier.

The *Manta* turned, transmitted, "Fight me or I'll blow up the Life Ship."

"Reid, I can't—" But even as I spoke I fired a beam at him.

I might have winged him, but he was gone so quickly I couldn't tell. I checked my scanners. The *Manta* is nearly tracker-invisible. I saw multiple ghosts. Were any or all of them Reid?

I lurked around the Life Ship, watching all quarters for Reid, waiting for a trick.

Or was this the trick? He wasn't coming back and I was caught here looming over a peaceful vessel.

I reached for my com to try to raise the Life Ship.

Computer defense sprang to life. My ship dove, my stomach in my throat. Detonation off the port side. Flash and spray of shrapnel. Tiny one pierced the hull. Computer told me I had a slow leak, commenced draining the cockpit atmosphere.

Can't get a sight on Reid. Can't even see him. Me in a twenty-five-year-old KR-22.

There he is. Sight locked on him. Fire torpedo.

Beam from the *Manta* rides my sight back and pushes the torpedo back into its bay.

Manual eject! Curl up and hug my legs.

Ship cracks open like an egg.

I uncurl cautiously. The computer is still working. The ship is bent and I am looking through a gaping rent in the hull at the stars. Damage is all structural. The engines still function, but directionals are useless. The crumpled ship doesn't know which way it's facing.

There is the *Manta* coming in for the kill.

I told you Reid was the best. I was done. I opened the rocket engine shrouds. When they blow, they'll blow big, like a flare, I hope. About to jettison this record out the blind side and hope it is found by anyone but Reid. If I am to have any hope of being recorded as something other than an Erden terrorist destroyed while making an attempt on the Life Ship. Someone find this and tell the story right.

I wait for him to finish it.

Something ripped through one of the *Manta*'s soft wings. A ghost that wasn't a ghost hurtled past. It wasn't a weapon. Reid had been rammed.

The attacking ship came back for another pass. No wonder it didn't shoot. It had no guns. It was an *ambulance!*

The *Manta* attempted evasion. The ambulance matched it zig for zag, blitzed past within touching distance, ejected something, raced on. An explosion ripped the *Manta* open.

The shredded remains wheeled; the black rags of its soft body looked as if they should have been fluttering, but of course they weren't.

The end had come so fast I needed to replay it slowly and even then ask my computer what actually had happened.

The ambulance had deposited compressed oxygen tanks, filled overfull, inside the *Manta*'s deflector field. In the sudden vacuum of space, the canisters exploded.

The ambulance moved in again cautiously, probed the wreckage for a survivor.

Meanwhile a tug came out to tow my ship into the Life Ship. I was met in the dock by an emergency medical crew, but I was quite healthy, and I pushed past them, demanding to see Maggie.

A voice behind me said, "The captain has taken a ship out to investigate a hostile presence."

I spun. "She—?"

Maggie! It was Maggie out there taking on the *Manta*. With an ambulance.

Yes, that sounds like my wife.

My wife.

I waited for her at the ambulance dock. As her ship put in, the emergency crew poised in readiness, but the spry little pilot jumped down from the hatch, signaled negative, no survivors.

She pulled off her helmet, shook out a tumble of gold fluff.

My heart jumped, but Maggie regarded me passionlessly. She had something in her hand, tossed it to me. "You dropped something."

I caught it. It was this recording.

My wrath boiled up. "I'm here, Maggie. In Tannian space. What was it you wanted to say to me?"

"What makes you think I have anything to say to you?"

"My mistake," I said. "I misinterpreted all those 'Come home' messages. I had this bizarre idea that we were married. But I get it. You got tired of waiting again and found someone better."

Her eyes blazed, their natural color, light blue-gray. "No, Anthony. You did. You gave me up for Erde."

"That's not how it went. I refused to abandon Erde. You were the one who decided you and Erde were mutually exclusive."

She was still tiny, thin as a willow sprig. She was looking sprightly for just having given birth.

I said, "Where is my baby?"

"My baby is in an incubator."

"Where?" I wanted to see it.

"Tannia."

"Not here? Fine. If you don't want it, I do." It. I hated calling children it. "What is it?"

She laughed. "Oh, that's a good one, Anthony. The good father has come to rescue the baby from the negligent mom. 'What is it?' "

I stared at her as she laughed. I saw how people could murder those they once loved.

Something in my gaze. She stopped, rethought, and blanched. "Oh. I'm sorry, Anthony."

"No you're not."

And we're screaming again, hitting in the ambulance bay. Maggie was doing the hitting. She'd always been quick with her fists.

No one intervened. Even the MPs stayed wide. I overheard one: "Don't get in between that. They'd turn on you sure as shit."

Maggie screamed, "You got out of Occo and you went

to Erde! You went to Erde! You went to Erde! You went—''

''I know that, Maggie. What *about* it?''

''You're gone most of a year, you're free at long last, I'm on Tannia and you go to Erde!''

''I see. I did something you didn't like and you decide unilaterally that it's grounds for divorce. That's all it takes? One wound? That's real commitment, Maggie. At this moment I don't very much feel like being married to you either, but I'm not going to run to divorce court every time my feelings are hurt.''

''You don't need to. We are divorced.''

''And I ought to just say fine. But I can't, because I don't give up on a commitment as easily as you. I went to Erde because if I didn't I wasn't sure I'd ever be able to again. And I am an Erder and I owe my country my loyalty—''

She broke in snidely, ''You're up for office—''

''I was drafted. I walked out of the hearings, and that's irrelevant. I didn't realize that my wife would be so unyielding that she would cut me off because I didn't abandon my country in its urgent need, because I didn't come to her the moment she called. Well, I haven't given up on my mean selfish unreasonable wife yet.''

''You had better! You're out! God forbid you shackle yourself to such a spiteful creature as me! Don't torture yourself!''

I couldn't talk anymore. I had nothing to say, nothing civil. I started to go, said on the way out, ''When you're ready to talk like an adult and not squawk like an Occon animal, maybe we can meet somewhere and get something settled.''

A deck boot whizzed over my shoulder. ''Settle that! You're so fucking smug superior with your name-calling. I know why I divorced you!''

I stopped. ''You do? Sounds to me like your reason changes every five seconds. You divorced me because I didn't come home. You divorced me because I'm smug. I'm getting everything but the real reason.''

''Oh, right, Anthony.''

''You aren't a touch angry because you're guilty as hell?''

She sneered. Too sarcastic. "Of *what?*"

Of what.

Her baby was in an incubator. It should not be in an incubator; it should have been full-term by now. If it were my child.

And besides convenience, there was another reason women put their babies into incubators instead of carrying them to term. Abortion is illegal on both Erde and Tannia. If a woman wants the unborn baby out of her life, the state takes it and puts it into an incubator and gives it to an adoptive family.

"Whose baby is in the incubator?"

She went white. After a dead pause she said, "Not yours."

I already suspected—which did nothing to lessen the shock.

Maggie mumbled, "Not mine either anymore. I gave it up."

Silence. I had nothing to say. She burst out, "Don't you dare call me a whore for that—"

"Oh no, I slept with one of those on Occo. Only I wouldn't call her a whore either. She was a nice individual."

"You had to get that in, didn't you?"

Yes, I did. "What happened to my child?"

"It wasn't. It was a 'nonviable fetus.' "

Oh God, who makes up these terms?

"Three weeks," she added in a whisper. "It just . . . quit."

Power drained away, the raging wind died, and I was left empty and ridiculous.

I paused. "I guess that's it."

I walked back to the docking bay which had received my ship.

My poor KR-22 lay broken in a hangar. Bent the way it was, it barely fit in. It could not take me home. I feared the Life Ship would put in at a Tannian station where I would be arrested, but the medic who was looking after me said we were moving to neutral space, whence to hail Erde to come get me. Tannia did not want to detain an Erder any more than I wanted to be detained.

The medic was an Erder, still serving Tannia but with sorely tried loyalty. He was deferential to me.

Having given this message, he remained in my presence, awkwardly, with something unsavory left to say.

"What?" I prompted.

"The official report gave you an assist on that kill out there."

Reid. I see.

So it was a case of an Erder killing an Erder, not a purely Tannian deed. To his great relief, I nodded. It was less incendiary this way.

The medic, positively reverential now, showed me to a private compartment where I could wait for my ship.

It wasn't until I was alone that I started crying. A three-week-old little bundle of cells I had built into a child who gurgled for me and spit up on my shirt and woke me up in the middle of the night for something besides mining lapis lazuli. I should not be so upset. Three weeks' worth of nonviable cells. No big deal. In olden days Mag wouldn't even have known she was pregnant when she lost it. Happens all the time, more often here than it did on Earth.

Why did none of that make me less distraught?

A knock on my compartment door. The medic leaned his head in. "Sir, it's your wife."

"I don't have a wife."

"That is what she called herself. It's Captain Collier. What should I tell her?"

I almost said for him to tell her to stick her head in a bucket of heavy water.

"Send her in."

The compartment was dark when Maggie came in. She did not turn up the dimmer.

"Anthony, I'm such an ass."

I nodded.

She came nearer, laid her hand on my cheek, brushed wetness.

I said, "They're not for you, darling. Don't be touched."

She sat next to me sheepishly with her toes turned in. "Just how committed are you to your mean selfish unreasonable guilty wife?"

"I don't have a wife."

"You want to fight, I'm walking out."

"No, I don't want to fight. Are you hungry?"

"No, but I can pretend."

We went to the commissary to get something to eat.

"I forgot to thank you for saving my life," I said.

"Don't," said Maggie. "I came out to kill you. We didn't see the *Manta.* We only saw you. So I came out. *You* saved *us.*"

She was prettier than ever, the lines of her face firmer, less babyish, an adult imp. She hadn't lost her taste for fancy clothes. She was wearing a pale blue silk jumpsuit, blue heels, and a blue necklace, which was sodalite, but I couldn't stand it.

"Please please please don't wear that."

She yanked it off and tossed the strand of blue beads over her shoulder. "It's gone."

We had to reconcile. If we who love each other cannot settle, what hope of peace can there be between planets? I had the peculiar feeling that if we did not remarry war was inevitable.

Ship captains no longer have the power to marry; voyages are too short, so the need is gone. Anyway, Mag *was* the captain, and she could not exactly marry herself. But there was no shortage of chaplains of every faith on board the Life Ship, all eager to perform something other than last rites. And Maggie and I remarried before the Erden ship arrived to take me home.

We don't see each other as much as we'd like, my wife and I. I was elected Kommissar upon my return. Maggie visits between tours of duty.

I almost lost Maggie her command of the Life Ship—the "doubtful association" specter again. This time the doubtful association was a Kommissar. I sent a communiqué to the Tannian military command saying in effect that if the Erden government was considered an ill association then we could break off all relations right now. It was a bluff, of course—I was not going to war over this, or over anything but my dead body, but Tannia bought it and backed off. And that was the last saber I ever rattled.

So Maggie visits me on Erde. I can't leave. I can't resign. I have to stay and block the warmongers.

I remember my night in the sweatbox with the *asha!a'*, liking to think we would have done better had we only authority and power to act. Suddenly I *have* it.

There are seven Kommissars, whose unanimous vote is required to declare war. I am one of those votes.

If ever another war breaks in this system, it's going to be an undiluted horror. And God help us then. Or perhaps in a blink we'll all be gone. Those new machines are beyond me. I can't keep up with the advances. There's nothing like a war to accelerate technological development. I am now conversant in antiques.

And what shall we do with our new powers? When we were so malignant with the old? What Occo and we did to each other is monstrous past my ability to say.

It ends now, the violent answers. It must end.

If there is another war, someone else will have to write it, because it happens over my dead body indeed, which I am coming to believe is a very long step.

About the Author

Rebecca M. Meluch graduated from the University of North Carolina at Greensboro with a B.A. in drama. She also has an M.A. in ancient history from the University of Pennsylvania and a black belt in *tae kwon do.* She worked as an assistant in the classics department at Greensboro. She has also worked as a data processor, artist, and fashion model. She is involved in the theatre and active in a playwrights' workshop sponsored by the Ohio Theatre Alliance, and has helped inaugurate a Readers Theatre program at Beck Center for the Cultural Arts. She travels at any excuse and has worked on an archaeological excavation in Israel. She has a passion for World War II fighter aircraft. Two of her other novels, *Jerusalem Fire* and *Sovereign,* are also available in Signet editions. Her next book is entitled *Chicago Red,* and will be available in June 1990, along with her previous works, *Wind Dancers* and *Wind Child.* Miss Meluch lives in Westlake, Ohio.